Ride
BY YOUR
side

KRISTEN LUCERO

Book Cover by Cindy Ras

Edited by Ramona at Ramona Edits

Proofread by Brittany Ballin

1st edition 2025

CONTENTS

Playlist   VI

Dedication   VII

Author's Note   VIII

1. Veronica   1

2. Miles   11

3. Veronica   21

4. Miles   31

5. Veronica   40

6. Miles   49

7. Veronica   55

8. Miles   62

9. Veronica   70

10. Miles   77

11. Veronica   86

12. Miles   95

13. Veronica   102

14. Miles   110

15. Veronica   116

16. Miles   124

17. Veronica   130

18. Miles   138

19. Veronica   146

20. Miles   152

21. Veronica   161

22. Miles   168

23. Veronica   175

24. Miles   185

25. Veronica   194

26. Miles   202

27. Veronica   209

28. Miles   217

29. Veronica   227

30. Miles   237

31. Veronica   244

32. Miles   256

33. Veronica   263

34. Miles   271

35. Veronica   277

36. Miles   286

37. Veronica   294

38. Miles   302

39. Veronica   311

40. Miles   318

41. Veronica   324

42. Epilogue   333

Thank You For Reading   341

Acknowledgements   342

Ride
BY YOUR
Side
THE OFFICIAL PLAYLIST

1. LAST NIGHT'S MASCARA | GRIFF
2. I CAN DO IT WITH A BROKEN HEART | TAYLOR SWIFT
3. HOLD MY HAND | LADY GAGA
4. FIX YOU | COLDPLAY
5. VODOO DOLL | 5SOS
6. I LIKE ME BETTER | LAUV
7. I FOUND | AMBER RUN
8. IN TOO DEEP | WHY DON'T WE
9. ACOUSTIC | BILLY RAFFOUL
10. BED CHEM | SABRINA CARPENTER
11. GATEWAY DRUG | DANIEL SEAVEY
12. LITTLE BIT BETTER | CALEB HEARN, ROSIE

To my Naldo and the Grump to my Sunshine
Our love story will always be my favorite!

Author's Note

Ride by Your Side is book 2 in the Evergreen Grove Series. While this book can be read as a standalone, the main characters of Ride by Your Side do make an appearance in Book 1, Aisle Come Back to You.

Ride by Your Side picks up right where Aisle Come Back to You left off, so if you would like a deeper understanding of these characters and more background I highly suggest reading Aisle Come Back to You first, but of course, is not necessarily needed or required. The choice is yours.

I also want to make you aware, that while the majority of this book is pure fluff, sweetness, and witty banter, deeper topics do get brought up. If you get triggered by any of the following you may want to skip this book: Spicy and Open-door love scenes, explicit language, on page drinking, emotional and mental abuse by a partner, mentions of alcoholic parents, and mentions of absent and neglectful parenting.

1

VERONICA

G O AHEAD, CALL ME Julia Roberts. I mean, it is rather fitting given the situation. Today was supposed to be my fairy-tale wedding, complete with a white dress and a swoon-worthy happily ever after with everyone in town there to witness and celebrate. Instead? I've crammed myself and my big-ass poofy dress into the passenger seat of an old-school Ford Mustang, driven by none other than my best friend's older brother—who, by the way, can't stand me. Romantic, right? I should be driving off into the sunset with a man hopelessly obsessed with me. But nope, it's the irritated grump glaring at the road ahead like I've personally gone out of my way to ruin his day.

Runaway Bride was one of my favorite movies growing up, but my situation is far from romantic. Instead of having a salt-and-pepper dreamboat like Richard Gere sitting beside me, I'm stuck with someone who probably wishes I'd never been born. Miles Bennett has seen me as nothing more than the bane of his existence since we were kids, and despite trying every trick in the book, I've never been able to win him over.

Okay, so maybe not everyone has to like me, but I personally think they should—I'm a freaking delight. Sure, I have a reputation for stirring up trouble and drama, but coming from a place like Evergreen Grove, can you really blame me? This town is boring as hell—I can't help that I had to be the one to shake things up. Plus, who else is going to be the one to give the good people what they want and keep the gossip mill running?

I know I'm the architect of my own chaos and responsible for the rumors that make their way through town, but I've also been blessed with the uncanny ability to talk myself out of almost anything. Take, for example, the time I got caught red-handed painting the side of an old, abandoned storefront. *"I was only trying to make our town more beautiful with a mural for everyone to enjoy, Officer."* And guess what? My so-called *mural* still stands today—a little slice of accidental civic pride, courtesy of yours truly.

So yes, it could be said that I was a bit of a troublemaker, and I often got Miles's little sister—my best friend, Blair—in trouble with me, but it wasn't like we ever had to deal with any serious consequences. We always walked away with minimal repercussions, and if anything, he should just be happy that his sister found her platonic soulmate, since that's definitely what Blair and I are.

That's exactly why she was the one I ran to this morning, completely panicked as fear and the realization I was marrying the wrong person took over. She not only stepped up and gave me the courage to do what I needed, but also set me up with my own personal getaway driver—too bad it turned out to be Miles. Where is Richard Gere when you need him?

Most people might expect their best friend to brush off wedding jitters as nothing more than normal cold feet, but not Blair. After spending the last ten years jetting around the world as a concert photographer, she's become unapologetically blunt. Even though she just met my fiancé—or maybe now *ex*-fiancé—two weeks ago, she didn't hesitate to make her opinion known: Pete West is trash. If only I could have figured it out just as quickly and without all the messy feelings involved.

I tried to lie to myself and tell her that all the red flags she was picking up on in such a short amount of time weren't a big deal, and that he was different, but deep down, I think I always knew the truth. Maybe once upon a time, when our relationship was just starting out, he was a kind and charming man. But all that changed the second we got engaged. He transformed from the compassionate, empowering man who encouraged me to embrace my true self into a controlling jerk, molding me into his ideal Stepford wife and stripping away everything that made me who I am in the process

"So, what's the plan?" Miles's gruff voice finally asks. So far, we've only just driven past the town line, and while I know I need to figure this out, my brain refuses to give me any direction, as it can only focus on what I'd just done.

If I weren't busy channeling my inner Julia Roberts in *Runaway Bride,* I'd be just minutes away from walking down the aisle. The day would have unfolded into hours of photoshoots, speeches, and celebration. Then, by tomorrow, we'd be en route to our honeymoon, starting what was supposed to be the rest of our lives together as Mr. and Mrs. West.

I should be panicking, but all I feel is relief. The only thing weighing heavily on my conscience is the fact that I left the task of relaying the news of my cold feet to Pete, my parents, and the whole town in the willing hands of Blair, and our other best friend, Ford.

"Would you hate me if I said I haven't quite figured that out yet?" I ask, wrinkling my nose and biting down on my bottom lip, anticipating whatever snide remark he's about to make.

It's pretty well known that he enjoys throwing jabs my way, and despite my attempts to brush it off as harmless banter, I suspect he genuinely means it more often than not.

Instead, he lets out a loud sigh. "Well, just let me know when you decide."

Am I imagining things, or is he genuinely being kind and patient with me? Sure, there's a chance he's only helping out of pity, but something about his calm demeanor feels... sincere? It's oddly comforting, especially when I'm standing on the edge of what feels like a full-blown breakdown.

"I just—I don't really want to be in Evergreen Grove right now. I'm not quite ready to run into anybody and have to open up about what's been going on, but it's not like I can just go on our honeymoon. It wasn't even somewhere I wanted to go in the first place," I ramble, animatedly lifting my hands as I speak. "And what if he decided he wanted it to be his getaway plan, too?" I ask, trying to suppress my body's involuntary shudder. One more sign I'm making the right choice. Shouldn't I want to be around the person I'm supposed to be marrying?

"Where was your honeymoon supposed to be?" Miles asks, his tone laced with curiosity rather than judgment.

His question catches me off guard. I've been bracing myself for a sharp retort, expecting him to call me out for running away and say that if I was bold enough to run, then I should be strong enough to face the repercussions. And while he wouldn't exactly be wrong, I'm neither brave nor strong enough. I barely managed to run today, and that was only because of his sister's help and encouragement

"Paris," I admit, completely aware of how ridiculous I sound. Who doesn't want to visit the city of love? Plus, it isn't like I completely hated the idea of the trip. There are tons of museums there I've been dying to visit, and while they were on the agenda, for me, the idea of a perfect honeymoon is a place where you get to relax, have fun, and take advantage of the fact that you now get to spend some quality one-on-one time with your new spouse.

"And you didn't want to go there?" he asks, sounding surprised as he glances over with a raised brow. "That sounds like it would be right up your alley."

"I want to go to Paris, and it's on my bucket list for sure. But when it came to our honeymoon, I hadn't even been consulted. Pete just told me where we were going and had the entire itinerary planned down to where we were eating and staying with barely a second to stop and enjoy the fact that we were finally going to be Mr. and Mrs. West."

"Well, if it were up to you, where would you have chosen to go?" he prods. I never would've expected for him to care—or really give a damn—and I'm still not sure he does, but given everything going on, I'll take whatever distraction I can get.

"Honestly, I'm not that hard to please. A trip to Southern California where we hit up the beach and maybe a day trip to Disneyland, would have been more than enough for me. I don't need fancy. I just wanted to spend the days lounging and enjoying my time with my new husband, not rushing around a new country without a second to breathe." I'm aware I might sound ungrateful, but instead of judging me, the corners of Miles's lips quirk up into a grin. "What?" I ask, not blind to the fact that *something* is going on in that brain of his. This seemingly nice-guy act of his can only last for so long—I've known him for too damn long to believe anything different.

"Please tell me you aren't one of those Disney Adults. I know you loved Disneyland growing up, given how often you and your family took Blair along with you, but for your honeymoon? You'd seriously choose Disney over Paris?"

I let out an indignant scoff. "There is nothing wrong with an adult enjoying some Disney magic. Even Walt Disney himself said that Disney is a place for children and adults to enjoy together."

"Right..." He nods, though I can hear the judgement in his tone. Still, of all the things he could have teased me about, this is one I can easily handle. "So why not go and do that instead?" he suggests.

Now it's my turn to be confused as I furrow my brow. "Do what?"

"Take the honeymoon you dreamed of. Go to California. Hit up the beach, go to Disneyland—live it up. After everything you've put up with from him, I'd say you deserve it," he says, his voice steady as he continues to stare at the road ahead.

"I guess I could." I muse, my lips turning to the side as I tilt my head. "I just don't know if I have the balls to go alone. I suppose I could ask Ford and Blair, but I'd hate to ask Ford to take more time off work. And with Blair, well... I don't exactly want to pull her away from what she and Ford *finally* started up."

"So that's for sure a thing, then?" Miles asks.

"What? Blair and Ford? Yes. I would definitely say that is a *thing* now." While I can't exactly take credit for playing matchmaker, my wedding festivities finally catapulted them back together. And with both his ex-wife and Blair's rockstar ex out of the way, they were finally able to act on their feelings for one another.

I'm sure almost everyone in town, Miles included, always knew they were destined to end up together, but no one knew it better than me. Growing up as a friend group of three, I had a front-row seat to their ridiculous denials as they constantly claimed to be *just friends*. Sure, I did my share of matchmaking and nudging to speed things along, but I also understood their hesitancy.

While both were my best friends in the entire world, things could've gotten messy if they decided to give it a shot and it didn't work out. Sure, I've always seen them as soulmates, but even I couldn't help the intrusive thoughts about what would happen if things went wrong. I'm only human, after all, and there was no way I'd ever be able to pick between them if things came crashing down, and thankfully I'd never been forced to.

"I guess it's about time," he agrees with a shake of his head. "And since I'm pretty sure we both want what's best for Blair, if you really don't want to go alone, I suppose I'll go with you."

My jaw practically hits the floor, as I blink in disbelief. He could've told me pigs were parachuting down from the sky, and I'd buy that before believing that *Miles fucking Bennett* is willingly agreeing to accompany me on my impromptu runaway bride adventure.

"I can't ask you to do that. What about your job?"

"It's my shop. I'm the boss, remember? I can do whatever the hell I want, and since I've yet to take any vacation since I bought the place, it's about time I give myself a small break."

"And you'd seriously use your first break to voluntarily spend time with me?" I blurt, sounding a little more incredulous than I'd like. But who could blame me? In all the years I've known Miles—which, by the way, is a lot, considering Blair and I became attached at the hip all the way back in kindergarten—he's never once willingly chosen to spend his free time in my company. So yeah, it feels like a valid question.

"Of course I know that. But we both know Blair wouldn't want you going alone, and since we both agree she deserves to be happy and spend some quality time with Ford, it just makes sense. Plus, I'm already here. So why the fuck not?"

"Are you sure?" I should just accept his offer and tell him no takey-backsies, but this feels... different. This is Miles we're talking about.

"Yes, I'm sure," he says, easing his foot off the gas pedal as he slows the car before pulling to a stop on the side of the road.

With the area completely deserted, he easily turns us around and begins the drive back toward Evergreen.

"So uh, why exactly are we going back then?" I ask, still trying to make sense of what's happening here. But honestly, I'm still in shock that Miles, of all people, is doing something nice. In fact, him being my getaway driver was probably the first kind thing he's ever done for me, but *two* things in one day? Who is this person and what has he done with the real Miles Bennett?

"To pack. Or did you plan on wearing your wedding dress to Disneyland?" he asks, glancing over, his bright blue eyes scanning me in all my bridal glory.

I look down at my dress, smoothing the soft satin fabric of the skirt with a wistful sigh. "Well, maybe I'd consider it if adults were actually allowed to dress up. I have always dreamed of being a Disney Princess, after all."

"A Disney Princess, huh?" he asks, amusement clear in his tone.

"Oh, please. Every girl dreams of being a Disney Princess—it's practically in the rulebook," I say with a dismissive wave. "Hell, I can even remember playing princesses with Blair growing up, and even *she*—Miss Too Cool for Everything—willingly played Aurora. So back off."

"Whatever you say, princess," he quips with a sarcastic edge. Instead of wasting my energy on a useless comeback, I let it slide. I close my eyes, letting the warm spring breeze whip around me as we drive back toward Evergreen with the top down in his red 1967 Ford Mustang.

Today may not have gone according to plan, and while I'm still unsure about Miles being my travel buddy, at least I can die happy knowing I didn't just make the biggest mistake of my life by marrying the wrong man. Going on a trip with one? Sure, that I can handle. But getting married to one? Not so much.

2

MILES

I BREATHE A SIGH of relief as we pull into the hotel parking lot. As someone who's always had a passion for cars, driving is pretty much second nature to me. It certainly helped that we spent most of the drive with the roof down and the wind in our hair. For once, I wasn't bothered that we had no concrete plans. It just felt nice to be out on the open road. Yet, despite being so in my element, I never could quite shake my worry for the woman sitting beside me.

She's not my favorite person and is someone I usually choose to avoid, but one thing I know about Veronica Prescott is that she never shuts up. She constantly has to be babbling on about *something*, and while I know I should be grateful, the fact that she isn't saying, well, *anything* is concerning.

I wasn't exactly expecting her to be yapping the entire drive or anything like that, but still, I expected more than the few words she muttered here and there. I probably should've taken over and asked if she was okay, but, number one, that's not me. And number two, the last thing I want to do is force her to talk about the traumatizing day she just had. The lady just ran away from the altar, that has to be normal, right?

One can't exactly expect someone who just ran away from everything she ever knew to be thrilled about it. While I suspect she made the right choice, that doesn't mean it was the easiest one to make. If anything, I'm sort of proud of her—not that I'd ever admit that out loud.

I'm sure the last thing she needed was my opinion anyway. Plus, every time I stole a glance in her direction, she looked far away, lost in her own little Veronica world, her legs curled up on the seat and her knees tucked close to her chest as she gazed out at the passing scenery.

With the car finally in park, I unbuckle my seatbelt. "I'm going to go and get us checked in," I announce, pulling her out of the fog she's seemingly been lost in.

"I can check myself in," she insists, stepping out of the car and stretching her arms above her head.

"Don't worry about it. Consider it a wedding gift," I say, but as her face contorts into a worried frown, I immediately backtrack. "I'm sorry, that was a bad joke. Either way, I've got it. Tonight's on me."

"You sure?" she asks, the crease between her brow deepening.

"I promise," I call over my shoulder as I head toward the entrance. It's not like I picked some fancy-ass hotel, anyway. While the town we've landed in looks somewhat small, it's bigger than Evergreen Grove, so that has to count for something.

Back home, there's only one place to stay: a small bed-and-breakfast. Here, there at least seems to be a few familiar chains, along with some unknowns. Playing it extra safe, I opted for one of the bigger and more well-known brands.

Heading inside, check-in is easy and I get us each our own king-bed suites. I suppose we could have saved some money by sharing a two-queen-bed suite, but I'm pretty sure both of us have had enough of each other's company for one day.

Plus, it's clear she's going through something, and if she's teetering on the edge of a full-on breakdown, I'm not sure I want to be there for it. I have a sister. Pretty sure I've dealt with enough of those moments to last me a lifetime.

With the newly acquired keys in hand, I make my way back outside, where she's leaning against the passenger side door, phone in hand as she seems to be typing.

"I got our rooms," I say and she snaps to attention before shoving her phone into the pocket of her jean shorts.

"You know, I really could have gotten it myself," she reminds me, walking around the front of the car before holding out her hand.

I pass her the key card and set it gently in her palm. "I know, and like I said, I've got it. If you really want to pay me back, you can fill up the first tank of gas tomorrow."

"You've got yourself a deal." She smiles, but it doesn't quite reach her eyes, and I hate that I notice. Normally, I wouldn't give Veronica's moods a second thought—whatever trouble she's gotten herself tangled in is usually her own doing and well-deserved—but today, I can't help it. Maybe I should've let her bring Blair instead. She'd know the right things to say to make her feel better. Me? When it comes to Veronica, she's as much of a mystery to me as why anyone would willingly order pineapple on a pizza.

"So, after we settle in, do you want to grab some dinner?" I ask. While we'd stopped for some McDonald's a few hours ago, I noticed that she'd only picked at her fries, leaving her burger completely untouched. With it now being almost eight o'clock at night, I have to assume she's starving. I know I am, and I actually ate my entire meal.

"I'm actually not feeling all that hungry," she admits, reaching into the backseat to grab her packed duffle bag.

My brow furrows. "You sure?" I'm not usually one to care about others' eating habits, and she's probably telling the truth, but just because she isn't hungry doesn't mean she shouldn't eat.

"Positive. I think I just want to lie down and sleep away the rest of this awful day," she explains. I quickly reach for my bag and follow her inside, toward our rooms on the bottom floor.

"So, uh, I guess I'll just see you tomorrow morning for breakfast?" I ask once we reach our rooms, which are side-by-side.

"Sounds good." She nods, tapping her key on the keypad before disappearing inside.

I tell myself not to worry about it. She's not my problem, but I know that's not quite the truth. While Blair likes to say that she's a grown woman and can take care of herself, as her older brother, I've made it my duty to be there for her. And I know her well enough to understand that making Blair happy means keeping her best friend happy, especially after such a crazy day.

Walking into my own room, I'm at least relieved to see I didn't pick out a total dump. In fact, it's kind of nice. Sure, it's your standard hotel setup with a bathroom immediately to the right, a bed dressed in a loud, overly patterned comforter, and cheap artwork adorning the walls. But it's clean, and right now, that's about all I really care about.

I set my bag on the dresser across from the bed before collapsing onto the comforter with a loud 'oof.' Okay, so the bed could use some work. Maybe I'm just spoiled since my bed back home is much softer and way more comfortable, but this should work for one night.

I reach for the remote on the nightstand and turn on the television, casually flipping through the channels. While I want nothing more than to relax and shut my brain off for the remainder of the night, my mind betrays me as my thoughts once again drift toward Veronica.

Settling on a random baseball game I hit mute before reaching into my pocket to pull out my phone and begin typing out a message to my sister.

> Miles: We found a hotel for the night in some small town in Utah. Just wanted to let you know we got here safe.

Almost instantly, my phone lights up, the familiar three little dots appearing on the screen letting me know she's already typing a reply.

> Blair: Good. How is Ronnie doing?

> Miles: Not sure. She hasn't said much and went straight to her hotel room. She's also barely eaten anything.

Blair: That's not like Ronnie. That girl loves to eat. I'll send her a text, but I think you should make her go out tonight whether she wants to or not.

Miles: I'll take her wherever, but I'm not forcing her to do anything. It's already weird enough. Just text her and keep me updated. I'm sure she'd much rather talk to you than me anyway.

I assume she takes my advice as my phone goes silent for a few minutes, until my phone buzzes once more.

Blair: She told me she's too tired and doesn't want to go anywhere. She wants to spend a night in, so just go grab her some dinner and bring it to her. I'll Venmo you the money for it.

Miles: Don't even think about Venmo'ing me. I've got it.

After sending me one final 'thank you' text, I reach for my wallet and keys and make my way out. Apparently, a getaway driver's work is never done.

With a Taco Bell bag in hand, I knock on Ronnie's door. I hear some shuffling, followed by what I assume is her looking through the peephole before I hear the locks being undone and the door opens.

It's clear she wasn't kidding when she said she just wanted to relax. The T-shirt and jean shorts she'd been wearing are now replaced with a big, white fluffy robe that she's holding tightly around her. Her short, shoulder-length wind-blown brown hair has also been pulled up into a ponytail, with a few tiny strands escaping to frame her face.

"What are you doing? Is everything okay?" she asks, folding her arms across her body.

"Brought you dinner. Blair said you're a sucker for a Crunch-wrap Supreme and a bean and cheese burrito, so here you go," I announce, lifting the bag.

She purses her lips and shakes her head but eventually gives in with a small sigh. "Blair just couldn't help herself, could she?"

"No, no, she couldn't," I agree. "But I couldn't either. I know today was shit and that you're going through it, but you have to eat something."

"Well, if it helps put you two at ease—since I'm sure you'll be reporting back—just before you got here, I made a quick trip to the front desk's little gift shop and treated myself to a bag of Skittles."

I shake my head, less than impressed. "Candy is not food."

"Sure it is. It might not be the healthiest food choice, but it is, in fact, food. Red food dye and all," she proudly proclaims, lifting her hand under her chin as she wiggles her fingers.

"Well, I guess Taco Bell probably isn't the healthiest of choices either." I slightly give in, doing my best not to smile at her ridiculous assessment. "But I think it's better than straight-up sugar, so will you please just eat it?"

She lets out a small huff as she motions for the bag. "Fine. I'll eat it. But even Taco Bell sounds a bit rough right now, so if I get sick and you have to spend the entire drive tomorrow stopping at every rest stop you'll only have yourself to blame."

"Oh shit," I curse, handing it over. Why does she have a point? And why did I let Blair make me think Taco Bell was the perfect choice for tonight? The woman had it wrong—Taco Bell is not the food of the gods and is, in fact, *not* the ultimate cure for a broken heart.

"Yeah, see. Taco Bell may be the food of the gods, but it must be chosen wisely," she tsk-tsks.

"Fuck, you and Blair are way too alike," I mutter, shaking my head. "But I still stand behind it being better for you than Skittles, so just this once, can you do the reasonable thing and go with it? Humor me for a change."

She scoffs. "Nothing is better for me than Skittles. A food that is dedicated to tasting like a rainbow? Come on now. They're magical."

"Oh, for the love of—" I groan, raising my hand to rub at the bridge of my nose. "I take it back. You two aren't alike—you're way more annoying than Blair," I declare, doing my best to fight off the fresh wave of annoyance. This is exactly why I've always gone out of my way to ignore her. Sure, she's undeniably gorgeous—practically a bombshell who could rank a solid ten on any scale, and not just by small-town standards like Evergreen. But looks can only go so far.

"Oh, come on, you know you love me," she says, playfully pinning a hand on my chest and giving me a light shove. "And hey, maybe my delightful personality will rub off on you during our little trip, and you'll finally stop being a boring old man."

I raise an eyebrow. "A boring old man?"

"Yes, a boring old man. Seriously, what do you do besides go to work and come home every day to your dog? Not that there's anything wrong with Bubba, because Bubba is a perfect little angel who..." She trails off before her eyes go wide. "Oh shit. Bubba!"

"Bubba is fine," I quickly assure her. "Blair agreed to look after him while we're gone."

Relief visibly washes over her as she places a hand on her stomach. "I'm glad you thought about it, because earlier the only thing on my mind was getting out of Evergreen as fast as I could. Hell, for a moment there, I sort of felt like Blair."

I let out a genuine laugh. Evergreen has always been home, but it hasn't always been easy. Growing up with a mother who ran off and a father who preferred the bottle to raising his kids, my sister and I ended up being cared for by our deadbeat grandma—until we lost her too. Despite everything, that town still holds its roots deep in me.

For Blair, though, Evergreen was a place she couldn't wait to escape—at least until recently. After rekindling old feelings for her childhood friend during all the wedding festivities these past few weeks it seems as though we might have her back for good. If nothing else, at least one good thing came from all this mess.

"But, uh. I should probably get to eating this. There's nothing worse than soggy Taco Bell," Veronica says, holding up the bag one final time.

"I could think of a few worse things," I reply, feeling compelled to disagree with her a bit more—it is our way after all. "But I'll leave you to it," I add. Nodding toward my room before turning to leave.

"Miles," she calls after me as I tap my electronic key to the door pad.

"Hmm?" I hum, looking back in her direction as the light on the door blinks green and I turn the knob.

"Thanks. Not just for the food, but for driving and coming with me. I know I'm a pain in the ass, but it really means a lot."

"Yeah, sure. Whatever. It's no big deal." I shrug, even if in many ways, it kind of is.

Is this how I imagined spending the next few weeks? Hell no! Especially considering the wrench it's thrown into my carefully planned schedule at my shop. But deep down, I know I'm exactly where I need to be.

3

VERONICA

DID I GET ANY sleep last night? Probably some, but it certainly doesn't feel like it. Between all the crying sessions and the panic attacks about how I just messed up my entire life, there really wasn't much time for anything else, and that includes sleep. I was hoping blocking Pete's number would help, given the millions of texts he's already sent, but if anything, it only made my guilt intensify, twisting it tighter in my stomach, so much so that the thought of eating made me absolutely nauseous.

It was nice of Blair and Miles to try and force-feed me, but I just couldn't do it. After taking one bite of the bean and cheese burrito, my nerves had me throwing it up in record time. However, my body didn't seem to reject the sweet and tangy bag of red Skittles, so I'm counting that as a win. Take that, Miles Bennett.

Not that I told him. The fact that he's clearly worried about me says a lot, since most of the time I assume he couldn't care less whether I live or die. But at least I now know he does, in fact care, even if it's more for Blair's sake than mine.

However, despite the dark circles under my eyes from the lack of sleep, I'm determined to enjoy this time away. When we get back and I'm forced to face the consequences of my actions that's when I'll let myself worry. That's future Ronnie's problem. She's the one who gets to deal with the fallout, and this Ronnie gets to live in the present and let go of all her problems—or at least that's the plan. Whether I can actually do it is the question.

"Looks like you got some of your appetite back," Miles notes as we walk through the aisles of the local gas station after not only filling up the car with gas, but also getting some snacks for the road.

Not only did I devour a heaping bowl of Fruity Pebbles this morning, but I also polished it off with a tall glass of orange juice—pure, vitamin-packed perfection. And just to prove I'm practically a health aficionado now, I followed it up with an even bigger glass of apple juice. That's practically two whole fruits in one morning. Of course, Mr. "Health Expert" didn't agree, rambling on about too much sugar this and too much sugar that. Honestly, what doesn't he understand? Sugar is the elixir of life, or at least my life.

"And none too soon, either. What's a road trip without stuffing your face full of food?"

"I personally prefer the interesting and unique views," he disagrees.

I roll my eyes. "You would say something lame like that. Sure, the scenery is great, but it's like when you go to a movie. Of course, the movie is the main attraction, but how are you supposed to enjoy the movie without a drink and some popcorn?"

He lets out a small scoff as we head toward the back of the small convenience store to get some drinks. "Do you always talk this much about food?"

"Of course I talk about way more than just food. Plus, in my defense, you were the one who kept pushing the subject yesterday, and you're the one who brought it up again just now. I'm just very opinionated about the best kinds."

He, of course, goes straight for the water, while I reach for not only a blue Powerade but also a Diet Coke. I can tell he's judging my choices, but I'm judging his right back, so I suppose that makes us even.

"Well, remind me not to bring it up again. I'm not sure I can take much more of this," he decides as he follows me into the candy aisle.

I, of course, start reaching for a wide variety from Skittles to M&M's, making sure to grab a little of each. "Sorry, Bennett, but I just don't see that happening. I'm a verified foodie, and if we're going to make the most of this trip, we're going to be eating out a lot. I mean, are you really going on vacation if you don't hit up all the best local hole-in-the-wall places?" I continue, but he doesn't seem to hear me as his vision focuses on all the treats I've managed to stuff into my arms.

"Think you got enough there?" he asks, eyebrows raised and eyes wide. Does he have to look that disgusted? It's not like I'm planning on eating it all in one sitting... or at least, probably not.

"Nope," I reply, popping the p. "In fact, would you mind going and grabbing me one of those little baskets near the front?"

"You're ridiculous." He huffs, but instead of forcing me to carry it all, he begrudgingly does as asked and makes his way over before returning, basket in hand. I plop the small bag of green sour straws that I'd just reached for inside, and instead of grabbing the basket like I'm sure he expects, I dump my small haul inside.

While I know it's something he can handle, given those strong muscles of his, especially visible in that tight black top, he seems surprised by the sudden action as he falls forward. "No, no way. This is your candy haul. You take it," he insists, but I just keep walking, ignoring his request as I grab a Carmello and toss it into the basket. "Veronica," he calls after me, and while he could easily drop the basket and refuse, he continues to follow.

"What?" I innocently ask as I walk around the aisle, ready to add some salty snacks into the mix.

"You're seriously not going to carry this?" he asks, stunned.

"Why would I carry it when I have such a *big, strong, manly man* like you to carry it for me?" I tease, laying on a Southern Belle accent as I place a hand dramatically over my chest and bat my lashes. "Oh, bless my heart, the very thought of lifting it myself," I add, raising my hand to fan my face, "it's just too much to bear!"

He isn't amused as he shoots me a deadpan stare. "Okay, you can cut the helpless act you've got going on. I've seen you in action. You're more than capable of taking care of yourself," he shoots back, raising a challenging brow in my direction.

"Okay, fine. *Maybe* I just don't *want* to carry it." I casually shrug as I grab a bag of Lays potato chips and toss it into the basket. "Plus, weren't you the one yesterday who was so worried about my eating habits? Shouldn't it make you happy to see that my appetite is back and that you're playing such a vital role in making it happen?"

"Maybe that would be true if this wasn't exactly like the whole Skittles debacle from yesterday. What's the point of eating if you're only going to fill your body with garbage?"

"Well, you know what they say," I casually add, grabbing some Salt and Vinegar chips to add to the mix as well. "One man's trash is another man's treasure, and junk food is definitely my treasure."

"How do you even plan to eat all of this?" he asks, his eyes glancing between me and my basket of goodies.

"It's not like I plan to eat it all today." I scoff, as if he's being so ridiculous, and honestly, he kind of is. Who wouldn't want to fill up on yummy food and snacks on their vacation? It's practically a rite of passage. "This is for the whole trip, or at least until I need to make another pit stop," I add in jest, nudging my hip into his.

"You're ridiculous."

"Nope, you're the one who is ridiculous," I tease, giving his chest a playful poke. "If you think for even one second I'm going to share any of this with you after all those snarky comments, you're out of your mind. I highly suggest you grab a snack or two for yourself before we check out; otherwise, you're going to have a pretty depressing drive."

"Fine," he grumbles, reaching for a bag of pretzels.

"Oh my God." I laugh, shaking my head. "That's really what you chose? Actually, you know what, it all makes sense." Sure, there are likely healthier choices than pretzels—he could have gone for a protein bar or something similar, but out of all the snacks, he actively chose pretzels. "You truly are the most boring person on this planet. You are doing very little to dispel me from thinking you truly are an old man in a hot dude's body."

"Okay, come on now. I'm sure there are plenty of people more boring than me out there," he huffs, seeming to ignore the rest of what I just said, and likely for good reason.

"Not really. Then again, you are a dog daddy, so I suppose you have that working in your favor," I concede, reaching for a bag of dill-flavored sunflower seeds. "But I'm not sure that totally invalidates the fact that you absolutely refuse to have fun or even smile."

"I smile," he challenges, clearly defensive. "And I know how to have fun. Just because my form of fun doesn't involve doing something illegal doesn't mean I don't know how to have it."

"Okay then, Mr. Ball of 'Fun,' what exactly does Miles Bennett do when he's out there having this so-called '*fun*?'"

"Hanging out with my buddies, watching games on TV, going to concerts, driving around, fixing cars..." he trails off, clearly trying—but failing—to come up with more.

"Fixing cars?" I smile, turning to face him. "That's your job. And while I'm glad you're doing something you love, if that's on your very short list of what you find fun, you're clearly not a very fun person." Okay, so maybe I'm being a little mean here, but until yesterday, I could count on one hand the number of times Miles Bennett had done or said something nice to me.

Plus, he's a certified grump. While I can understand some of his need to be standoffish and broody, given what I know about his childhood from Blair, I don't think that gives him the right to be mean or, oftentimes, outright cruel.

I know I got his sister into trouble from time to time, but it's not like we ever ended up in jail or faced any serious consequences. It was all just silly, harmless fun. What else do you expect from a bunch of kids and teenagers stuck in a small town? When there isn't much to do, you have to create your own entertainment, and we definitely did just that.

"Oh, so you don't enjoy your job?" he challenges.

"I love my job," I happily admit. Being an art teacher is a dream come true for someone who has always had a passion for creating and sharing that joy with others. "But that doesn't mean when someone asks me what I do for fun, I'd say teaching at the high school."

"Well, that sounds like a you problem," he says, walking past me toward the register, clearly trying to nudge me toward checking out without grabbing anything else. "Plus, it's not just working on other people's cars that I enjoy. I also enjoy rebuilding them for myself. That car out front that we're driving," he says, nodding toward where we left the car parked, "I fixed it up myself."

"Really?" I ask, reaching for one last bag of beef jerky before chasing after him.

In many ways, I can't say I'm surprised by what he just told me. While the two of us happily avoided each other, I do remember him sticking around after school to work in the auto body shop. Then as soon as he turned eighteen and graduated, he went straight to working at the local mechanic shop before buying out the owner when he retired.

As someone who's always had a lifelong love for the arts, I completely understand choosing a career that sparks joy and fuels your passion. It makes all the difference, especially when all those minor inconveniences crop up that make you want to quit right then and there. But I suppose I never realized just how deep his passion went.

Then again, Evergreen does have quite a few old clunkers driving around, even if none look as good or are in as pristine condition as his. Plus, the fact that many of those cars you see still driving around are likely only doing so because they have Miles there to fix them and make it all possible.

Given that Miles and Blair's parents weren't the most beloved people in town—Mrs. Bennett ran off before Blair's second birthday, and Mr. Bennett made a fool of himself as the town drunk—a lot of people looked at the two Bennett children and saw nothing but a problem, especially when I did little to help Blair's case, as the two of us made a point of becoming known as the town's notorious trouble-makers.

Obviously, none of the stuff we did was malicious, but still. I can see why most people chose to look negatively on her instead of me, especially when my dad was the well-known and beloved town mayor. It really isn't much of a surprise that Miles took the opposite approach and has gone out of his way to show that he's nothing like either of his parents. Sure, he's perpetually grumpy and broody, but everyone knows he's the go-to guy for any of your mechanical needs.

"Yeah, but don't go thinking I'm looking for you to see me differently or that I'm fishing for some sort of compliment. I'm just trying to prove a point. Just because I fix cars for my job doesn't mean it's not also a hobby. Come on, you can't tell me you never work on any projects outside of work?" he presses.

I twist my mouth to the side and wrinkle my nose. He's got me there.

"Okay, fine. Maybe I dabble a little here and there," I lie, because art is my life. While I didn't have as much time to fully dedicate to my passion as I would've liked when Pete and I were together—especially not when we were engaged—it was something I would've loved to focus on more.

"Yeah, sure." He half-laughs, half-scoffs as we move up in line and he starts to unload our huge haul onto the counter.

It's fairly obvious the clerk is judging us, and even as Miles sends me an annoyed glance I don't let it deter me. I'm finally starting to feel like myself again, and if buying a shitload of junk-food is what's going to make me happy, then I'm going to do it.

I let Pete squash my happiness for far too long, and while I don't think it's his intention, I refuse to let Miles do it as well.

"Alright, that will be seventy-eight sixty-three," the cashier says, doing his best to put all the snacks into one bag, but clearly failing as he's forced to pull out a second one.

"We're really spending seventy dollars on snacks?" Miles asks, still stuck in disbelief at the total.

"No, *I'm* spending seventy dollars on snacks, and *you* will be sitting there all sad and depressed the entire drive with your sad little water and pretzels," I hush him, tapping my card on the small reader to pay.

"Wait," he says, grabbing my hand to stop me, but it's too late as it dings to let me know the payment was accepted. "I wanted to take care of this."

I turn to face him. "I get that you feel bad for me, Bennett, but you gotta stop. I'm the one who left him, not the other way around. In fact, I'm starting to think I'd almost prefer it if you went back to hating and being annoyed at every single thing I say," I admit, gladly reaching out for the bags as the cashier hands them over the counter. "You paying for my hotel was more than enough. Hell, putting the miles on your car is already way too much. I'm just happy that you're here. So please, let me pay for things, too."

That thankfully has him relenting as he follows after me. I head toward the entrance door and hold it open for him as we step outside. "Fine, but it did only feel fair, given that you just paid for the gas," he mutters. "And for the record, you annoy me, but I wouldn't go as far as saying I ever hated you," he casually suggests as he heads toward the driver's seat while I take my spot as the resident passenger princess.

"Well, you've never road-tripped or been forced to spend more than a day or two around me, so let's save your opinions on how much you hate or dislike me until the end of our little adventure. There's still plenty of time for me to change your opinion on that one," I playfully advise as I set the bags to the side and buckle myself in.

"True, but one thing I can promise you, princess. If you spill any of that shit or stain the interior of my car, I will *definitely* hate you."

"Noted."

4

MILES

As yet another Taylor Swift song blares through the car's speakers, I do my best not to groan. Veronica had told me that she didn't want me to feel sorry for her or offer her any special treatment, but at the time, letting her pick the next playlist felt like the least I could do.

I guess I didn't fully realize what I was signing up for. But, honestly, that's on me. I should've at least suspected, since Blair's also been obsessed with Taylor for years. The two even throw personal listening parties for every new album release—even if many of the more recent ones had to be over video calls. I guess where I really went wrong in all this was assuming that some of Blair's more eclectic musical taste would rub off on her best friend. Blair has spent the last decade traveling with some of the biggest, most influential bands in the world—so, naturally, I thought her friend might develop a slightly more adventurous musical palette. But apparently, I was wrong.

Unfortunately, I don't see her switching it up anytime soon as I glance over and see her singing—or rather, screaming along—to *I Can Do It with a Broken Heart*, her hair blowing majestically in the wind, her hands moving artistically to the melody. I'd probably find it kind of cute if it weren't so damn annoying all at the same time.

My mood worsens when a car full of men—probably fresh off a weekend of questionable decisions in Las Vegas—slows down in the fast lane of Interstate-15 and the men start dancing and leering at her like they're auditioning for the world's sleaziest boy band.

She might find it amusing as she shimmies her shoulders their way, but I'm nowhere near as entertained. Lifting my foot from the pedal, I let our car slow down, forcing them to officially pass us.

The assholes aren't the only ones disappointed as she turns to look at me, mouth open in shock, as she brushes some of her snarled strands behind her ear. "What was that for? We were having fun." She sulks, my eyes dipping toward her pink pouty lips before I force my attention back to the road ahead.

"Those guys were probably a bunch of married assholes with nothing better to do than stare at a gorgeous woman. I did you a favor," I assure her.

Her open mouth closes, and her lips curl into a smile. "A gorgeous woman, huh?" she smirks, nudging her elbow into my arm.

"Oh, come on. You know you're stunning. It's the rest of you that needs some work," I shoot back, mostly joking, but I see the way my words land as she falls back into her seat, her excitement from earlier evaporating.

I know I shouldn't feel bad, but I do, and I fucking hate it. Then again, I'm used to feeling this way around her. She's always found a way to get under my skin, and while she should already know she's not my favorite—she even pointed it out earlier—I'm also not looking to be intentionally cruel, especially when yesterday was likely one of the worst days of her entire life.

"Hey, I shouldn't—" I start, but she interrupts.

"Oh my God, there it is! We have to stop!" she shouts.

My eyebrows furrow. "What?" I ask, turning my head to look at her. We're in the middle of the desert—what could possibly be worth stopping for?

She rolls her eyes as if I'm the densest person in the world. "The world's largest thermometer. We have to stop and take a picture next to it. It's a Prescott family tradition."

"That thing?" I ask, feeling less than impressed as I spot a giant white figure in the not-so-far distance. "That looks like some old piece of shit."

"It is, but that's what makes it so wonderful all at the same time. Please," she begs, reaching out and wrapping her hands around my bicep. While I'm fully aware of the touch, she quickly seems to think better of it and folds her hands back into her lap. "Come on. We have to stop."

I let out an annoyed breath, but once again, I find it impossible to say no to her. "Fine. We can stop. But don't even think about somehow turning this into another excuse to grab more snacks."

Most of the drive has been her blasting Taylor's music, but when she wasn't doing that, she was making her way through her collection of snacks. I know I shouldn't let it get to me, but damn, it was annoying as hell. Every time she opens a new bag, she grabs one or two pieces, pops them in her mouth like some kind of sample, then moves on to the next as if the previous one never existed.

"Party pooper," she shoots my way, sticking out a playful tongue in my direction. Instead of being annoyed like I normally would be, I press my lips together to suppress a smile as I roll my eyes once more.

"Oh my God, was that a smile?" she asks, in mock shock.

I press my lips together even tighter. "I don't know what you're talking about. You aren't even funny," I say, finding it much easier to insult her. Thankfully she can see right through the sarcasm, as her smile only grows.

"Oh, I never claimed to be funny, but I just made *the* Broody Bennett smile, and for me, that's a win. In fact, I think my next road trip game is going to be seeing how many times I can break through that tough-guy facade of yours and make you smile."

"Hey, I smile," I say, defending my honor. Okay, no, I'm not exactly the smiliest person out there, but that's not my fault. If anything, it's the world that's screwed me over and never given me much of a reason to want to smile.

I also can't help that I have whatever the man's version of resting bitch face is. It's just how my face looks, and beyond that, when it comes to the life I was dealt, I don't exactly feel as though I was given the easiest hand. If I had something worth smiling over, I would, but most of the time, I just don't.

"Then why did you stop the moment I called you out on it?" she challenges, reaching into her giant bag of goodies and pulling out a Red Vine as she taps me on the shoulder with it.

I grunt in response before letting out a small huff of air as we near the exit of her world-famous thermometer. "Are you really serious about stopping?" I ask instead, nodding toward the thing that looks even more ridiculous and junky the closer we get.

"Of course I'm serious. That thing is a true landmark, and it must be admired for its grandeur and beauty," she declares before biting into her treat, which I'm sure is also filled with way too much red food dye and sugar.

This has to be one of the most ridiculous things I've ever considered. It feels like a complete waste of time, but given that we're not on any sort of schedule... What the hell, why not? At the very least, taking this detour puts more distance between us and those creeps who were leering at Veronica, so there's that.

As we hit the exit, I feel a new smile tugging at my lips as her excitement seems to build. She's practically bouncing in her seat, and as much as I hate to admit it, her energy is strangely contagious. "Oh, come on. Admit it," she pressures. "This is exciting, and you know you're dying to stop."

"I wouldn't go as far as calling it exciting, but I suppose I am interested in getting a bit closer to see what all the fuss is about."

"You're going to love it. I promise," she says. But as I look at the rundown town of Baker, I'm even less sure what she sees in this place. To me, it looks like a total dump, but as much as I hate to admit it—even to myself—if this puts a genuine smile on her face, I'll do it.

Pulling into a small rundown lot, I put the car in park. "So, what now?" I ask, still completely unimpressed, especially since, as we stare up at it, I can actually see that it is, in fact, a giant-ass thermometer.

"We get out," she says, unbuckling her seatbelt before running to get as close to it as she can, given the small fence around it.

I follow her lead and unbuckle. "This is seriously the weirdest fucking thing I've ever done in my life," I mutter to myself.

"Oh, come on, you love it," she calls back to me over her shoulder as she continues to race toward it.

"Quite the opposite, actually. I hate it," I deadpan.

She giggles, turning to face me as she stands next to the fence. "You know you fucking love it. Actually, I'm pretty convinced this is going to be the highlight of our entire trip."

"I hope not, because if that's the case, you're not exactly selling the rest of this vacation."

"Come on, Broody Bennett, can you at least pretend to enjoy this?" she asks, jutting out her hip as she places her hand on top of it.

"No," I say, especially since not only is this large-ass thermometer not living up to the hype, it's also windy as hell here, evidenced even more by the fact that her hair is blowing all over the place. But unlike me, she doesn't seem to mind as she pulls out her phone and begins to snap a selfie.

As much as I want to head back toward the car, I stick around and let her have her fun as I place my hands in my pockets and watch.

"Would you mind getting a picture of me?" she asks, pouting her lips as she looks up at me from under her lashes.

I let out an annoyed breath as I pull my hand out, phone and all. "I'm only taking one. I'm not Blair, and I'm not going to sit here looking for the perfect light and angle. You get what you get," I warn, turning on the camera app on my phone.

While I love my sister to death, I have nowhere near the same kind of patience that she does. She sees pictures as a form of art, but taking or even standing for photos just isn't my thing and it's something I avoid at all costs.

I suppose I can somewhat understand the need to capture a memory that you can hold onto forever, but given my history, I have very few memories I care to preserve. Even more so, standing in front of a weird hunk of stone that doubles as a giant thermometer is yet another thing I don't see myself caring to remember.

Posing for the photo, Veronica raises her hands above her head and smiles, a magnetic one that almost makes me want to smile back at her, but I resist. I click the small circle on my phone to capture the image before sliding it into my pocket. "Alright, got it."

Her face falls, looking less than amused as her hands drop to her sides. "You're not even going to let me see it?" she asks.

"No, because I'm not going to chance you hating it and somehow convincing me to take another."

"Oh," she starts, tilting her head as a devious grin appears on her face. "So you're saying that you could, in fact, be convinced?"

"No," I promise her, realizing just how much that particular word keeps popping out of my mouth. But while I've done my best to be nice, a guy can only do so much.

"Fine." She sighs, thankfully giving up. "But what about posing next to me and the two of us taking a selfie to commemorate the moment? I mean, how else in the world would I ever convince anyone that I got you to stop and take a picture in front of such a ridiculous landmark?"

"You know, you aren't exactly selling this to me, especially since *if* you did somehow convince me, there's no way I'm letting you post that anywhere. I don't do social media."

While a huge part of my sister's career is posting pictures and images on various accounts, I've done everything in my power to stay off that particular grid. Sure, like most other people out there, I've created an account, but for viewing purposes only. You'd never catch me dead posting on any of those sites.

"Okay, fine, this one will be for my own private collection," she agrees. I raise an eyebrow and she rolls her eyes. "Not like that, you perv. This spank bank is completely full."

While I'm tempted to laugh, I do my best to keep it in, even as a smile tugs at the corners of my mouth.

"Plus, come on. You know Blair would love it, and it'd likely earn you a few more bonus points in her eyes."

"I don't need bonus points," I assure her, even as I take a few steps forward. "I'm always going to be her favorite, but if this gets you to shut up about it, let's just do it and get it over with."

Miming the action, she pretends to zip her lips as she waits for me to join her. "You're going to have to get closer than that," she scolds, as I leave an inch or two of space between us. However, instead of waiting for me to do it, she slides in next to me and presses herself into my side. "Now smile," she demands, holding the phone down low to grab a picture of not only our faces but the large thermometer in the background.

"No," I tease her once more, but ultimately she wins this battle as she wraps her arm around my back and pokes me in the side with her hand.

"Hey," I call, but in doing so, the makings of a smile appear on my face just as she hits the button to capture the moment.

"Perfect!"

5

VERONICA

"BEHIND EVERY CLOSED DOOR *lies a story waiting to be unearthed. Join us in our relentless pursuit of truth, as we navigate the murky waters of deception, intrigue, and murder. Tune in next week for another chapter in the ever-unfolding saga as we seek justice for Marissa Wheeler. Until then, stay curious, stay safe, and keep questioning the narratives. The truth is out there, waiting to be discovered. You just have to be brave enough to look for it. Until next time, truth seekers.*"

"You really enjoy this shit?" Miles asks as the episode of my true crime podcast wraps up.

Shocked, my mouth drops open. "You don't?"

"Listening to people talk about the misfortunes of others, all while being reminded of how shitty and fucked up this world is? No, thanks."

My lips curl into a subtle pout. "So, I take it this means you don't want to listen to the next episode?"

Not only am I dying to find out what happens next, but it also made the last hour of our drive fly by. It was especially handy since this portion of the drive isn't exactly my favorite as we pass through the vast California desert.

"No, I really don't. This part of the drive is depressing enough. The last thing I need is to listen to the gruesome details of how someone went missing and is likely gone forever. What I don't get is how someone like you can be into all this."

I arch an eyebrow. "Someone like me?"

"Yes, someone like you. Little Miss Bubbly Princess with constant sunshine shooting out of her ass isn't exactly who I'd peg as someone who enjoys hearing about death and murder."

While part of me questions whether that should be taken as a compliment, I smile despite myself. "You know, women are pretty interesting creatures and are actually known for enjoying a diverse array of things. We're perfectly capable of loving Disney movies with their sweet love stories and happily ever afters, just as much as we enjoy the feeling of our hearts racing in anticipation as we listen to mysteries and unsolved crimes. If anything, we need this shit so we can better learn how to protect ourselves."

"I don't know. I still don't understand getting enjoyment out of listening to something so sad and depressing. For me, it only ramps up my anxiety since all I can think about is something like that happening to Blair."

I frown. "First off, nothing like that is ever going to happen to Blair. There's something about you badass Bennetts that gives off an air of 'don't mess with me or else,' and I'm pretty sure most people would be afraid to mess with Blair. And if someone did, we'd both go Liam Neeson on their ass and hunt them down," I remind him, doing my best to lighten the mood and ease his worry. "Secondly, I wouldn't necessarily say I get enjoyment out of it. It's sad and depressing a lot of the time, but I think it's important to know about these things and not forget that these kinds of tragedies do exist. These people deserve to be remembered, and their killers brought to justice."

"I don't know. It's still not my thing." He shrugs, focusing on the road while I rummage through my stash, reaching for the bag of Red Vines.

"It wasn't Pete's thing either," I admit, going against what I'd told him earlier as I offer one of the red sticks in his direction.

He looks over at me, his gaze drifting toward the candy, and while I think he's about to decline yet again, he ultimately lifts one hand from the wheel and accepts.

"You know, I'm not sure I like hearing that I possibly have something in common with your ex-fiancé," he says with a grimace before taking a bite.

I chuckle softly. "No worries there, because that's probably the only similar thing about the two of you."

While Miles has that tall, muscular blond thing going on, with a body to rival a Greek god, Pete feels like his exact opposite. Not that Pete's bad-looking—his warm brown, always neatly styled hair and green eyes make him the kind of handsome you'd proudly introduce to your parents and friends. But let's face it, if you were to line up Miles and Pete side by side, most women would gravitate toward Miles, even with his signature broody glare that practically screams, *I'm emotionally unavailable, but good luck resisting me*. Of course, that only adds to his appeal. Who doesn't want a mysterious bad boy who looks like he could bench-press you with one arm?

Okay, so maybe Miles isn't your textbook bad boy. Truth be told, I probably racked up way more detentions and made a million more questionable decisions in my teenage years than he ever did. But that certainly didn't stop the good people of Evergreen from painting him as some kind of rebel-without-a-cause. It's funny how being quiet and having sharp cheekbones can instantly make you more "dangerous" in a small town. Okay, that, and his family's stigma. But even with him doing absolutely nothing to warrant such a reputation, everyone seemed to go out of their way to avoid him.

"I guess I should feel relieved about that. Dude's a fucking loser. I still don't understand how you almost got married to him, let alone dated him," he says with a small shiver.

"I don't know," I say, barely above a whisper, doing my best not to let his words sting as my smile instantly falters. Sure, he has a point, but that doesn't mean the pain isn't still a little too fresh.

He looks over at me, his face falling with realization. "Vee," he says, remorse written across his features. "I'm sorry. It's none of my business. I shouldn't have said anything."

"No, it's fine. I *was* stupid. I don't even know why it took me so long to see just how wrong we were for each other—"

Before I can say another word, he cuts me off, his voice sharp as his blue eyes burn with intensity as he glances my way. "You shouldn't think like that. None of this is on you, not one bit. This is all him. He's the one to blame. He's the one who's broken. That guy couldn't be right for anyone, not now, not ever, because he's a selfish, narcissistic asshole who's been that way since we were kids. He doesn't care about anyone but himself, and he never will."

My brows furrow in surprise. I figured Miles would jump at the chance to chew me out and tell me how stupid I've been. After all, he's never had a problem calling me out for all the dumb choices I made while growing up.

"I just wish I hadn't missed all those early red flags," I carefully answer. Clearly, Miles would love to put all the blame on Pete, but *I'm* the one responsible for my own decisions, and *I'm* the one who chose him as a partner. This is on *me*, even if I wish I could place the blame elsewhere.

"You think you're the first person he ever manipulated?" he asks with a loud scoff. "I may not have put myself out there in high school, but I watched and kept a close eye on the people and things going on around me, and he's fooled plenty of people over the years. I'm sure that's exactly why he does so well in politics. He's good at showing people the persona he wants them to see, when in reality, he's got his own sick ideas and agenda going on behind the scenes."

I bristle, sitting up straight, and feeling oddly protective. "You know, not all people in politics are horrible. My dad's a genuinely good guy and wants nothing but the best for the people of Evergreen Grove."

"Your dad is the exception. Most people aren't like him," he explains, and I can feel a gradual smile returning to my face. But as my thoughts linger on my dad, the smile quickly fades, replaced almost immediately with a frown.

"Ugh, I don't even want to think about this anymore. As hard as it is to think about Pete, I feel even worse and guilty about how I left. I didn't even tell my parents what I was doing before I ran. Can you believe that?"

"I don't think you need to worry about them," Miles tries to assure me, reaching out to give my knee a light pat. But his words do little to ease the anxiety bubbling inside me.

"I let them pay for an entire wedding just to bolt. I can't even imagine how they're feeling," I say, my voice trembling as I turn to stare out the window, tears stinging the corners of my eyes. Sure, I managed to send a quick text to let them know I was okay and safe, but I've yet to bring myself to pick up the phone when it rings. The thought of hearing their voices—hurt, confused, disappointed—feels like way more than I can handle.

"If your parents are as amazing as Blair says, I'm sure they're more relieved than anything. You're lucky. Not everyone has parents who give a shit about them, and if they've seen the side of Pete that I know he's shown the rest of us, then I'm sure no amount of money is worth the relief they must feel at not having to watch their daughter marry some asshole."

Great, now I get to feel horrible about this too. Here I am complaining to the guy with the world's shittiest parents. Sure, he could be wrong, and my parents could be fuming over the amount of money that was put into my wedding, but even with the guilt eating me alive, deep down, I know without a doubt that my parents still love me. They're probably disappointed, maybe even resentful right now, but eventually, they'll come around. Not everyone has that kind of certainty, and for that, I'm blessed.

"And please don't use this moment to apologize to me too," he says, apparently reading my mind. While I'm used to having this kind of connection with his sister, I can't say I ever expected Miles Bennett to know me just as well. "I'm not looking to get into a game of who has it worse. All that matters is I have Blair, and she's all the family I need."

"What if I wasn't going to apologize, huh?" I ask, deciding to go the immature route as I take an over-exaggerated bite of my Red Vine. "Maybe you don't know me as well as you think you do."

"You were Blair's shadow growing up..." he starts, but pauses, taking a moment to correct himself. "Or maybe she was yours, but just like I said, I've always been good at paying attention to the people around me. That's precisely why every single time the two of you got yourselves into trouble, I knew it was you at the helm, even if everyone else always liked to pin the blame on Blair."

"You know that was never my intention, right? To get her in trouble, I mean. I love Blair, and I'd never do anything to purposely hurt her or make her life harder."

"It may not have ever been your intention, but sometimes when you make shitty choices, you have to deal with the consequences. In fact, I think that's always been your problem. You don't think things through, you just do it and deal with the repercussions later," he says, a clear sense of bitterness lacing his tone.

I open my mouth to argue, but it's hard to deny that he has a point as my chest tightens, the guilt nearly suffocating me. "I'm sorry I hurt you, and I'm sorry I've hurt Blair," I say, my voice shaking. "God, and I'm so fucking sorry for dragging you into my mess and forcing you on this stupid road trip with me. If you want, we can turn around. Or just—just drop me off at the nearest airport or car rental place. I'll figure it out from there," I add, my emotions reaching their breaking point as they finally spill over.

"Stop, Veronica," he commands, his jaw hardening as he shakes his head. "This is exactly what I'm talking about. You don't always have to make such rash decisions based on temporary feelings that are bound to change. And sorry to break it to you, but you're not getting rid of me that easily. We're going on this goddamn road trip, and I'm going to Disneyland with or without you," he continues, the corners of his mouth lifting into a smile as he attempts to lighten the tense atmosphere I've created.

"You actually want to hang out with me now?" I ask, not even remotely convinced.

"I wouldn't go *that* far. I'm in it for the rides, the ocean, and those amazing Disneyland churros you've been raving about. You're just the consolation prize."

"If you say so." As glad as I should be that he's not chomping at the bit to get rid of me, all my brain can focus on is how he just psychoanalyzed me—and the worst part is, he was dead on.

"You want to listen to some more Taylor, or maybe another episode of that weird-ass podcast?" he asks, clearly trying to cheer me up.

"No, you pick," I say, letting my head rest against the window. "I think I might try to take a nap."

"You sure?"

"Yep," I say, closing my eyes.

I need a break, and I'm sure he needs one from me as well. Just because he's attempting to be nice doesn't mean he actually cares. This conversation only reminded me that the two of us aren't actually friends, nor does he probably want to be. He's only sticking this out because he feels like he has to. That, or he really does want to explore California, and I'm his excuse. Like usual, I'm nothing more than an inconvenience who continually makes his life harder. Apparently, some things never change.

6

MILES

I'M AN ASSHOLE. THE worst part is, I actually feel guilty this time. I've never cared about hurting someone's feelings, especially not Veronica's. It's not that I don't stand by what I said, but I get that now isn't the time or place.

Do I think she needs to be coddled for life? Hell no. However, she does deserve a break before shit totally hits the fan. With us living in a town where everyone feels entitled to have opinions about everyone's lives and misfortunes, she's going to get plenty of that when she gets home. She doesn't also need that from me, especially not when she's so obviously trying to run away from all of it.

I need to apologize, but it's clear she's done with this conversation and I'm not sure she's even in a place where she can be apologized to, or if she'd even accept it. She's beating herself up, and while I believe she totally brought all of this on herself with her horrible decision-making, I'm not looking to make things worse.

As her eyes close, it's hard to ignore the weight behind the gesture. This so-called "nap" is less about rest and more about shutting me out, and honestly, I can't blame her. I'd been a complete asshole. I try to focus on the road, but my attention keeps flickering back to her. Her breathing finally evens out, soft and steady, signaling that despite everything going on, she's somehow managed to fall asleep.

As I glance over once more, I can't help but notice how adorable she looks, curled up on the seat with her legs tucked into her stomach. While I've never let myself see her in that light, I get why people do. She's like a modern-day Disney Princess with her big, round brown eyes, petite button nose, and perfectly plump, kissable lips

Not that I want to think about her or her lips.

Not only is she Blair's best friend, but she's been nothing but a constant source of irritation throughout my entire life. Veronica Prescott is not my type.

If things were incredibly different and I was looking for nothing more than a one-night stand like I do in my normal day-to-day life, then sure, maybe it could happen. I could've found myself drawn in by her outgoing personality, but given who we are and how much I know about her, she's not only not my type, but most importantly, Blair would kill us.

Okay, maybe she wouldn't go that far—after all, there was a time long ago, back when we were just kids in elementary school, where she joked about Veronica and me getting married so she and her best friend could officially be sisters. But those days are long gone. Now I'm pretty sure Blair's main concern would be the fallout if I ever so much as thought about hurting her best friend.

I know Blair loves me and we're as close as two siblings can be, but without a doubt, if I were ever to truly hurt her best friend, she'd one hundred percent take Veronica's side.

Thankfully, those thoughts are interrupted as the view changes and we return to civilization. I consider waking Veronica up to show her the new scenery, but her peaceful expression stops me. I know she didn't sleep well the night before, and I'm guessing sleep is more important than watching us drive through some random Southern California cities.

Without my co-pilot to guide me, I turn on the GPS on my phone, eventually getting the alert that we're only ten minutes away from the ocean. While I'm sure she'd be fine missing out on the rest, I have to imagine this is something she'd actually be excited for. I know I have a tendency to hide my excitement, but I'm strangely stoked to see the ocean for the first time.

It actually feels somewhat monumental, which is why I do my best not to startle her as I place my hand on her shoulder. "Vee," I say softly, my voice barely more than a whisper. She exhales slowly, her eyelids staying shut as she gently tilts her head away from the window.

How does she somehow look even cuter, especially as her perfectly plump lips pout out in her sleep. I shake off the thought, quickly regaining my composure as I clear my throat and tap her shoulder a little harder. "Vee," I try again, and her eyelids slowly flutter open. "Morning, sunshine," I say, noticing the brief moment of confusion on her face as she returns from whatever dreams had overtaken her for the last part of our drive.

"How long was I out for?" she manages, her voice rough with sleep as she reaches up to wipe the sleepiness away from her eyes.

"A couple of hours."

"Are you serious?!" she asks, sitting up straight in her chair as she looks out the window.

"Yeah, I think your body needed the rest. That, or your body needed a break from eating all that junk you've been consuming," I tease, hoping to start things off on a fresh note. Yes, I still feel bad, and I want to apologize at some point, but right now, I just want to see her to be happy and excited again, especially as we near our destination.

"Ha, ha!" she scoffs, saying the words as if to somehow prove that my joke wasn't funny, despite the fact that she's got a giant smile on her face that says otherwise. "So where are we, anyway?" she asks, her head swiveling from window to window as she tries to place our location.

"Uh, I'm not entirely sure," I admit, since unfortunately trying to navigate all these freeway changes on my own has me all mixed up. "But according to the GPS we should be arriving at the ocean in... eight minutes," I say after checking once more.

"Oh my God, are you serious?!" she loudly squeals, and I scrunch my forehead at the noise. Given that I've lived with a younger sister for a lot of my life—who acts an awful lot like the one next to me—one would think I'd be used to that kind of reaction. But nope, still annoying as hell.

"Yep." I nod, doing my best not to look over again, especially since the traffic here is insane. In Evergreen Grove, two people meeting at a stoplight at the same time is considered a traffic jam, so for a small-town guy like me, this is a bit overwhelming.

I've, of course, driven to Denver and attended some sporting events and concerts there. I've even traveled to some of the bigger cities to spend time with Blair when she was working, but in those cases, I flew and was ultimately driven around. This is definitely a whole new ball game and something I never could've truly prepared myself for.

Luckily, with Veronica now awake, she takes over as the navigator, making my life much easier as she tells me when and where to turn.

"Aw, there it is!" she squeals again, pointing the short distance ahead, and this time, even the high-pitched noise can't bring me down. Driving down a hill, the sight of the endless blue ocean merging with the sky on the horizon creates a mesmerizing view.

I wasn't sure what to expect, but this is pretty damn amazing.

"You know, you don't always have to do that," Veronica says, eyeing me with a giant smirk on her face.

My eyebrows knit together. "Don't have to do what?"

"Try to hold back your excitement. It's okay for you to smile and be happy every so often," she says, casually shrugging.

"I don't do that. I just don't usually have any good reasons to smile." I grumble, sitting up straighter as my hands tighten on the wheel. Okay, so maybe there are times where it feels weird to be happy, and like I need to hide it. It just tends to feel like the second something good happens in my life, it immediately gets taken away. I've long since learned to not let myself get excited about anything.

Much of my life has been filled with disappointment after disappointment, leading to the unwavering belief there's no point in seeking happiness, since it never lasts for long anyway.

"Seeing the ocean for the first time is more than enough of a reason to smile," she suggests. As we get closer and Veronica opens her window to let the ocean breeze drift in, I surprisingly find myself agreeing with her for once.

"Well, let's just get there first and then I'll decide what I really think," I offer. While this feels like a bucket-list moment, from what I've heard, the Pacific Ocean gets pretty cold this time of year, not to mention the sand getting everywhere. Knowing my luck, this will be yet another disappointment in my life.

Thankfully, she doesn't press the issue, and focuses instead on giving directions until we reach a parking lot by the water.

Veronica wastes no time, swiftly getting out of the car, lifting her feet one after the other to pull off her shoes, and tossing them into the sand as she runs toward the water.

Maybe it's the fact that she took a nap, but I have nowhere near as much energy as she does. I take my time, stretching before following her out. Continuing to take my time, I undo my work boots, and remove my socks before carefully setting them aside and I follow her out onto the sand.

I've walked in a sandbox before and felt the sensation of the soft, grainy sand between my toes, but this sensation is truly unique, and like nothing I've ever experienced before. Between that, the warm salty breeze, and the sound of waves crashing, I can't help it—I'm truly happy and very little could ruin this once-in-a-lifetime opportunity.

Veronica was right—this moment is everything.

7

VERONICA

THERE IS A SPECIAL kind of magic in witnessing some-one's first encounter with the ocean. As the car got closer to our destination, I watched him slip into his usual Broody Bennett routine, but seeing him walk on the sand and feel it beneath his feet for the first time is truly awe-inspiring.

I wonder if this is like one of those moments that parents always brag about. The kind where they say Christmas is great, but you don't truly get to experience the real magic of it all until you see it through the eyes of a young child. I'm not sure how true that is, but I have to say, if it's anything like this, maybe they have a point.

While I can't exactly remember my first trip to the ocean, I've seen the pictures of my parents holding my hands as they walked with me on the sand. I also remember all the other fun trips my family took as I got older, each of those memories holding a special place. But I have a feeling this trip will now hold the top spot in my heart from here on out.

He looks genuinely happy, something I'm not sure I've ever seen from him. Sure, it's easy to tell that his smiles are hardly ever fake when he's around Blair, but that's been about it.

The beach isn't completely deserted; a few random people are scattered about, but as the evening approaches and the temperature dips, I'm grateful for the chance to enjoy this moment with just the two of us in our own little area.

"So, are you actually going to put your feet in, or what?" I call out to him as I walk backward, feeling the cool, wet sand cling to my skin with each step as I near the water.

"I'm coming. I'm just—taking it all in."

With a small nod and a smile fixed firmly in place, I watch him do just that. But for me, it's him I can't seem to take my eyes off of.

When he reaches me, he glances down at his jeans with a hint of regret, clearly weighing the battle between keeping them pristine and getting them wet. With a dramatic sigh, he bends and rolls them up over his muscular legs as high as they'll go. I can't help but feel a tiny pang of gratitude for my own foresight, having chosen a pair of orange and pink striped shorts, leaving most of my legs bare. Not to mention, I'd even taken an overly long shower the night before—most of which I'd spent in tears—and made sure to shave. Small victories!

"You know you didn't have to wait for me," he suggests as he stands, once again taking in the vast ocean in front of us.

"I get it, but experiences like this are always so much better when you have someone to share them with," I admit, carefully leaving out the part about how I've been far more captivated by him, than the actual ocean.

He appears skeptical but shrugs, choosing not to call me out on it.

"Whatever you say," he says before finally walking to the edge of the sand, where the first small wave breaks on the shore, only inches away from our bare toes.

"Come on," I say, no longer able to stand his slow pace. I reach for his hand and yank him toward the water, just as another small wave breaks nearby, its foamy water skirting up and covering the tops of our feet.

It's comical, as we both react to the shock of the cool water. I let out a loud screech while he intakes an audible breath of air as we jump back together.

"Shit, that's cold." He chuckles as we watch the water retreat back out to sea, before a new fresh wave comes barreling toward us. Luckily, we're both a bit more prepared this time.

"Well, it's still a bit early in the season for most people to want to swim, but don't worry, you'll get used to it," I assure him. While a few other brave souls are in the water, the majority of the crowd is smart enough to enjoy the rest of the evening lounging on beach chairs and towels. "It'll be even better tomorrow when we come earlier, while the sun's still out."

"I don't know, this is pretty fucking cold. I don't think I can handle much more than this," he insists, just as a larger wave crashes in. We scramble to inch back, but the water splashes over us, soaking the rolled-up bottoms of his jeans.

"Oh, come on, Broody Bennett," I tease, realizing that our hands are still interlocked. Instead of dropping it, I do my best to inch him further out, as the water moves from covering the top of my feet to my ankles.

"No way. I didn't come dressed for this," he insists. However, he doesn't release my grip; instead, he weakly fights back, lightly tugging me toward him.

"Come on. Your clothes can dry. This is your first time at the beach. You need to take advantage of this monumental moment," I beckon, and he finally gives in, taking a step forward.

"Can't we just come back tomorrow?" he whines, still not entirely sold on this, even as we inch even deeper into the water, our clothes getting a bit more soaked as another wave crashes over us, with a few more droplets of water hitting my bare thigh.

"Oh, we're coming back tomorrow, but you only ever get one first time at the beach," I encourage. "Come on, don't tell me you're afraid of a little water," I tease, finally dropping his hand as I lean down to splash some water toward him, the droplets hitting the bottom of his shirt.

"Seriously, Vee?" he asks, using the nickname that I've only ever heard him use once before, and only on this trip. I don't know why he refuses to go with Ronnie, like most other people in my life, but weirdly, it sounds surprisingly nice coming out of his mouth.

I shrug. "I mean, you're already more than a little wet. Just embrace it, Bennett."

He purses his lips, less than pleased, but I can see something going on in that brain of his, and part of me already suspects that I've poked the wrong bear.

"Embrace this," he finally says, lunging toward me.

I let out a loud yelp as his strong arms effortlessly wrap around my waist, and before I can even process what's happening, he hoists me up and slings me over his shoulder. "Miles

Bennett! What in the world do you think you're doing?" I squeal, half-laughing and half-panicking as he casually strolls deeper into the water.

"It's like you said, you're already wet. Just embrace it." And with the water now at his thighs, his hands grip my waist once more before tossing me into the water as I come down with a loud splash.

I'm sure I look like a wet dog as I thrash my way up and spit out the water that went into my mouth. Once I regain my composure and reorient myself, I narrow my eyes in his direction.

"You could have at least eased me into it. It's freezing." I laugh, despite the fact that I just got thrown into the fucking ocean. Maybe I should be mad or annoyed, but truthfully, it's sort of nice to watch Miles transform into the silly and carefree person he never gets to be.

"Honestly you should be grateful. Now you don't have to worry about slowly easing into it. Your body should now be used to it," he offers with a smug grin. I'm sure he knows exactly what he's started, because as soon as the words leave his mouth, he takes a step back, but I'm on him in seconds as I do my best to imitate a linebacker as I lunge toward him. With my arms wrapping around his middle, we both go crashing backward. Luckily this time, we're both more prepared as we anticipate the fall.

As the war between us escalates, everything else disappears. It doesn't matter that the water is freezing, or that the sun is setting. All that matters is that we're both laughing and finally letting go, releasing the heavy weight we've both seemingly been carrying for far too long.

It's only as we make our way back to the shore that we realize that many mistakes were made tonight. It's only April, after all, and while the sun is still setting, creating a beautiful spectacle of reds, oranges, and pinks across the massive sky, so has the temperature also dropped, and it's not just the water that's cold anymore.

Worst of all, we hadn't fully prepared for this impromptu beach trip by bringing any towels or blankets. Knowing that we were headed to California, I probably should've been smart enough to pack a beach towel or two, but since I'd been so paranoid about Pete stopping by to confront me, I packed as quickly as possible—beach towels and other necessities had, sadly, been left behind.

"Please tell me I'm not the only one having some major regrets right about now," Miles begs, and I have to admit, it's pretty comical to see him soaking wet. Not only is his tight white T-shirt practically see-through as it sticks to his skin, but I can't help but notice the way his blond locks cling so perfectly to his forehead and neck.

"You know what? No regrets. That was fun, and I can't say I ever expected to see that side of you," I decide, wrapping my arms around myself, and doing my best to wipe away the goosebumps forming as I run my hands up and down my arms.

"Oh, come on, you've seen me have fun before," he argues, rolling his eyes.

"Not like that. That was an entirely new Miles I saw out there. I think I even heard a true and genuine laugh," I add as we approach our shoes, neither of us eager to put them on. Instead, we grab them and continue our walk toward his car.

"Well, I'm not laughing anymore," he grumbles as we reach his parked Mustang. "Shit. We're going to ruin the interior."

"A little water won't hurt it. Plus, we'll just drive to the nearest hotel and check in there. We won't be in there for long."

He lets out one last, defeated sigh. "Fine, but if anything happens to my car, you're paying for it," he warns, pointing at me over the top of the car before sliding into the driver's seat.

"Just add it to my bill." I exhale, and while I do already feel like I'm going to be owing him, my parents, and quite a few others after this little trip, it all feels worth it.

Yes, I may be cold, wet, and shivering, but this was easily one of the best days I've had in quite some time, and was much needed after everything that happened with my wedding. And as for Broody Bennett? He can keep up this little act of his and pretend all he wants that we didn't have fun, but as I settle in and glance over, even he can't hide the happiness written all over his face. He's having a blast, and I plan on making sure the two of us continue to have the best vacation ever. We deserve this.

8

MILES

I'VE NEVER BEEN MORE grateful for a hot shower. I'm not sure what the people at the front desk thought when they saw two waterlogged individuals trudging into their fancy-shmancy lobby, but thankfully, they seemed to take pity on us. They were even kind enough to offer us a two-bedroom suite. But while I'm slowly finding Veronica less annoying, I'm not quite ready to take our friendship to that level. At least with the connecting room they offered instead, we still have some semblance of privacy.

Plus, it's probably best that we take a small break from each other. Sure, she's less annoying, but after spending an entire day in the car together, I feel like we've had more than enough quality time.

Emerging from the steam-filled bathroom, I rummage through my bag and retrieve a black short-sleeve button-up shirt and a fresh pair of jeans. It would have been more convenient had I unpacked first, but I was too damn cold to think about anything else as I hurriedly stripped out of my wet clothes where they're still sitting in a sopping wet pile in the middle of the bathroom. I decide to leave that problem for future Miles to deal with and grab my phone to check the latest text message from my sister.

> Blair: So, I got the picture Ronnie sent. Looking good. Although, I have to know how in the hell did she convince you to get in the ocean completely dressed?

> Miles: Oh, there was no convincing. I was all but forced as she pulled me in.

> Blair: Still. I'd be dead if I so much as tried to pull that, and I'm guessing since she was the one who sent the picture, that she's still alive... So once again, I have to ask how the hell did she manage that?

> Miles: The only thing keeping her alive at this point is the fact that she's your best friend and that, when wet, she looked like a sopping wet kitten. Even I have morals, and you know I can't kill a drowning cat.

Okay, so maybe that's not entirely true. It's starting to feel like I'm beyond just playing nice for Blair's sake or because of how her wedding day ended. Maybe that's how it started, but now I find myself doing whatever I can to see her smile, especially when it feels so damn good to know that I was the one who put it there.

Blair: Hmm, I'm not sure how she'd feel about being compared to a drowning cat. So, what else is on the agenda for tonight?

Miles: As long as the sensation comes back in my hands and feet, I think the plan is to go out for dinner. My body is craving something other than burgers and all the candy your friend force-fed me.

Blair: Are you really complaining about burgers and candy? You must be a load of fun. But seriously, though, it sounds like a blast.

Blair: Oh, and please keep the pictures coming. They're the only thing making me feel less guilty about not being there.

Miles: I'll try.

Even after I send the text, I know I won't actually be trying all that hard. Pictures aren't my thing, and I'm certainly not going to be the awkward lunatic in the middle of a crowded restaurant taking pictures of my food. I'll leave that to Veronica.

Plus, I'm pretty sure there will be no time to stare at my plate, since I can already imagine that the second I get some actual food in front of me I'm going to scarf it down. I'm starving, and I wasn't exaggerating when I told Blair about what we'd actually eaten on the road.

While Veronica had been fine munching on sweets all day, I had reached my limit before we finally stopped and went through a McDonald's drive-thru. However, a McDouble can only go so far, and I'm definitely looking for something less greasy and more sustaining.

Despite feeling hungry, I also feel oddly bloated and am eagerly looking forward to taking advantage of the on-site exercise room to go for a quick run tomorrow. Or who knows, maybe I'll go for a run on the beach. When in Rome, right?

Fully dressed and ready to go, I flop onto my bed and wait for Veronica to finish getting ready. Growing up with a younger sister taught me to always expect delays. No matter how much time you think they'll need, always plan for at least fifteen more minutes.

Then again, Blair has always been known for her perpetual lateness, so maybe Veronica will actually surprise me. However, with the two of them being so close, maybe it's best I don't hold on to any extra hope, even if my growling stomach is currently wishing for the best.

Trying to distract myself, I keep busy by doing something I promised I wouldn't do: Checking in with my work emails. There isn't much to look at, since it's just a mechanic shop in a very small town, but a guy can dream. I should be relieved that business seems to be carrying on as usual without me, and that the guys are holding down the fort while I'm away. However, something to distract myself with would've been nice, especially as another small grumble escapes my stomach.

A timid knock breaks the silence as I reach for my wallet and keys, stuffing them into my pocket before answering.

While I know exactly who to expect, it still shocks me to find Veronica standing in front of me. She looks stunning in a white sundress, with a light-blue sweater thrown over it, casually slipping off one shoulder. Her short brown hair is perfectly styled, half of it pulled back and fastened with an oversized white bow.

It's obvious she's wearing little to no makeup, with freckles visibly lining her nose. But as my eyes scan her from top to bottom I find it difficult not to stare. How big of an idiot did Pete West have to be to fumble this bag so badly?

Perhaps it's only because the last time I saw her, she was nothing more than a waterlogged mess, but now it's impossible to ignore the fact that she looks incredible. I know I need to look away, but I just can't get myself to follow through.

"So, what do you think?" she asks, clearly amused by my reaction as she lifts the ends of her dress and shimmies from side to side. "Am I still giving drowned cat?"

I roll my eyes. "Of course Blair would tell you."

"Duh! What did you expect? She tells me everything. Believe me, Broody Bennett, I know all your dirty little secrets," she teases with a wiggle of her eyebrows, even though I actually find myself wondering how much of that is the actual truth. Those two were attached at the hip growing up, and I wouldn't put it past Blair to share both the good and the bad with her best friend.

"Can we just go and get some dinner? I'm starving," I say, choosing to ignore the fact that she likely knows more about me than she should as I shut the door behind me. Plus, I'm not particularly in the mood to tell her just how good I think she looks. That's not the type of relationship we have, and I plan to keep it that way.

"Fine, but for the record, I'd say you clean up mighty nice there, too, but I don't know..." she trails off, following after me. "For you, I kind of liked the whole soaking-wet look you had going on. Who knew you had all those muscles underneath that shirt of yours?"

Once again, I decide to ignore her words and start the trek down the long hallway. I'm way too hungry for this.

"You really expect me to eat *that*? It looks like something Bubba threw up." I all but gag as I watch her pick up the oyster and slide the meat into her mouth.

"They're amazing. Seriously, just try it," she encourages after finishing, then grabs another one and pushes it toward me.

I'm sure I look like a little kid as my mouth twists in disgust, but can anyone truly blame me? That doesn't look like something that should go into *anyone's* mouth, let alone mine.

"Seriously, Bennett?" she asks, shaking her head. "Come on, I ate these when I was a little kid. Surely you can stomach one now as a thirty-one-year-old man."

"That's the thing. I'm no longer a kid who just puts anything in his mouth. I know what I like and what I don't, and just by looking at that, I can tell it's something I'll hate."

Maybe I should give it a chance, but given the visceral re-action I'm having just by looking at those things, I can only imagine the ammo I'd give her if I tried one. I'd likely not just gag, but also puke.

"Fine. More for me then," she happily decides as she sets the oyster back down on the platter, moving the whole thing closer to her. "But you know, they say that oysters are a natural aphrodisiac."

I'm not sure why she thinks that's some kind of draw, and my face says it all as I raise an eyebrow once again in her direction. "Are you planning on getting some action tonight?" I ask, my gag reflex tested all over again as I watch her slide yet another one into her mouth.

"Who knows?" she says, shrugging one shoulder, a wicked smile appearing on her face. "I'm a single woman now. Plus, they say the best way to get over someone is to get under someone else, so maybe that's exactly what I need to be doing."

My lips curl into a frown. "You really think that's a good idea?" I ask, raising my glass of wine to my lips. Sure, I was the one who brought it up initially, but now that she's actually considering it, the idea starts to annoy me more than I expected.

"Why not?" she asks, clearly not on the same page as she dismisses my worries. "I'm supposed to be using this time to forget about my troubles back home, and letting go with a good orgasm sounds pretty tempting right about now."

My eyes go wide as I do everything in my power not to spit out my drink. I definitely don't need to be thinking about Veronica having any kind of orgasm. I suppose I can understand the pleasure and relief an orgasm brings, especially when you're looking for a much-needed distraction, but I think I'd much prefer she find another way to stay distracted.

I clear my throat. "But why complicate things by bringing a complete stranger into the mix?" I ask, before lifting my glass once more.

This time, it's her turn to lift a questioning brow. "Are you volunteering as tribute?"

I can't fight it anymore and actually choke on my wine as I attempt to regain my composure. "N-No. Of course not," I stutter, my cheeks and ears turning a bright shade of red.

"Chill." she giggles, shaking her head as she reaches for her own glass. "I was only kidding. Can you even imagine? Blair would kill us."

I wish I could laugh this off as effortlessly as she does, but I struggle to find the humor, especially when the joke comes at my expense. And worst of all, despite what she'd just suggest-ed—joke or not—she's still as poised as ever, while I look and feel like a damn clown.

"Good, because I can assure you, something like that will never happen between us."

"Promise?" Her lips curl into a teasing grin as she swirls the liquid in her glass.

"I can promise you, Vee. Nothing is ever going to happen between the two of us."

Sure, she may be sexy as hell, but I don't ever plan on crossing that line with her, and I'm positive that she feels the same way. We hate each other, or at least I sort of do—she's weirdly grown on me these past few days, even if she still insists on stuffing weird and slimy food into her mouth. I thought the candy was bad, but those suckers are a million times worse.

9

VERONICA

HIS LIPS PEPPER FIERY kisses on my neck, trailing down to my collarbone before making their way even lower. My fingers sink into his soft blond locks as his mouth works its way down south, making a sudden detour as they stop at my bare breasts. One hand reaches up to palm one, meanwhile, his mouth expertly takes in the other, flicking my pebbled nipple with his tongue before teasing it with a soft nip of his teeth.

"Fuck, Miles," I cry, savoring the way the pain only adds to the aching pleasure between my thighs. "I need you," I pant, breathless, but just as he looks up at me with that wickedly sexy smile of his, a knock sounds at the door.

"Just ignore it," Miles insists, his lips traveling even lower. As much as I want to listen to him, the knock grows even louder, finally pulling me out of my dream as my eyes shoot open.

The absence of a warm body above me should bring relief, yet the persistent ache in my core tells an entirely different story.

"Vee, are you okay in there?" Miles's actual voice calls out, softly muffled by the shut door between our adjoining rooms.

"Oh God," I mutter to myself. What if everything I'd just said hadn't only been said in dreamland?

Pushing myself out of bed, I don't even stop to consider how crazy and frazzled my hair must look as I move to unlock and open the door that separates our rooms.

"Yeah, I'm fine. What's up?" I try to ask as casually as possible, praying to whatever God exists that my rosy cheeks don't reveal the truth of what had just been happening in my delusional dream. Seriously, that's where my brain went?

"Oh, uh," he says, his eyes looking me up and down as he clearly takes in the white silk and lace teddy with matching panties that I'd specifically picked out for my honeymoon.

When I'd done my packing for this trip, to consolidate and save time, I'd kept much of what I'd been planning to bring on my honeymoon and brought it with me here on this trip. I'm not sure if it was those traitorous oysters or something else, but last night, I felt like dressing up a bit before bed. After all, why waste a perfectly good pajama set? I deserve to feel like the beautiful, sexy woman I am.

"Eyes up here, Bennett." I direct, pointing two fingers at my eyes, glad to reclaim at least a little bit of power as he seems to feel some semblance of shame about where his gaze had just gone.

If I'm being honest, I like the way he's so obviously taken in my bare legs and chest—both on full display and perfectly accentuated by the well-placed lace bodice. Unfortunately, I can no longer blame that side effect solely on the oysters; it's more likely due to the lingering memory of Miles's lips on my skin from my dream.

"Sorry," he apologizes, clearing his throat. "I was just planning to go for a run on the beach this morning and wanted to see if you wanted to come."

Oh Miles, I definitely wanted to come. However, I send that dirty thought right back where it came from.

"Me? Run?" I ask instead, placing a hand over my barely covered chest. He can't be serious. I'm someone that loves a good yoga or Pilates routine, but you'd catch me dead before you caught me running. "Don't be silly."

"Well, in that case, I'll let you, uh, get back to... um, bed," he says, somehow needing to clear his throat yet again.

"Wait," I say as he takes a step back and I reach out for his arm—though I quickly drop it when his gaze drops to where our bodies are now linked. "I said I didn't want to run. I never said anything about not wanting to join you at the beach."

I have no desire to run, especially on such challenging terrain like sand, but that doesn't stop me from wanting to find any excuse I can to be out near the water during our stay.

"Oh, yeah. Duh, of course. I guess I'll just let you change, and then you can meet me out front?" he suggests, throwing a thumb over his shoulder.

"Sounds good, Bennett," I say, giving him a final smile before shutting the door behind me and leaning my back against it.

I know I managed to keep myself composed during our conversation—and hopefully I came across as unbothered as I tried to be—but damn. My body is still in complete disarray, especially with that tortuous ache lingering between my legs. It certainly doesn't help that I'm ninety-nine percent sure Miles Bennett just checked me out.

One would think that walking along a nearly empty beach with the calming sound of crashing waves and the smell of the salty ocean air would calm my nerves, but nope. It's quite the opposite as I walk side by side with Miles.

Having known each other for so long, he's given me more than enough reasons to feel uneasy around him. It's not as if he's ever been all that good at hiding his dislike for me, and now, as we walk, the uncomfortable silence between us grows even thicker. Have I really gone and messed things up all over again, ruining the already fragile friendship we've been trying to build?

I'm not stupid enough to believe we'd ever end up besties or anything crazy like that, yet he's been strangely kind to me these past few days. Even when he made fun of my food choices last night, we managed to have a good time. I'd even managed to bring out a few more of those ever-elusive smiles of his.

However, today is feeling a bit more like our usual interactions, with him quietly trying to ignore my presence—which seems a bit silly considering he was the one who invited me out this morning.

"I think I'm going to set up here," I decide as I pull the towel off my shoulder and drop it onto the warm sand.

He nods. "Alright. My plan is to run down to the edge of that cliffside and back a few times. Just let me know if you need anything."

"I think I'll be alright," I assure him, leaning down as I unfold the towel until it lies completely flat. "You convinced me to be a good girl and do some yoga this morning," I explain. "Gotta work off all that candy somehow," I joke, though I'm not entirely kidding, especially since I definitely plan on using this vacation to pig out even more.

Plus, a little yoga and meditation is likely what I need to clear my mind of all these ridiculous thoughts swirling through my brain. Okay, so maybe Miles checked me out earlier, but that doesn't mean anything. I'm pretty sure any sane person would have looked, given what I was wearing—or rather what I wasn't wearing—and how much skin I'd been showing.

Plus, as much as I'd like to forget about my worries back home, it's a little hard to do when my ex-fiancé has been blowing up my phone, even going so far as to switch numbers. I've done my best to block each new one that pops up, but it's all so damn exhausting.

"Yoga?" he asks, lifting a brow.

"Why not?" I shrug as I stand back up. "It's good for both the body and the soul." While I may have personally been a bit skeptical at first, when Maeve, one of my co-workers and recent bridesmaids, had started teaching a class three times a week at our local community center and asked me to join, I'd done it and realized rather quickly how good it left me feeling. "Plus, you should see how flexible I am now," I add with a wink, deciding to forget, at least briefly, that I'm trying to be good here.

His jaw tenses. "I'll take your word for it," he says, reaching behind his neck with one hand before tugging at the back of his shirt and lifting it up and over his head.

I know I shouldn't be staring, but that's precisely what I'm doing as I take in his newly exposed chest. Never in my wildest dreams did I imagine I'd be checking out my best friend's older brother, yet here I am, doing just that.

I always knew he wasn't some scrawny guy, especially since he's always given off the vibe of someone who works out and isn't someone you want to mess with. Still, in my head, I always figured a lot of that was attitude-based. I never actually expected to take in a muscular, built body, especially as my eyes fall to his six-pack abs. And why, oh why, are his gym shorts riding just a little too low on his hips, drawing my gaze to the lines leading down toward his...

Okay Ronnie, you are officially going to stop your mind right there, I tell myself, especially as I feel my teeth sinking into my bottom lip. Now it's my turn to clear my throat as I attempt to look away, hoping Miles doesn't realize what a nosey creep I'm being.

"Do you mind if I leave this here?" he asks, thankfully breaking my thoughts from that ridiculous direction

"Um, what?" I ask, bringing myself back to reality for the second time today. I take in his freshly removed shirt that rests in his hands and he glances down toward it as well. "Oh, yeah, duh. Of course." I nod, answering before he can say anything else. "I promise to keep it safe."

His brow furrows as he looks me over, and I can only assume he's making sure I'm actually okay and in my right mind. After what feels like an unnecessarily long pause, he slowly nods. "Alright. Just give me a shout if you need anything," he reassures me one last time before jogging leisurely toward the water's edge and running parallel to the crashing waves.

I let out a loud breath as he picks up speed and heads toward the rocky cliff he mentioned. "Ronnie, get it together," I mutter under my breath, willing my eyes to stop following the delicious view in front of me. "You're not allowed to look at Blair's older brother like that," I remind myself. I mean, seriously, God really outdid himself when he made that one. Those back and leg muscles? It's like he's chiseled out of marble.

While it may have never been something I've needed to consider before, brothers are officially off-limits—right?

10

MILES

MAYBE VERONICA IS RIGHT and there's something to be said about yoga's ability to calm the mind, because I'm experiencing the exact opposite as mine is a trainwreck of thoughts as I continue on my run.

The salty air, the crashing waves, the gorgeous blue ocean—running by it should feel completely euphoric, an experience that will stay with me forever, yet I can't seem to enjoy it the way I should.

I've always been a runner. As a child, I watched and longed for the camaraderie of playing on some sort of sports team, but despite all my begging, my dad and grandma never signed me up, leaving me to sit on the sidelines while all the other kids played. I had to learn the hard way that the only basketball or football teams I'd be playing on would be the ones on the playground.

Running was something I could do for free and provided an amazing escape not only from the confines of the tiny, dirty apartment I'd grown up in but also from all my troubles. While my sister found solace from hers through music and photography, I'd found mine through running, and of course tinkering with things, which eventually turned into my love of working on and fixing up cars.

However, I'm completely off my game today, and it all started when Veronica opened that damn door this morning wearing... well, whatever the hell that revealing outfit was, showing way more skin than I ever cared to see on my little sister's best friend. I don't want to see her like that. I don't want to notice how perky and full her breasts are, or how soft and smooth her skin looked under that thin, sheer fabric.

I wouldn't say I see her as a sister, especially since I've always made a point to avoid thinking of her like that—or really, thinking of her at all. She's very much cemented herself as my sister's obnoxious, pain-in-the-ass best friend.

Sure, she's undeniably beautiful, but even as we grew older, I still always found it easier to dislike her than to ever think of her as someone I'd want to look at in that way.

There's no denying, though, that the past few days I've gotten a glimpse into what my sister sees when she looks at Veronica. Her constant energy might be exhausting, and while I don't consider her my friend just yet, I've surprisingly grown to not totally hate every second I'm around her. I'm actually starting to enjoy her company, at least when she isn't trying to force feed me nasty-ass seafood or candy.

However, dinner and what we ate last night are the furthest things from my mind as my feet hit the sand beneath me—Veronica is all I can think about now. One would hope I'd be able to let my mind break free from that strange little encounter this morning. I've seen women wear far more risqué lingerie and outfits.

Fucking hell, even now, all my brain can think about is her current outfit—those tight yoga pants that cling to her perfectly round ass and the sports bra that, while it covers the important parts, leaves a nice peak of cleavage. Not to mention the fully exposed skin of her tight stomach.

Pete fucking West is truly one of the dumbest men I've ever met. While I'd made it a point to spend as little time with him as I could, I'd unfortunately, had a front-row seat just days before their would-be wedding as he attempted to body-shame her for wanting to eat some donuts. While I called him out that night, I'm even more worked up now. What the hell could he have possibly disliked about how she looks? Her body is perfect—each and every curve—and I'd do just about anything to run my hands all over it.

God, why the hell can't I stop thinking about her damn body? And worse, I shouldn't want to look at it, let alone touch it.

I force myself to keep running, but a quick glance over my shoulder pulls my attention away as I slow my pace. I can see Veronica, but I also spot a group of men, two of whom are making their way toward her.

I'm ninety percent sure she isn't in any danger, especially since the man doing most of the talking is casually tossing a volleyball up and down in his hands. Before I can stop myself, I turn around and run straight toward them.

"Hey Ronnie!" I call, my voice straining to be heard from this distance, but thankfully she seems to hear me as she glances over her shoulder with a smile. "Are you ready to head back?" I ask, more winded than I should be, but I hadn't exactly paced myself given how fast I high-tailed it back here.

With a sharp wrinkle of her brow and a scoff, she dismisses my idea with a slight wave. "We haven't even been out here for a full thirty minutes." She shushes me before looking at the two men, who seem to check me out and assess me exactly like I'm doing with them. "And Jace and Benson here just invited me to play volleyball with them."

"Oh, yeah?" I ask, doing my best to control my breathing as I close off the rest of the distance between us. I stand up straight as I walk directly behind Veronica and place a protective hand on her shoulder.

Okay, so usually I'm not the type of man to feel the need to mark my territory, but right now, I feel oddly protective. And okay, maybe she isn't exactly my territory, but considering she just broke off her engagement only days before, these men definitely need to take a step back.

"You're more than welcome to come and join in too," the taller of the two males nods as I fully take him in. He's got at least two or three inches on me and clearly has no problem being shirtless, as it shows off his broad chest and muscles, but I'm not the least bit intimidated. Then again, not much intimidates me—I've had an unwavering determination and fighting spirit, since I was a kid—hell, I've been fighting my entire life. I just can't stand his smug grin, nor the way the shorter skinny guy is practically drooling over Veronica. Doesn't he get how pathetic he looks?

"You really want to play?" I ask, turning my attention to Veronica instead of acknowledging the invite to join.

"Why not?" She says, shrugging as she meets my gaze.

"I just never took volleyball to be something you'd be interested in."

I choose to keep my annoyance to myself that these men are a bunch of young college students, likely here for spring break. I'm not saying there's anything wrong with it, but she is twenty-eight, after all, and these guys look barely legal. They're pretty much babies and would probably have no idea how to handle a woman like her. Then again, maybe I shouldn't trust her judgment, given that she'd somehow fallen for Pete West, of all people.

"Oh, come on. How often does one get to play beach volleyball?" she asks with a small giggle before turning back toward the guys. "I'm totally in."

"That's the spirit," the smaller of the two cheers as he reaches out and gives Veronica a high five. I do everything in my power to keep my eyes from rolling to the back of my head.

"I guess that means I'm in, too."

Playing volleyball with a bunch of horny, immature college kids is the last way I want to spend my afternoon, but I'm not about to let any of these men take advantage of Veronica in any way.

"Oh my God, I suck at this," Veronica whines after trying to serve the ball over the net but failing as it falls toward the sand, not making it even halfway to the net.

My first instinct is to tell her it's her fault for wanting to play in the first place, but as I watch the kid from earlier, the taller one who I've since learned is named Jace, and who can't seem to stop flirting with her inch toward her, I beat him to the punch.

"Here, I'll show you," I volunteer as I move to stand next to her. "Hold the ball like this in your left hand, and move your right hand back like this." I demonstrate, and while she attempts to mimic what I just showed her, her stance is completely off. "No, like this," I explain, moving behind her as I take hold of her arm and move it into position before I adjusting her other arm as well. "And pull your leg back to get some more momentum behind your serve," I continue, tapping her leg before taking hold of her left hand one final time as I wrap my hand around it to turn it into a fist.

It isn't until I look down at her face to check for understanding that I realize how touchy I've gotten. Her warm, chestnut eyes lock onto mine, wide with attention, as her lips part just enough to tease a playful smile, drawing my annoyingly hungry gaze along their delicate curve.

What the fuck is wrong with me? I'm not supposed to be looking at Veronica Prescott's lips. Worse, I'm not supposed to know or think about how soft her skin feels against mine.

I let out something resembling a cough as I clear my throat and step back. "You got it?"

She wordlessly nods before turning to look toward the net. Letting out a visible breath, she follows my instructions, stepping forward and hitting the ball, which then sails perfectly over the net.

"I did it!" she shrieks as she jumps up and down, and while I'd just inwardly cringed not too long ago at that Benson guy offering Vee a high five, I find myself doing the same. Instead of high-fiving me back, though, she leaps toward me, wrapping her arms around my neck, utterly oblivious to the fact that there's still a game going on. Thankfully the college frat boys seem to keep the ball going back and forth over the net.

"You did. That was amazing, Vee," I congratulate as I peel myself out from underneath her. I've never seen myself as someone that wanted to hug Veronica, but given the way my body is reacting to her touch, I know I can't let it happen—at least not until I get myself and my mind under control.

Luckily, I'm saved when the ball lands on the sand on the other side of the net, scoring a point for our team. Cheers erupt as they celebrate, and I should be celebrating with them, but my heart sinks as Jace scoops Veronica into his arms, her laughter echoing through the air as he twirls her around.

"Look at you, Ronnie. From barely being able to get it over the net to scoring us a point." He chuckles, and this time I do roll my eyes. Sure, she served the ball and got it over the net, but it wasn't like she was the one fully responsible for the actual point. I don't say that, though. She looks genuinely happy, and after the rough couple of days she's had, I'll do whatever I have to in order to keep that smile on her face, even if it means another man gets to put his hands all over her.

Reaching for the shirt I discarded before my run, I try to ignore Veronica's laughter as she waves goodbye to the guys.

"Looks like you had fun," I comment, my voice tighter than intended. I shouldn't care that she spent the rest of the game flirting with Jace. She's newly single and has every right to do whatever—or *whoever*—she wants. But knowing that didn't stop the sharp twist in my gut that came every time I saw her lean in close to him, laughing at whatever dumb joke he made. Even now, the memory causes my hands to involuntarily curl into fists at my sides.

"Yeah, I did," she agrees as she reaches down to retrieve her towel and stuffs it into her beach bag. "I don't even have to ask about you though, you looked like you were in pain the entire time." She giggles, nudging her shoulder into mine as we start the trek back toward the car.

"Did I have fun? No, but come on, I didn't look that bad."

A small, dismissive sound escapes her lips. "Are you kidding me? You looked absolutely miserable. It was also pretty obvious that you couldn't stand any of the guys. I actually thought you were going to take a swing at Jace when he asked for my number."

"Can you blame me? The only thing going on in that small neanderthal brain of his is beer, boobs, and sex."

I decide to leave out the part where today, my brain may have been having some of those same exact thoughts.

She glances up, tilting her head to the side. "You really think that's all he thinks about?"

"I was young like them once. I know exactly what's going on in their minds, especially when they all kept looking at you like you were nothing more than a piece of meat."

She rolls her eyes. "Young? They were twenty. They were men. Good-looking men at that, and who cares? It's not like I actually gave him my number."

I hold my hands up. "Hey, you're free to do whatever you want. If you want to give him your number, then you're free to do it. However you choose to move on is fine with me." As soon as the words leave my mouth, I know they aren't true. I do care, and I'm feeling oddly relieved to know that she didn't actually give out her number.

"Whatever you say, Broody Bennett." Veronica smiles, her eyes twinkling as she seems to see right through me as she leans against the side of my car, waiting for me to unlock it. Looks like I'm not the only one who's not buying what I'm selling.

11

VERONICA

I'M IN HEAVEN—OR AT least my version of it—now that I'm back in my happy place. Yesterday's beach day was fun, and I won't lie, it was a little ego-boosting having those frat boys blatantly flirt with me. The crazy thing is, my favorite part wasn't their cheesy pickup lines or how they tried to flex like they were auditioning for a *Baywatch* remake. Nope. The real fun came when Miles and I went back to the beach later that afternoon. Turns out, hanging out with Broody Bennett of all people is way more satisfying than being hit on. Who knew? Definitely not me.

There was something downright magical about convincing him to ditch his serious side and dive into the waves with me. We spent the entire afternoon splashing around like kids, body surfing and laughing so hard my cheeks hurt. But honestly, the real bliss came later when we stretched out on the sand, soaking in the last rays of the sun while I sketched away. Lying out turned into lazy chatter as he opened up more than I'd ever heard before as we watched the sunset side by side.

However, nothing compares to the magic that is Disneyland. Sure, there may be lots of loud voices, the occasional cry of a young kid, or the sound of a parent who's finally lost it as they yell at their children, but all I can focus on is the cheerful Disney music, the swooshing and whirring of rides, and the mouthwatering smell of candy, ice cream, and churros.

"Are you kidding me? They seriously expect us to pay almost six dollars for a fu—" I lift a hand to cover his mouth, but he thankfully stops himself before he can use the word that would have a thousand angry parents glancing in our direction. "Churro," he corrects himself instead. "What are they making it with? Golden cinnamon dust?"

"It might as well be. You'll see. You might've had a churro before, but you've never had a *Disneyland churro*. They're in a league all their own." As the people in front of us move aside, we step up to the counter. I quickly order two churros and slide my card over before he has the chance to argue. "My treat," I say with a sickeningly sweet smile, knowing full well he's annoyed given the way his jaw hardens. I'm still surprised I somehow managed to stop him from paying my entrance fee earlier. What I don't get is why he wanted to, especially since the entire morning all he did was grumble about how this place is nothing but a giant overpriced scam.

Everyone knows Disneyland is expensive, but the chance to truly escape reality, be myself, and let go in a whimsical world makes it worth every penny, even if it is a whole lot of pennies.

As the cast member hands us each our churro, I nod for Miles to follow me down the pathway toward the iconic Matterhorn, with its rugged, snow-dusted peak. I can already hear the sound of gleeful screams echoing with each passing bobsled, and while I fully intend to make him climb into one later as we go in search of the great abominable snowman, right now, I have something more important planned.

"Well, go ahead. Take a bite," I encourage with a nod, holding off on my own gratification since this is another first of his that I'm dying to witness.

He lets out a sigh, seemingly put out by my request, but reluctantly, he lifts the cinnamon stick to his lips and takes a bite. As usual, he's as stoic as ever as he chews, giving no indication of what's going on in that thick, hard-headed skull of his.

"Well?" I ask, spinning my free hand, beckoning him to give his opinion.

"It's fine." He nonchalantly shrugs, but as he brings the churro up to his mouth for a second bite, I see the slight grimace on his face, and I know that I've got him—no one, not even Broody Bennett can resist a Disneyland churro.

"Psh." I brush him off. "You know it's more than fine. I can see right through this little tough-guy act of yours and I know you already plan to get another one later, perhaps even one of the funky specialty ones."

"Would I say no to getting another one?" he asks, still doing his best to hide the smile that so desperately wants to break free. "No, but I also wouldn't go around claiming this is the best thing I've ever eaten."

"And what is the best thing you've ever eaten, Bennett?" I ask, realizing just how flirty and suggestive that sounded—but even so, no regrets.

It's clear from his widened eyes that he wasn't expecting that kind of question from me, but he recovers quickly. "I'm not sure I can answer that, since I'm not so sure the answer is appropriate for a little Disney Princess like yourself," he teases, nodding toward the pair of Mickey ears on my head, which are currently Snow White-themed.

While I hadn't had a ton of time to plan, I'd luckily been able to Disney-bound my outfit to look like Snow White. Despite my lack of foresight, I had already packed a red tank top and a short, flowy royal blue skirt for my original trip. Then, as soon as we hit Main Street and stepped into the Emporium, I saw these ears, and knew they had to be mine.

It's all so fitting, especially as I lead him toward Snow White's Wishing Well. "I may be a Disney Princess, but I can promise you, I'm not as innocent as you may think." I smile, chin held high, before taking a bite of my churro.

"I'm honestly not the least bit surprised, but I'm also thinking this may not be the best place to discuss this sort of thing," he says, his eyes darting around the area. Given all the kids and families running around, I'm thinking he may be right—at least this time.

The one good thing, though, is that while a few people are lingering in this area, this particular part of the castle always seems to be a little less crowded than others. It tends to be one of those places many people overlook, and today, I couldn't be more grateful.

"That's okay. I don't think you could handle what I'd have to tell you anyway." I shrug, loving the way I seem to make him uncomfortable all over again as his jaw clenches. It may be a little mean, but he makes it way too easy.

"So where are we heading next?" he asks, in what I assume is an attempt to change the subject. Given that I've been dragging him from ride to ride since the rope drop, I'm not surprised he knows I already have our next destination picked out.

"Right here, actually." I say, nodding ahead toward the small well only a few short feet in front of us.

"This feels like a bit of a letdown, especially after just getting off Space Mountain and Star Tours."

I let out a soft laugh. "Well, nothing can really compare to Space Mountain, but I figured we could use a short break from the rides. Plus, not only is this one of the best places to get an amazing photo near the castle, but it's tradition. Every time I come, I have to make a wish."

"Great," he says, rolling his eyes. "You are aware that I'm not Blair, right?"

"Oh, believe me, I know you're not Blair, and the photos I've already made you take make that incredibly obvious. But since you're all I've got, I kind of sort of need you, Miles," I plead, making sure to pout my lips as I flutter my lashes at him.

"Ugh, let's just get this over with," he says, shoving the last bite of his churro into his mouth before wiping the excess sugar off his hands onto his khaki shorts.

"Not yet. We have to make our wish first." I scoff, as if he's so ridiculous.

"Let me guess. You're going to wish that I was Blair and that you'd have brought her over me."

"No," I smile proudly. "I mean, sure, I miss Blair and would love to be at Disneyland with her again, but I kind of enjoy being here with you," I admit, shrugging as I inch closer to the well and look down at all the other coins and wishes that have already been made. "You're actually not half-bad company, Bennett."

"Even with me continually complaining about the prices and long lines?" he asks, skepticism lacing his tone.

"Even with all the complaining. I wouldn't have it any other way," I tease before holding out my churro for him to hold. Despite looking put out, he does as asked as I slip my bag off my shoulders and reach in for my wallet, finally pulling out two pennies. "Here, switch me back," I request, grabbing my churro with one hand while dropping a penny into his.

"You really expect me to make a wish?" he asks, tilting his head downward as his brows inch toward his hairline.

"Yes, I do." I confidently nod. "There's nothing wrong with believing in a little bit of magic and happily ever after from time to time."

"Even after everything that happened with Pete?" he asks, and although he sounds rather disbelieving, I can hear the effort he's making to be understanding, which, coming from him, is sort of touching.

"Yes, even after dating and almost getting married to someone like Pete. Plus, I'm pretty sure most princesses have to kiss a couple of frogs before they find their prince charming anyway." I dismiss, brushing him off since my ex is definitely the last thing I want to be thinking about today. "Now, stop stalling and start thinking of a wish," I command.

"Fine," he gives in and takes a step toward the well.

His lack of enthusiasm is evident, and I can't say I blame him for not wanting to do something others might consider silly and childish, especially at our age. Maybe I should stop guilting him into things, but part of me knows I should milk this for all it's worth. I have a pretty strong feeling that the moment we step back into Evergreen Grove, reality will hit as we sink back into our old lives, and he'll go right back to disliking me as much as he always has.

"So, am I supposed to wait for you to say some kind of magical words or do I just toss it in?" he asks.

It's impossible to resist the urge to smile as I look over at him. "Look at you, indulging me," I tease, but it's not just sweet—it's irresistibly attractive as he leans over the well, a stray lock of blond hair falling into his piercing cornflower blue eyes. How in the world is it fair that someone as grumpy as him gets to look like a real-life Disney prince?

"I only ask because I'm sure you have more pennies in there, and if I didn't, you'd make me do it all over again. I just want to get this done and over with," he explains, his mouth quirking into a grin.

"You're not wrong. So how about this: I'll count, and on three we both toss them in?"

He nods in agreement.

"Alright, one," I begin as I close my eyes. "Two. Oh, wait," I say, my eyes popping open as I use my hand with the penny inside to point a threatening finger in his direction. "You're making an actual wish, right? You're not just going to toss the penny in and waste it?"

His head rolls to the side in frustration, a disgruntled sigh escaping his lips despite the playful smile also stretching across his face. "Yes. I'm making a wish."

"Okay, good," I relent, closing my eyes once more. "One. Two. Three," I continue, holding my hand over the small well releasing the penny, letting it drop toward the bottom.

"So, what did you wish for?" he immediately asks as I open my eyes.

"Can't tell you, otherwise it won't come true."

"Isn't that just for birthday wishes?" he asks, feigning irritation. Yet, once again, the faintest hint of a smile lingers on his way too handsome face.

"Nope. It's the universal rule for all wishes. So no telling me your wish either," I warn, letting my now empty hand trail along the stone as I close the distance between us.

"Well then, how am I ever going to know if this so-called magic you speak of is real if I don't know if your wish ever comes true?" he asks, pushing himself off the well, and straightening up as I get closer.

"Well, when it comes true, it won't need to be a secret anymore. So I promise, when my wish inevitably comes true, I'll tell you," I assure him.

He lifts a brow. "And what if it never comes true?"

"Oh, believe me, this wish is coming true. All Disney wishes have to come true," I assure him, tapping a finger on his chest.

That, I am sure of. Things may not have worked out with Pete, and while I have every reason to believe that fairy tales and happily ever afters are just things you read about in books, I know that one day I'll find my true prince charming. And that was exactly what I wished for when I threw my penny into the wishing well.

"Now," I begin, letting my hand trail toward his before I yank him toward the castle. "Take my picture, and I'll reward you with another churro," I tease, figuring that when it comes to Miles, bribery is definitely the way to go.

"I suppose there are worse ways to get paid than with churros," he relents, surrendering with a smirk as I pass him my phone. With a playful twirl, I make my way toward the stone wall beside the castle, striking my most princess-like pose, churro in hand, completely ready for my royal close-up.

"Say cheese," he directs.

"Cheese." I smile, a giant grin that I'm sure will be plastered on my face for the rest of the day. Not only am I at the happiest place on earth, but I'm also genuinely happy to be here with Miles of all people. From the look of it, he might actually be enjoying himself with me too. I guess what they say is true—Disney miracles do come true.

12

MILES

WITH THE OCEAN JUST minutes away, I could've easily spent our entire vacation at Newport Beach. I probably would've even agreed to spend another day at Disney—even with the insane crowds and overpriced snacks—not that I'll ever admit that to Veronica. Then again, it's possible it wasn't the place I enjoyed, but the person I spent the time with.

Okay, so maybe the food and the rides weren't *that* bad either, but what made the day truly worth it was watching her face beam with constant excitement as she rushed us around the park, completely lost in the moment, without a care in the world. I know for a fact there's no way I would've had as much fun going by myself or with anyone else, for that matter.

She's the one calling the shots, though, so when we drove back to the hotel after another long day at the beach and she suggested we pack up tomorrow and spend the day driving down the coast before continuing our road trip, I didn't have it in me to argue. Sure, it's my vacation too, and I'm the one with the car and the keys, but the truth is, I didn't want to say no. Veronica needs this vacation way more than I do. After putting up with Pete West for as long as she did, I'd say she's more than earned it.

Plus, she was right. With the Pacific Coast Highway stretching out before us, the wind whipping through our hair, and the salty scent of the ocean filling our lungs, it's hard to feel anything but pure joy. Without a doubt, this was precisely what my car was made to do.

"Let's stop here for dinner," she suggests, her voice breaking through our carefree silence. We'd occasionally exchanged words about the passing landscape or a special landmark, but the overwhelming beauty of the drive transcended the need for conversation, as we both seemed to get lost in this once-in-a-lifetime memory.

"Yeah, sure." I nod, taking the exit.

Taking charge again, Veronica decided that a picnic was the way to finish off our time in California. We'd stopped at a small grocery store, grabbing supplies for sandwiches, along with chips, and fresh fruit.

I drive into a small, nearly empty lot and pull my car into a stall. Reaching into the back, she pulls out one of the blankets we'd bought since arriving in California, while I grab the bags of our recently purchased food.

"Ahh! This is beyond perfect," she practically squeals, reaching for my arm and giving it a quick, excited shake. "And we're just in time for the sunset."

I nod, taking it all in. The sky is awash in a soft, ethereal glow of orange and pink, reflecting over the vast expanse of the dark blue ocean beneath it. It really does feel fitting—a stunning sunset on its way to bid us a final farewell from our time in California.

Reaching the sand, we remove our shoes, and she lays out the blanket for us to sit on. I drop the bags and eagerly sit down, but she takes her time, carefully settling in as her flowy blue summer dress spills around her.

My stomach protests waiting any longer as it lets out a soft, hungry growl. I reach into the bag and work on building myself a small sandwich, while Veronica opens the clear container of prepared fruit and pops a green grape into her mouth with a soft crunch.

"I'm going to miss this," she says, closing her eyes and seemingly savoring the moment. I don't blame her—I feel the same exact way.

Despite the setting sun, the slight breeze, and the fact that I'm only wearing a pair of khaki shorts and a black T-shirt, I can still feel the residual warmth of the day on my skin.

"Our mountains back home are pretty great, but nothing compares to this. I think I may now understand why Blair loved living here so much and why she chose this over me. I'm starting to think I might choose California over going back home," I joke.

She waves me off, reaching into the bag to grab the Salt and Vinegar chips she'd picked out for dinner. "Oh, hush. She didn't choose *this* over you," she says firmly, but her voice softens as she continues. "We both know she was running away from her feelings for a certain someone. 'Exploring the world' was just an excuse. Hell, the only reason she ever came back to visit was because of how much she missed you. And let me tell you, that says a lot, considering how stubborn she was, especially over these past two years."

"Maybe." I sigh before taking a bite of my sandwich. I don't fault my sister for wanting to escape our tiny town, but I can't deny that her moving so far away stung. Luckily, based on her recent texts, it looks like she might truly be settling down for good.

"Plus, you wouldn't want to live here full-time, anyway. I'm pretty sure the thing that makes this place so special and magical is that when you're here, and for only a short time, you get to enjoy all of this," she explains, waving her hand out toward the ocean, "without it ever getting old. I don't think I'd ever want to live in a place that would make me take this view for granted."

I bob my head up and down as I ponder her words, wondering if she's right. "Maybe that's why I'm not finding you as annoying as I normally do," I say with a teasing smile as I glance her way, meeting her narrowing gaze. "Maybe California really does make everything better."

"So you're saying that as soon as we get back to Evergreen Grove, you're going to go right back to hating me?"

I furrow my brow, staring down at her with a stern expression. "Not this again. You know I don't hate you. I just don't usually appreciate you. But who knows? Maybe there's a chance I've somehow been wrong about you this entire time."

Her eyes light up. "Really?"

"I wouldn't go as far as saying you're one of my favorite people, but hey, at least you aren't my least favorite anymore."

"You know," she says, after biting into a chip. "With you? I'll gladly take that. But now I'm curious—who's taken the lead for least favorite?"

"Pete," I reply with little thought and no hesitation as I lean over, reach into the bag she's holding and grab a small handful of chips.

"You can't steal my answer," she insists, her voice thick with indignation, even as she leans the bag closer to make my attempt easier.

"I'm allowed to hate whoever I want, especially someone as fucking insufferable as Pete West. Seriously, what kind of idiot lets someone like you get away?" I ask before I can think better of what I've just admitted. Did I really just say the quiet part out loud?

"Someone like me, huh? And what exactly is he missing out on?"

I close my eyes, letting out an exasperated sigh. "I don't know. You're fun, and not horrible company. I'd maybe even go as far as saying I now get what Blair has seen in you all these years."

"He's missing out because I'm fun?" she asks, poking my arm playfully as I flinch back, feeling the need to avoid her touch at all costs. I'm clearly not thinking straight, and her close proximity is already doing a number on me. The last thing I need is her touch sending my mind into another confusing spiral.

"Among other things," I mutter, the salty and tangy taste of the chip being a much-needed distraction from the conversation I'm desperately trying to avoid. Sure, she's been less irritating as of late, and I find that I'm not only starting to enjoy being around her, but also enjoy looking at her—not that I can say any of that, or rather, I'm not going to. There are some things that are just better left unsaid. Now if only I could make these thoughts stop happening altogether. Now *that* would be helpful.

"And you're not planning on sharing what those other things are?" she asks, reaching over to snatch the half-eaten sandwich I'd made for myself and taking a bite.

My mouth drops open. "Are you serious?" I ask as she casually shrugs her shoulders, savoring the taste. "Well, in that case, I take back what I just said. You're just as annoying as I always thought," I smugly reply as I retaliate by grabbing the bag of chips and placing it in my lap.

"Nope. No take-backs. Now that you love me, there's no going back. It's just the rules," she says coolly, her gaze steady as she looks out toward the water. I shake my head in annoyance and dig into the bag, pulling out another small handful.

"You keep thinking that," I say before tossing two chips into my mouth.

"They don't call me the delusional queen for nothing, so believe me, I will," she says, giggling and clearly enjoying herself.

I'm pretty sure no one calls her that, but luckily, we don't have to keep fighting about it, as we both get distracted by the gorgeous scene unfolding in front of us. I've seen many gorgeous sunsets in my day, especially those with the sun setting behind the mountains, their peaks turning a fiery orange and red, but this view, with the sky ablaze in a riot of color, beats all of them. In fact, I'm not so sure I'll ever see anything like this again.

A strange urge compels me to look over—as if something inside me aches to see this view through her eyes. As I give in, I see her smiling up at the scene, her expression mirroring my own.

I know how much she loves to point out that I don't smile enough, but for me, I've only cared to smile at things I deem worthy of smiling for. I refuse to fake a smile just to appease someone or make them feel more comfortable. I need a reason to smile, and right now, I have one—especially as my eyes trace and take in her delicate features.

Despite the wind, her short brown hair looks stunning as it frames her adorable face, blowing gently around her. My chest tightens as I take her in, the realization hitting me like a freight train: much like this view, when it comes to Veronica Prescott, I'm not sure I've ever seen something so breathtakingly beautiful.

As the thought sinks in, I quickly avert my gaze toward the setting sun as it lowers over the horizon, the glow fading as it leaves behind nothing but a dark-blue expansive ocean.

I'm not blind. I've always known that Veronica is a good-looking woman, but now I'm forced to face the terrifying realization that I'm more than simply attracted to her—it runs so much deeper than that. I'm undeniably drawn to her, and this is just the beginning. We're only a week into our little adventure, and I have no idea what the rest of this road trip has in store for us. Heaven help me, because I'm going to need all the help I can get if I can't get these feelings under control.

13

VERONICA

A s MUCH AS I wanted to linger and soak up every last moment at the beach, the sun's warmth was replaced by the bitter bite of the evening breeze, signaling that it was, unfortunately, time for us to say our final goodbye to the ocean.

"So I'm thinking if we still want to get a good start toward our next stop in Las Vegas, we could stop in Barstow for the night. Although, if you're not up for the drive, we could stop sooner. I know I'm getting kind of tired, and it is still a few hours away," I explain, deciding to leave the choice up to him.

"I'm not tired. I can make it to Barstow," he assures me.

My brow creeps upward. "You sure? I can always pick somewhere closer," I offer again.

"No, I got this. Believe me, it won't be a problem," he confirms, his eyes darting to mine for a split second, as if to emphasize his seriousness, before returning his gaze to the road ahead. "Just put the information on the GPS and I'll be fine if you want to nod off for a bit."

"No way. I may be the passenger princess here, but I take my duties seriously. There's no way I can leave you to drive for a few hours all on your own," I argue. However, almost as soon as the words leave my mouth a yawn follows.

He shoots me a pointed look, and I shrug sheepishly.

"Okay, so maybe I wasn't lying earlier when I said that I was getting tired."

"Seriously, Vee," he says, using the nickname that only he uses—and one that weirdly has my stomach tying up in knots. "Just go to sleep. You know me; I've always loved driving, and it's not a problem. I don't mind. I promise," he reassures, placing a hand on my knee.

However, as soon as I feel the heat of his hand on my skin, the fleeting touch is gone just as quickly, leaving only a lingering warmth as he returns his hand to the steering wheel.

"Fine, but if we end up lost or you fall asleep and crash the car you love more than life itself, I take no responsibility. This is all on you," I tease, before reaching out to set the coordinates on his GPS.

Wanting to plan ahead—at least a little bit—I pull out my phone and book us two rooms at a hotel, since the last thing we need is to drive all the way there only to find no rooms available. While this car might work for a quick nap, there's no way we'd both be comfortable if we tried to sleep in it for the night.

With that, I put my phone away, lay my head against the side of the car, and close my eyes as the world quickly fades away.

I hadn't been lying when I said I was tired and I'd somehow fallen asleep quicker than I'd thought possible. Despite the top being up on Miles' car, blocking out most of the sound, the gentle drumming of rain against the window and the roof is enough to rouse me from my sleep.

With a gentle groan, I tilt my head from side to side, trying to ease the stiffness in my neck, and squint through the haze of sleepiness as I attempt to make sense of my surroundings.

"Where are we?" I ask, because even with his windshield wipers on high, it's impossible to see through the rain-streaked glass, let alone read any passing signs.

"We're almost to Devore," he explains.

My brows fuse together. "Really? I guess my nap was a lot shorter than I thought."

"No, you've been sleeping for quite a while, but right after you fell asleep, it started to rain, and it's only gotten worse, so I was forced to take it slow."

"Why didn't you wake me?" I frown, turning to glare at him.

"I didn't know I was supposed to. Plus, it's fine. I know how to drive in a rainstorm," he assures, but the confidence in his voice is immediately drowned out by a loud popping noise. He does his best to stay calm as he turns the wheel, correcting the car's out-of-control trajectory and thankfully preventing us from careening into the other lane, or worse, veering off the road entirely. While his hands clench tightly around the wheel and his knuckles turn white, his face remains cool and calm until the car comes to a complete stop on the side of the road.

"Fuck," he curses loudly.

My eyes widen in alarm as I turn to him, my voice shaking. "What was that?" Despite the terrifying event, he somehow remains surprisingly composed, even though most of the color has drained from his face.

"We got a fucking flat," he swears, hitting his palm on the wheel before blowing out an annoyed breath as he moves to unbuckle his seatbelt.

"Shit!" I panic. "What do we do? Do we call Triple A?" I ask, reaching for my phone as I force myself to remember what my dad taught me to do in this kind of emergency.

"No," he grumbles. "We don't need Triple A. I know how to change a damn tire."

"Oh right." I try to laugh, attempting to find some humor or relief about our unfortunate predicament. Despite being with a professional mechanic, the heavy rain pounding on the roof of the car is a constant reminder of the relentless storm outside, making it difficult to feel any sort of comfort in our current situation.

"Just stay inside and I'll take care of it," he assures me, opening his door. The crashing rain immediately drowns out all other sound. Obviously, I knew it was bad out, but it truly hits me how crazy this storm is when a loud crack of thunder roars from above us, one that I can practically feel in my bones.

He slams the door shut, leaving me alone with my thoughts as I nervously pick at my thumbnail. I want to find comfort in the fact that he knows what he's doing, and while I'm sure he's changed many tires in his day and knows how to do so quickly and efficiently, I also have to imagine he's never been forced to do so in a downpour like this.

Before I can overthink it, I'm undoing my seatbelt, opening the door, and heading outside to help. Huge, icy pellets of rain batter my body, immediately soaking through my clothes as I rush to join him at the back of the car where I find him struggling to change the tire.

"What the hell are you doing?" he shouts, pointing toward the passenger door. "Get back in the damn car, Vee."

I should probably do what he says, since, from the look of it, he seems to know what he's doing, but I'm not about to be shouted at by anyone. I recently ended things with someone who constantly put me down and made me feel small, and now that I'm free, I won't let anyone do that to me ever again—not even Miles.

"No," I say, planting my hands on my hips. "I came to help, and I don't appreciate being talked to like that."

I can see my words have had their desired effect as he seems to think better of the way he'd just shouted. He closes his eyes and tightens his fists, and it's obvious he's still fighting with himself not to do it again. His face contorts with barely suppressed rage, and his jaw clenches with the effort.

"You're right. I shouldn't yell, but I've got this," he attempts to apologize. Standing up, he quickly walks toward me, placing a hand on the small of my back as he ushers me toward the front seat of the car. "It's just... it's a fucking shit show out here, and there are a lot of people who don't know how to drive in this kind of weather. The last thing I need to worry about is you standing on the side of the road, someone hydroplaning into us, and something happening to you," he explains as he opens the door for me to climb inside. "So please, just stay in the car so I don't have to worry about you, too," he pleads, his icy blue eyes all but begging me to comply.

I'm feeling utterly useless, but I'm also not looking to make this job harder on him, so I regretfully slink back into my chair. "You don't even care that I'm getting your seats all wet?" I joke, despite knowing now probably isn't the right time. Then again, I've never been known for my good timing or tact.

"If you staying safe means getting my seats wet, I'll deal with it. Just stay in the car, please," he begs once more.

"I will. Promise."

He gives me one last, lingering look that I can't fully decipher before shutting the door and disappearing behind the car once again.

I try not to worry, but the relentless drumming of the rain against the glass and the roof only seems to grow louder, sending shivers down my spine with each small thud. My original worry had been being stuck on the side of the road all night, but now all I can think about is a car swerving into him, just like he'd worried about for me.

I've always been aware of his lukewarm feelings towards me, and I learned long ago not to let it bother me. Really, the blame is on him since he's always made himself such an easy target, making it way too easy for me to get on his nerves. However, as I sit, I'm hit with a newfound protectiveness. I can't let anything happen to him and it's driving me absolutely crazy that I can't help. So for once, I fight my natural instinct and stay out of his way, even if that's the last thing I want to do.

After what feels like an eternity, the door swings open and he collapses inside, slamming it shut behind him. "Fuck, it's cold out there," he shivers. He reaches up to wipe the water from his face before running his hands through his thick blond locks, shaking them out as tiny droplets fly everywhere.

I know I shouldn't be thinking anything other than being grateful for his safe return, but seeing him soaking wet, his shirt clinging to his body and revealing the perfectly defined muscles of his toned physique, sends my mind to dangerous places. Not to mention the water droplets falling down the side of his strong jaw. The mere sight of it sends a jolt of pure desire through me, urging me to lean over and lick them off, but I quickly push the thought away. Now is *not* the time to be thinking about that.

We're in a dangerous storm. Pull yourself together, woman! I shake my head, trying to focus. I mean, what the hell? This is Miles Bennett. He's my best friend's older brother, for God's sake.

"Will you turn the heat up?" he asks, pulling me from my thoughts as he turns in his seat to reach for a tucked away towel in the back of the car, using it to dry off.

I waste no time and blast the heat on high. "So, what do we do from here?" I ask. Maybe the answer is obvious, but as someone who's never had to deal with a flat tire—and someone who clearly doesn't handle emergencies very well—I'm very new to all this.

"I'd rather not have to drive too far tonight with the spare on, especially in this kind of storm, so I think our best bet is to find the closest hotel and stay there for the night until we can get a new tire tomorrow," he explains, putting the car into drive, and slowly pulling back onto the road before taking the first exit we come to.

All that seems to be around is some hole-in-the-wall gas station and what looks to be a pretty cheap motel, but right now it looks absolutely heavenly. My nerves are completely shot, and given where my head had just gone, I could probably use a little space from Miles.

I'm sure tomorrow, when he's no longer playing the sweet knight in shining armor concerned about my safety and no longer resembling a rain-soaked Adonis, things will go back to normal.

14

MILES

"WHAT DO YOU MEAN you only have one room left?" I ask, doing my best to hide the rising panic.

"I'm sorry, sir, but the storm has brought in a lot of travelers. We normally have plenty of availability, but for tonight, all we have left is one king," the man behind the counter states, looking as equally annoyed with me as I am with him.

"It's fine. We'll take it," Veronica cuts in from beside me.

"Are you sure? We can keep driving and look for another hotel," I offer.

She shakes her head. "In this storm? I don't think that's a good idea. And what if all the other hotels are booked up too? I think the best decision is to just take this room before someone else does," she says, playing the voice of reason, but right now, I'm not so sure I want to be reasoned with.

The man behind the counter taps his fingers against the front desk, waiting for me to answer. Unfortunately, Veronica is right. There's no guarantee we'd find anything else tonight. Even if it's a shared room in the middle of nowhere in a shitty ass motel, at least it's better than trying to find a way for both of us to sleep comfortably in my car.

"Fine, we'll take it," I relent, bitterly slapping my card on the counter before Veronica can step in and do it herself. It's my car that got us into this mess—the least I can do is cover this ridiculous expense.

Opening the door, we both walk in relatively slowly, assessing our room for the night. While I'd been hoping the rundown look on the outside wouldn't follow us in, clearly, I was wrong. The air is heavy with a muggy, damp smell. Not only that, but it's obvious the furniture has seen better days, especially with a hole greeting us right there on the comforter, which is likely from all the way back when this motel first opened decades ago.

Veronica's eyes follow mine. "Well, luckily, we don't need this. They say you should never sleep with the big comforter anyway," she says, a failed attempt at being positive as she lifts it from the bed and tosses it to the side. "And hey, why don't you use the bathroom first?" she suggests. "You're the one that got hit with the brunt of the storm. I'm sure a nice, hot shower is just what you need."

While I appreciate the offer, I shake my head. "No, you go. With a place this sketchy, I want to bring everything inside. So while I do that, you should just go, get warmed, and cleaned up."

"I'm not useless Miles. I can help bring the bags in," she sulks, folding her arms across her chest.

"I know you're not, but there's no reason for both of us to get wetter. Hell, I'm already soaked through, so what's a little more?" I ask. As her eyes sweep over me, lips slightly parted, a primal part of me wants to move forward and see what those sweet pink lips taste like when pressed against mine, but I brush the thought away. "Just... go and shower," I tell her with a dismissive wave, slipping the keycard into my back pocket and retreating out of the room before she has the chance to argue.

This is exactly why I didn't want to share a room with her. These thoughts are getting harder to control, and I'm starting to wonder how long I can keep them in check before I do something stupid. I may be seeing her in a different light, but I'm pretty sure those feelings only go one way. There's just way too much history between us, and I know for a fact that I've never given her any real reason to like me back. I'm a self-proclaimed asshole, and I need to remind myself of that. She's way too good for a guy like me.

Rather than soaking the bed while she showers, I take a seat in the nearby chair, idly scrolling through my phone. I make sure to send Blair a text, purposely leaving out the part about the tire, and instead letting her know our location and that we're safe for the night. I also decide to leave out the part about me and her best friend sharing a room.

It's probably all done in vain given how close they are. Veronica will probably spill the beans, but I'm not in the mood to hear it from my sister right now—I've had enough stress for one evening.

"Hey," Veronica's tentative voice calls out, making me look up from my phone. Despite my best efforts to look elsewhere, my gaze travels along her exposed legs, up to where the towel barely covers her thighs, before it's secured just below her cleavage, leaving very little to the imagination.

I swallow. "Um, hey," I finally manage, before clearing my throat and doing the gentlemanly thing by averting my gaze back toward my phone screen.

"Sorry, but with all my bags in here, I didn't exactly have anything to change into," she explains, quickly scurrying over to where I've set her bag on top of the dresser.

"No, don't worry about it. It's not like I've never seen a woman in a towel before," I stupidly answer, scrunching my eyes closed before lifting a hand to pinch the bridge of my nose.

"Oh, I'm sure you have, but I'm going to assume I'm likely the last person you'd want to see in one."

I want to say that's not true, but I think better of it. "You're probably right," I lie instead. "But, uh, I'll give you some privacy and head in for my shower so you can change in here."

While the hotel room isn't the nicest, it at least has a sink with a mirror and a long countertop outside of the bathroom, which means she can take care of whatever she needs to out here, while I enjoy my shower in peace without feeling like a complete asshole.

"Sounds good. But, oh, quick heads up, the water pressure sucks. But hey, at least the water is hot, so there's that," she warns.

"I'll keep that in mind."

She wasn't lying. The water pressure is weak, creating a pathetic drizzle as several spouts are entirely blocked, leaving only empty spaces where the water should be flowing. At least she'd been honest about the water's temperature. Normally, I relish the sensation of the flowing hot water, but this particular torture feels like it came straight from the depths of hell, its heat burning my now tender skin.

I wouldn't be shocked if I've now got some second-degree burns on my back. Despite setting the gauge to what felt like the perfect temperature, every so often, the water spikes unexpectedly, the heat rising along with it. Then again, it's probably for the best that this shower is keeping me on my toes, since, as I scrub my body, it's Veronica and her tight, perfect form that refuse to leave my mind.

With her having stepped out of the bathroom in nothing but a towel, she'd been the epitome of unadulterated sexiness without even trying. Despite my attempts to brush my feelings aside, my body seems to have other plans, reacting entirely on its own as the blood rushes south and my cock stands at full attention.

I shouldn't be the guy that gets off to the memory of his younger sister's best friend, but as my hand sinks lower, I can't help it as I wrap my palm around myself and begin to fuck my hand. I start slowly, closing my eyes and dipping my head backward as my body pleads for me to pick up the pace.

God, she really is beautiful. As I picture the image of Veronica wrapping her perfectly plump lips around my dick, and her round, sexy eyes looking up at me, it's almost embarrassing how quickly and intensely I come.

With my free hand, I steady myself on the wall, trying not to groan too loudly. The last thing I need is for her to know exactly what I've been doing in here. Sure, I could blame it all on the fact that it's been a while since I've had sex, but while there's no way in hell that I'd ever admit it to her or anyone else, it's ultimately her that has me so hot and bothered.

One would think that an old bathroom with dirty grout and tile, along with a shower head that barely works, is the last place anyone should be having any sort of inappropriate thoughts. Yet that's exactly what happened.

Even now, I still can't seem to get the image of her out of my head, and that's precisely why, instead of letting myself relax in the warm water, I yank the small knob, twisting it as hard as I can, and gasp as the icy water smacks against my skin. Yep, this is exactly what I need—and more importantly, deserve.

15

VERONICA

> Blair: So Miles told me that you guys stopped early for the night. How are you feeling?

> Ronnie: Yeah, it was a little scary for a moment there when the tire popped, but we're safe for the night. Or at least as safe as one could be at a motel in the middle of nowhere.

> Blair: Wait, you guys popped a tire? Miles just told me you guys stopped early because of the rain. WTF?!

I SHAKE MY HEAD and let out a soft sigh. Of course Miles wouldn't want to worry his sister.

"Time for some damage control," I say softly to myself as I type.

> Ronnie: Men! No, but seriously, it sounds scarier than it was.

> Blair: Well, I'm glad you're both safe, even if you are in a sketchy motel.
> At least you have Miles for protection.
> If anything, he'll likely station himself right outside your door to make sure nobody gets in. At least, that's what I imagine he'd be doing if I were there.

My eyebrow tilts upward. Did he also not tell her that we're sharing a room?

Okay, so it's not a big deal. It's just a room. A room with only one bed in it, but we're mature adults. It's not like either of us is going to insist the other person sleeps on the floor. In all likelihood, I imagine Miles suggesting he take that spot, but that's not going to happen if I have anything to say about it.

I should tell her the truth, but if it wasn't a big enough deal for him to mention, maybe I don't need to bring it up either. Sure, Blair and I share everything, but I know her well enough to know she'd likely blow this out of proportion.

Who knows? Maybe I'm the only one overthinking this. Instead of replying, I place my phone on the bedside table and reach for the remote, eager to drown out my overactive imagination with the familiar hum of the television. Unfortunately, the screen remains stubbornly blank, a field of white noise and gray squiggles no matter how many times I try to change the channel. So much for a distraction.

Maybe I should be careful what I wish for, as I'm given one in the form of Blair's older brother who saunters out of the bathroom. A sheepish grin spreads across his face, the fresh scent of soap and steam following after him. He's wrapped in only a towel, much like I had been earlier, but where mine had covered my chest, his is entirely bare, the towel sitting around his hips, and leaving much of his muscular legs exposed. It's also resting provocatively low, and I become all too aware once again that he has those sexy-ass lines that point downward like a beacon toward his cock—and that's exactly where my eyes go.

"Sorry," he apologizes, as my eyes quickly dart back to his, completely glossing over the fact that his well-sculpted body is on full display for me to admire. "One would think I'd have learned after you had to come out half-dressed earlier, but I also forgot to grab my clothes," he explains, his cheeks flushing as he heads over to his duffle bag and rummages through it for his pajamas.

I know I should show him the same level of respect and privacy he gave me earlier, but I'm completely captivated. My eyes are drawn to the smooth curves of his sculpted back. Is a back supposed to look that sexy? Because in his case, it looks absolutely immaculate.

"No problem," I manage, and I genuinely mean it. I'm savoring this view, and although I should feel guilty, that feeling is overshadowed by a warm shiver of delight. My body ignites with pure desire as my eyes continue to drink him in.

Fortunately, he appears completely oblivious to my prying eyes as he heads back into the bathroom to change.

As he moves out of sight, I lift my hands to my warm and flushed cheeks. Is it hot in here, or am I just being a complete and total creep? Letting out a breath of air, I push myself off the bed and walk over to the sink, where my toiletries are already scattered around.

"Pull yourself together, woman," I silently scold as I stare at my reflection in the mirror, willing my flushed cheeks to go back to their normal color, and fast.

The bathroom door opens, and my close proximity catches Miles off guard, his eyes widening as he sees me standing there. My gaze betrays me once more as my eyes trace the length of his body all over again. Is this man for real? He went from a towel to a pair of gray sweatpants. There is no way he isn't trying to mess with me. All he needs is a backward baseball cap, and I'd be climbing all over him.

"Oh, sorry. Did you need...?" he trails off, pointing over his shoulder toward the bathroom behind him.

"Um, no," I say, quickly shaking my head. "I was, uh, just finishing brushing my teeth," I lie, grabbing my discarded brush from earlier, even though I had actually done that already after my shower.

I've already done everything I needed to do to get ready for bed, but how do I explain that to him? '*Oh, you know, I was just trying to suppress my body's reaction to seeing yours in nothing but a towel.*' But nope. Sorry, that's not happening, which is saying something since I usually just blurt out whatever ridiculous thing comes to mind.

"Oh, okay," he says. While I wouldn't say he looks like he doesn't believe me, there's still something weird going on with him too—something I can't quite figure out.

He scoots past me, giving me a wide berth as he heads back toward his bag and grabs his own packed-up toiletries.

With my body still feeling incredibly warm, I move to check the thermometer on the wall, which reads seventy-five degrees.

For all I know, that could very well be the temperature in here, but it definitely feels hotter. Or it could be the fact that I've gone out of my way to dress in my least sexy pair of pink flannel pajamas, which have teddy bears and bows on them.

While I'd normally never wear this set in front of anyone other than Blair, it felt like the safest option. Given the hurry I'd been in to pack, most of what I brought along was lingerie that had been carefully selected for my honeymoon. While a part of me longs for him to see me in the same light that I'm currently seeing him, I'm not so sure that's a good idea right now, especially since I imagine Miles isn't looking to see that much skin.

Sure, he got a little sneak peek of me in them the other day, but that was likely one of the more modest pairs, or maybe I'm just once again overthinking it. He clearly isn't afraid to show off a little skin. He doesn't even seem worried that I'm seeing him shirtless, but then again, why would he? I highly doubt he ever thought he'd need to worry about his little sister's best friend checking him out, yet here we are.

For good measure, I turn the dial down and the old air conditioner near the window sputters to life with a loud, mechanical growl that fills the room. If I'm going to be expected to sleep next to the sexiest man in the world, then I need that air, and I need it quick.

"So," Miles starts, his eyes finding mine through the large mirror before he sets his toothbrush down and turns to face me. "What's the plan for tonight?"

"Well, I was figuring it would include us both getting some much-needed rest," I cheekily reply, sending him my most innocent smile as I take a seat on the side of the bed I'd already claimed while he showered.

"Okay, smartass," he scowls, folding his arms across his tanned chest while leaning against the counter. "I was referring more to the sleeping arrangements."

"What's there to figure out? It's a king-size bed. We can both fit." I shrug, doing my best to act like this isn't freaking me out as much as it is. Earlier, I'd brushed off the idea, telling myself it was no big deal, but now, with the reality of it looming, I can't ignore the nervous flutter in my chest. My body aches to be near his, and though this arrangement should be exactly what I want, it's actually quite terrifying.

"And you don't think it will be awkward?" he asks, his eyes studying mine way closer than I feel comfortable with.

"Not unless we make it weird," I say, averting my gaze and reaching for the lotion I'd placed on my bedside table, then pouring some into my hands.

"And what do you think Blair would have to say about the two of us sharing a bed?"

"I think she'd want us both to get a good night's sleep and not be weird about it. We're grown adults. I don't see what the problem is," I lie, rubbing my hands together before sliding the lotion up my wrists and arms.

I know exactly what the problem is, especially as the ache between my thighs continues to intensify. My eyes once again catch sight of those lines peeking out from the waistband of his sweats. I know where those lines are leading my gaze, and it's the very place I know it should never go.

"Alright," he says, unfolding his arms and pushing himself off the counter. "As long as you're good with this."

"I'm good with this," I lie to both him and myself. What other choice do I have?

Given how uncomfortable I had been the night before, I'm surprised by how refreshed I feel as I wake from my dreamless slumber. I can't remember the last time I slept this well, which is strange considering how long it took me to finally fall asleep. Perhaps Miles is one of those people that can fall asleep easily, but it didn't seem like it took long before his breathing changed, leaving me alone to toss and turn.

Even with the covers, or rather the thin sheet discarded from my body, I knew I needed to change as I quietly tiptoed toward my bag to grab a large oversized T-shirt.

After changing, I felt somewhat better, but it definitely took me longer than usual to fall asleep. However, as my eyes slowly open, I become acutely aware of why I feel so damn warm and comfortable.

I'm fucking cuddling against a bare-chested Miles Bennett, my cheek firmly nestled into his chest. I slowly lift my head and take in the sight of my leg carelessly resting over his, my thong-covered ass practically sticking out, his arm holding me close as the soft heat of its embrace warms my back.

At least I'm not the only one who should be embarrassed about this situation, especially as I realize my knee is only mere inches away from his very hard, alert member.

Fuck. Is *that* seriously what he's working with?

Then again, what does he have to be embarrassed about? Sure, he's got some morning wood going on, but I'd be hella proud and showing that thing off too if it belonged to me. Plus, it's not like I'm the reason it's risen to attention. That's just a normal bodily function for men, right?

Needing to extract myself from this embarrassing situation, I do my best to carefully untangle myself from around him, taking extra care not to move his arm and wake him in the process.

While it's not like I snuggled into him on purpose, it's also not a conversation I want to have, especially after I was the one who convinced him this was no big deal in the first place.

Finally free, I carefully scoot back off the bed, letting my feet quietly hit the floor as I scurry to where I'd discarded my pajama pants the night before and slip them back up my bare legs.

I'm not exactly sure what my course of action is here, but without overthinking it too much, I grab my purse, slip my feet into my sandals, and make my way out the door, careful not to let it slam behind me.

I know there aren't many places for me to go, especially since we're in the middle of nowhere. But wherever I end up, it has to be better than being alone in a room with the man I just woke up next to. I need to clear my head—and fast.

16

MILES

I'M AN EARLY RISER, but it's not my internal clock that wakes me up—it's the insistent sliver of sunlight cutting through the curtains that forces my eyes open. The faded, once-red curtains, though clearly meant to block out the sun, barely dim the morning light; they probably should have been discarded well over a decade ago.

With a light groan, I'm reminded once more of where I am as my back begins to ache. I may only be thirty-one, but the constant strain of working on cars and physical labor have certainly taken their toll, leaving it much stiffer and sorer than it should be.

Sitting up, my hand instinctively reaches for the sore spot on my lower back as I blink away the sleep, my eyes taking in the unfortunately now-familiar room. Glancing beside me, I expect to find a still-slumbering Veronica, but the spot is vacant.

Letting my feet hit the floor, I walk toward the sink. The least I can do is freshen up and brush my teeth before she comes out of the bathroom. Before I can even register the massive case of bed-head I have going on from sleeping with wet hair, I become all too aware of the fact that the bathroom door is wide open and the small room is dark, with no annoying little brunette in sight.

With creased brows, my eyes scan back toward the bed. Her phone is resting on the bedside table, still plugged in.

Fuck. Where the hell could she have gone? That woman has her phone attached to her at all times, only causing the panic to intensify. She wouldn't leave without it, would she? Plus, where the hell could she have gone? We're in the middle of fucking nowhere.

Spinning around, I spot my keys sitting exactly where I left them on the dresser. That means there is literally nowhere that she could have gone on her own. Panic claws at my throat, and my heart pounds against my chest. It seems nearly impossible that I could've slept through someone abducting her, but the fear still tightens its grip on me as I rush toward the door and yank it open.

I'm not sure if I should be relieved or annoyed when I see Veronica's wide, earthy eyes staring back at me, door key in hand, having been just about to use it to let herself in.

"What are you doing?" she asks first, her brows shooting upward in confusion.

My frustration builds. "What am I doing? What the hell are you doing?!" I snap, not able to keep my voice from rising.

"I was getting breakfast," she casually explains, inching past me with four packs of donuts in hand—two powdered and two chocolate.

"Fuck, Vee!" I curse, my voice sharper than intended as I exhale a ragged breath, huffing in sheer frustration. Slamming the door shut, I run a hand through my unruly hair. My heart is pounding so hard it's almost painful as the adrenaline still courses through my veins. "I thought—" my voice cracks, the words sticking in my throat as anger and relief battle for dominance within me. "I thought something happened to you."

"Like what?" she asks, a playful grin spreading across her face. She clearly has no idea what I just went through as the small haul she carries spills onto the bed and she casually settles down next to it, annoyingly clueless.

"I don't know, but we're in the middle of who the fuck knows where, and with you leaving your phone behind, I honestly thought someone had kidnapped you or something."

"Are you serious?" she asks, a soft laugh escaping her lips as she picks up a small pack of white powdered donuts and rips it open. "You really think someone could kidnap me without you knowing? I mean, come on," she continues, taking a donut out of the package. "You really think that low of me? You don't think I'd put up a fight?"

"With you, who knows? They'd probably only have to show up with some candy or a puppy, and you'd willingly hop into a sketchy white van, no questions asked."

She dips her head, clearly not impressed as she takes a bite, sending a dusting of white powder spilling over her lips. "I'm not that bad," she argues, speaking through the mess with a playful smirk.

"I don't know, you bought into what Pete West was selling, so I'm not exactly sure I trust your judgment," I counter, my words sharp enough to finally cut through her playful facade. It's clear I've crossed a line as an uncomfortable silence follows.

"Fine. I'm an idiot. Is that what you wanted to hear?" she asks, her voice barely a whisper, her frown deepening.

I let out a breath and move to sit beside her, gently placing a hand on her knee. "You're not an idiot, Vee. I shouldn't have said that. I don't know what's wrong with me. I guess I was just really freaked out and worried when I woke up this morning and saw that you weren't here."

While my words seem to placate her somewhat, there's still a tension in her posture. "Sorry, I was…" she begins, hesitating for a moment. "I was hungry, and I guess I just didn't want to wake you," she finally adds, her gaze dropping to my resting hand, where my thumb unconsciously brushes small circles over the fabric of her pants.

As the realization sets in, I quickly pull my hand away and stand up. "Well, I wish you had. I'm not sure I like the idea of you wandering around this place without me."

"You've made it incredibly clear that you don't trust my judgment, but I am, in fact, a grown woman and know how to take care of myself. I promise I didn't go around talking to strangers. And if it makes you feel any better, the only person I spoke to was Ralph."

"Ralph?" I repeat, not sure how hearing some random guy's name is supposed to make me feel any better. And a Ralph? Seriously? Who the *fuck* is named Ralph?

"Yes. Ralph. The front desk guy. And not only was he far from intimidating with his eighty-year-old frame, but he was also incredibly sweet, even helping me pick out what to eat for breakfast. Plus, I'm not sure anyone would want to approach me, given my *sexy* outfit," she adds, glancing down at her mis-matched self.

I finally take a moment to really look at her. She's still wearing the same pajama pants from the night before, but the matching button-up top is gone, replaced by an oversized band T-shirt that looks like it was probably stolen from Blair's closet.

"Wait, you changed?" I blurt out, somewhat confused. Sure, I can understand wanting to change out of your pajamas before going out in public, but why only change the top?

"Kind of," she says, a soft flush rising to her cheeks. "I got hot last night and ditched the top."

Nodding, I step forward and snatch one of the chocolate packs of donuts. It's not my typical choice for breakfast, but in a place like this—where there's no hot meal and only a small gift shop—it'll have to do.

"So, what exactly is the plan for the day?" she asks as she pulls another donut out for herself.

"Well, first things first, I need to figure out where the closest tire shop is. Then from there, we can figure out what we want to do. Were you still thinking we should hit up Vegas?"

"If you're still good with it, then I definitely say we head there next."

"Then Vegas it is." I nod, especially since, right now, I'd be willing to do just about anything for her. Plus, given how big of an asshole I just was, I'd say she more than deserves it now.

I know I went overboard, and I shouldn't have mentioned Pete at all, but lately, I can't help but feel more and more pro-tective over her. I'd truly do just about anything to keep her

safe and happy—even if that means sacrificing my own feelings.
God, what is this woman doing to me?

17

VERONICA

"YOU CAN'T BE SERIOUS, Vee," Miles says, sitting back in his seat with his head falling against the headrest.

"Of course I'm serious," I assure him, unbuckling my seatbelt to turn toward him. "We need to have fun and celebrate tonight."

"And I have to dress up to do that?" he asks, clearly skeptical.

"Come on. I packed a bunch of nice dresses for my honeymoon and I haven't gotten to wear any of them." I pout, pushing out my bottom lip for good measure.

"Yeah, because you're not going out with your fiancé, and for good reason."

"And we should celebrate that. Please," I add, linking my fingers together and holding my hands under my chin, pouting out my bottom lip even more. "I mean, you already drove all the way here. We should at least see what they have, right?" I ask, nodding toward the thrift shop I found on google just outside of Vegas.

With no need for fancy clothes, he packed accordingly, only filling his bag with the basics: worn jeans, comfortable shorts, and plain T-shirts. While I've enjoyed wearing my sundresses and shorts, I'm eager to switch things up tonight. Getting him to dress up with me has been priority number one throughout our drive today.

"Fine. But I'm not buying anything ridiculous, so don't even try to get me into some Elvis costume or anything stupid like that," he warns, pointing a finger in my direction before hopping out of the car. Pushing my door open, I scurry to catch up.

With his long legs, he's already walking through the door, and as I reach him—almost as if by fate, a few shiny Elvis costumes are right there at the very front.

"Don't even say it," he threatens as I press my lips together to suppress the giggle that desperately wants to break free. However, with how hard it was to get him just to agree to come with me today, I figure it best not to press it—at least not too much.

"You know," I finally say, unable to keep it in, "I happen to think you'd make a freaking sexy Elvis, but if you don't want to be the man, the myth, and the legend tonight, then I suppose I won't force you."

"Good, because I wouldn't do it anyway. You may have gotten me to do a lot of weird shit on this vacation that I wouldn't normally do, but this is where I draw the line. So pick wisely," he warns as he folds his arms. "So, how fancy are we talking, anyway?"

"Well, since it's a billion degrees here, I won't make you wear a suit or anything crazy like that, but I would like to go a little nicer than a pair of jeans," I suggest, immediately heading toward a rack of men's shirts. The colorful patterns and textures draw my attention as I pan through the small circle, taking a moment to really take in what I'm looking at.

"Well, I'll tell you right now: don't even think about picking something sparkly or flashy."

I roll my eyes, letting my fingers fall away from the shiny, metallic silver shirt I'd paused on. Sure, it would be a fun choice for Vegas, but even I can admit it's not exactly Miles' style. If I had to define his look, it would definitely fall under "motorcycle chic." Most of his shirts are simple, but they fit him like a glove, perfectly accentuating his sculpted chest and the muscles he's no doubt earned from long hours at his shop.

The funny thing is, his jeans are always incredibly stylish, with holes and distressing in all the right places. But I highly doubt he bought any of his clothes in that condition; it's all from daily wear and tear.

I'm the complete opposite. I have a very particular girlish style and closet that I've spent years working on and cultivating. I'm obsessed with anything feminine and girly, and I love the use of fun patterns and colors. While looking around this place for myself would be a dream come true, it's him I'm here for today.

"What about this?" I ask, pulling out a short-sleeved black button-up shirt that has silver lines running down it.

He shrugs, a noncommittal gesture that speaks volumes. "I guess it's not horrible."

"Not horrible? I'm not sure that's the vibe I'm going for here," I mutter as I move toward the next rack of shirts and begin to shuffle through them.

"Sorry, this just isn't my thing. I'm pretty sure the majority of my clothes come from Bob's Clothes Barn or the Target in Willow Creek. I'm not exactly well-versed in picking out anything fancy."

"While I think that shirt would have looked amazing on you, I want something that will wow us, or at least have you saying more than just 'it's not horrible,'" I tell him as I pull out a couple of different tops for him to try before heading over to the racks with pants.

I'm a woman on a mission, and I'm not leaving until I've made Miles the best-looking man in Vegas tonight. Then again, I'm starting to think that won't be too hard as I steal a glance at him. His blond hair may be a mess from the wind and him constantly running his fingers through it, but I can't help but think that this guy could easily grace the cover of GQ as one wayward strand falls perfectly in front of his eyes. The man is effortlessly handsome, and I'm not sure he even knows it.

Maybe I shouldn't be trying so hard, especially when I'm already having a hard time keeping my eyes off him, but I can't stop now, especially since I was the one who made this a big deal in the first place. Maybe Miles is onto something, and I shouldn't always be coming up with these outlandish and crazy plans.

Standing in front of the mirror, I snap a quick selfie and begin typing a message to send to Blair.

Ronnie: What do you think?

Hitting send, I turn back toward the mirror, taking it all in. I've gone all out tonight, and rightfully so. For my honeymoon, I picked out the perfect whimsical and romantic white dress—it's a plunging neckline, both front and back, with a hem that falls right about mid-thigh. The entire thing is outlined with a matching white, polka-dotted tulle overlay, accented with ruffled detailing on the shoulders. A satin waistband cinches in at the middle, perfectly highlighting my figure. I've paired it with white heels, each adorned with a matching bow on the back, and I topped it off with a matching bow in my hair, tying back some of my waved and curled locks.

I haven't felt this pretty since my wedding day, and it's very much needed. My heart had hammered all morning as I got ready with my bridal party, each carefully chosen detail of my appearance feeling wasted as it became even more glaringly obvious that I couldn't go through with it. But tonight, I can finally enjoy it and be proud of my look.

Maybe it's overkill since we're just going to a fancy restaurant and walking the Las Vegas Strip to take in all the sights and sounds that Vegas has to offer, but I've never needed something more. Sure, going to the beach had been fun, and Disneyland was incredible and as magical as always, but this feels like a different way of letting loose—and one I very much need.

Gazing into the mirror, I can't help but smile at the woman looking back at me, her eyes sparkling with a newfound sense of pride. For far too long, I let Pete dictate my every move, from the clothes I wore, to the way I styled and cut my hair, to the amount of makeup I dared to apply. Ditching my usual, more natural look, tonight I've applied a dark smokey eye—a perfect contrast to the sweet and girly outfit I've curated. I'm finally seeing a much-needed reflection of the person I truly am, and not the one Pete had envisioned or tried to create. I finally feel like myself again.

> **Blair:** Damn girl! You look hot! Too bad it's all being wasted on my brother.

Reading the message, I let out a nervous laugh and sink my teeth into my bottom lip. Maybe it's a waste, since I have absolutely no reason to believe he'll give even the slightest fuck about how I look or care about what I'm wearing. I know he doesn't see me that way, but there's still that delusional part of me that wants him to not only notice me tonight, but to also like what he sees when he does.

Luckily, I don't have to think about it for long as a knock sounds at my door. Glancing back at my phone, I check the time, and unsurprisingly, he's right on time. How he and Blair are related, I'll never know, since she's always perpetually late, but thankfully, those genes don't seem to run in the family.

I can't say I hate it, especially since I somehow managed to secure us a reservation at the Paris Hotel. While I may not be in actual Paris for my honeymoon, I can still somewhat enjoy what should've been. The best part is, the company is much better than the company I would've had if I'd been going with my fiancé.

With a shaky breath, I smooth the hem of my dress, desperately trying to calm my ridiculous nerves. As I open the door, I can't help but stare at the impossibly handsome man standing in front of me.

"Holy shit!" I exclaim, my mouth dropping open. "You look perfect."

Not only is he wearing the plain white long-sleeved button-down dress shirt, but the first two buttons are undone, giving the perfect glimpse of his chest. Sure, the black dress pants and shoes we picked out fit him just right, but it's the top that I can't take my eyes off. He's also wearing the black sunglasses—the ones he reluctantly bought after I insisted—giving him an extra sexy and mysterious look.

"You don't look too shabby yourself," he says, slipping off the sunglasses and hanging them on the edge of his shirt.

"Thanks." I smile shyly, glancing down at my dress and doing my best to hide the light flush of my cheeks.

"Actually, it's a little more than not too shabby. You look amazing, Vee. Truly."

I keep my gaze downward as I nervously kick out one of my heel-clad feet. "You don't think it's too much?"

"I didn't say that," he replies, a sly smirk working its way onto his lips. "But we're in Vegas. I'm sure you'll fit in just fine."

"Oh, yes. That's the dream," I say, feigning a dramatic pout as his eyebrow lifts questioningly. "To blend seamlessly into the background and just *fit in*. Truly, every woman's ultimate fantasy."

"Hey," he begins, holding his hands up. "I'm all about fitting in and not standing out. In fact, I'm pretty sure that's been my motto for the majority of my life."

For him, I suppose that does make sense. Given that he was one of the children of Evergreen's notorious town drunk, I can understand why he hadn't wanted to be noticed. His sister and

I, on the other hand, had always been the opposite—or at least I had. I loved being the center of attention and had always found a way to bring the spotlight onto myself.

"Well, too bad for you," I say, heading back into the room to grab my matching white clutch. "Because you look hot as hell, and there's no way you're going under the radar tonight."

"Whatever you say, princess." he half-grumbles, seemingly not believing what I'm saying, but I have absolutely no doubts.

"I know you don't tend to be a relationship type of guy, so maybe you haven't quite learned this lesson yet," I begin, closing off the distance between us. His eyebrows knit together in confusion, but that doesn't stop me as I reach out and un-button two more buttons on his shirt, leaving even more of his sun-kissed skin visible. "But us women are always right."

His eyes follow the movement of my fingers, his lips slightly parted as his gaze meets mine, a questioning look in his eyes.

"It's hot out." I shrug, but deep down, I know the sweltering Las Vegas heat has nothing to do with it. I'm not sure why it even matters—it's not like he's *really* my date tonight. But still, something inside me insists on helping him. Okay, so maybe a man as fine as him doesn't need my help to look undeniably attractive, but something about those undone buttons has me coming undone and I need more of it. "Now, let's go. Can't miss our reservation," I say, giving his chest one final pat before slipping past him and out the door. Not only do we have a reservation to make, but I need to get out of here before I'm tempted to undo even more of those buttons.

18

MILES

FUCK, IT'S HOT! AND I can't even blame the Las Vegas heat. From the moment I laid eyes on Veronica in her hotel room, my body's been on fire. It's not like I can fully blame my clothes, either. I've already rolled up my sleeves to just below my elbows, and thanks to Veronica unbuttoning my shirt, I'm getting a nice cooling breeze. But the more time I spend around her, the hotter, more bothered, and uncomfortable I get.

After we part ways tonight, I'm pretty sure I'll be heading straight to the shower. My hand and I likely will have date number two, thanks to the tiny vixen walking beside me.

"Where to next?" Vee's voice breaks through my thoughts as my eyes take in the breathtaking view—not the shiny, bright lights of Las Vegas, but the gorgeous woman walking beside me.

I place my hand on her shoulder and guide her to the inner side of the sidewalk, positioning myself as a shield between her and the bustling chaos of the Vegas Strip. The city's infamous party crowds are in full swing tonight. Rowdy laughter, flashing lights, and blaring music spill out from every corner. It's sensory overload for a small-town guy like me, but that doesn't mean

I'm not alert and ready to step in if anybody tries to mess with us, or more importantly, her.

"Wherever you want. This is your trip," I say, my eyes scanning the area, truly taking it all in.

She nudges my arm with her shoulder. "It's our trip. Plus, I want you to have fun too, especially now that I know you are, in fact, capable of enjoying yourself and having a good time. And what better place than Las Vegas to let go and fully unleash your wild side?"

I roll my eyes with a smirk. "Oh, I've always been capable of having fun. We've just never exactly agreed on what qualifies as *fun*."

While she found "fun" in stirring up trouble and causing as much chaos as possible in our small Colorado town, I preferred keeping to myself, diving headfirst into cars, and learning everything I could about them.

"Okay, well, in a place like Vegas, what exactly is your idea of fun?" she asks, raising a brow in my direction. I tilt my head from side to side as I mull it over, realizing I'm not quite sure.

"See!" She giggles, taking my moment of hesitation as an answer.

"I don't know. I've never been much of a drinker, as you already know..." I trail off, hesitating. Growing up with an alcoholic father, I've always tread carefully when it comes to drinking. I know I'm nothing like him, but even the mere thought of turning out like the notorious Bill Bennett sends a chill down my spine. "Sure, I'll hit up a bar or two outside of Evergreen every now and then, but this place?" I glance around, my unease clear. "It's more than a little out of my comfort zone."

"In a place like this, I'm sure we can find something interesting to do that doesn't involve drinking," she assures me. "But I will say, I am kind of tempted to try one of those big slushy-type drinks that I keep seeing people walking around with," she sheepishly admits, nodding in the direction of what I have to assume is a bachelorette party, as they walk in matching pink outfits with giant, wavy-like cups of what I assume is a blended alcoholic beverage.

"Then let's get one," I give in with a decisive nod.

She shoots me a skeptical look. "Really?"

"When in Vegas, right?" I ask, shrugging. Plus, it's not like I plan to let myself lose control. After years of practice, I know how to keep myself in check.

Okay, so maybe I let myself drink a little more than I usually do—or okay, let's be real—a lot more. That's the only way I can explain why I let her drag me to this nightclub. The throbbing music and flashing lights make it feel like an entirely different world in here. There's definitely nothing like it back in Evergreen, that's for sure.

"Come on, Miles. Please," she begs, pouting out her freshly painted bottom lip. *Fuck!* The buzz of alcohol courses through my veins, fueled by the sugary slushy, the cocktails we were served during our gambling session, and the shots we took just after arriving at the club. It's a thousand times harder to resist her allure now.

That's not the only thing that's gotten harder. I've had to adjust myself more than once in an attempt to hide what's happening down south, and all because of nothing more than being in her mere presence.

"You have to know that I'm not a dancer," I warn, praying my words are enough to keep her pleas at bay.

"Believe me, I never expected you to be one, but do you really want me out there on that dance floor all alone?" she asks, batting her lashes innocently as she links her fingers together, her chin tilted in a pleading gesture.

Clearly, she knew exactly what to say, because at that, I push myself off the red velvet couch where I've taken residence in an effort to give my body a break. I know my kind, and I know plenty of men would do practically anything to dance with Veronica, to get up close and personal with her. It really shouldn't matter what she does or who she does it with, but the primal part of me refuses to let that happen tonight—or, if possible, ever. I tell myself it's the alcohol talking, but I'm no longer sure.

The small buzz I usually get from a couple of beers is gone, replaced by a deep, burning warmth that courses through my entire body. I've never felt this bold before. The typical Miles would flat-out refuse to be seen on the dance floor, afraid of how people might view him, but this version? He couldn't care less.

With an excited clap of her hands, she grabs mine and pulls me along, practically yanking me toward the middle of the dance floor.

The energy of the club is nothing short of intoxicating—a living, breathing force that wraps itself around us like a warm blanket. Strobe lights slice through the darkness in vibrant hues of purple, blue, and pink while the pounding bass reverberates in my chest like a second heartbeat. The air is thick with a mix of sweat, perfume, and the faint tang of spilled drinks. I should be grossed out. I should want nothing to do with this, but instead, it's the exact opposite. I want more of it, and as she moves her body to the music, I find myself swaying along.

A smile blossoms on her face as she watches me, clearly impressed by what she sees, even if she has no reason to be. I'm a mess of flailing limbs as I attempt to keep up, likely appearing more ape-like than graceful, but she doesn't seem to care as she moves her body even closer.

Despite the alcohol swirling around in her own system, she moves with hypnotic grace and my eyes refuse to focus on anything but her. She places a hand on my shoulder, then lets it fall, her fingers tracing a slow, agonizing path down my chest, lingering on the bare skin before sinking lower. Only when her fingers brush the waistband of my pants does she pull them away, lowering herself and swaying in time with the music before rising and spinning around to press her back against me.

Shit. I shouldn't be enjoying this as much as I am, but as her ass presses into my already hard cock, I know I'm a goner—especially as she reaches her arms behind her and her fingertips graze my shoulders once again.

I shouldn't touch her. I should be putting a stop to this, especially since there's no way she doesn't feel my hardness pressing into her ass. But instead of following reason, my hands trace their way along her arms, savoring the goosebumps rising on her skin.

Soon, I drop my arms, letting them slink around her waist. My fingers do a little exploring of their own as I attempt to move in sync with her. One hand stays on her flat stomach while the other trails upward, barely grazing the bottom of her breast.

I should know better, but all sense of restraint vanishes as my hand slides higher, slipping beneath the plunging neckline. My fingers brush against the soft, supple skin of her breast, finding her nipple. Her breath hitches, and she presses her backside into me more firmly, drawing a groan from my lips. Thankfully, I don't have to worry about anyone noticing—or caring—since everyone around us seems lost in their own world.

As she leans her head back against my chest, I'm only encouraged to explore further. I carefully take her nipple between my fingers and give it a soft pinch, continuing to enjoy the feel of her ass brushing against my dick. *God, she feels good*. Before I can completely lose control, she turns to face me, her earthy-brown eyes hooded with lust, lips slightly parted as she drags her teeth hungrily across her bottom lip.

The temptation to bend down and drag that lip against mine is palpable, but I hold back. Instead I reach out and pull her into me—partly because I can no longer stand the distance between us, and also because if she's not in front of me, it's going to become pretty damn obvious just how much of an effect she's having on me.

I need to stop this. I know I do. She may be a twenty-eight-year-old woman, but it's always been clear that between the two of us, I'm the responsible one. Then again, I'm not so sure I deserve that title anymore as I snake my hands around her waist, one hand sliding down beneath the hem of her skirt to take in a firm handful of her round ass.

"Is this okay?" I manage to ask. Given the way she's pressing her body into mine, I assume I know the answer, but I still need to be sure. I may be drunk, but I haven't forgotten how to be a gentleman.

"You know what they say," she murmurs, leaning in on her tiptoes to brush her lips against my ear. "What happens in Vegas stays in Vegas."

Okay, so maybe that's not exactly an answer, but I know exactly what she means. We both know that this would never happen in real life—nor will it ever happen again.

That right there is all the reason I need to be the adult I always claim to be and pull away, but instead, I close the final distance between us, sliding my knee between her legs and press it into her warm core.

She seems just as desperate for this closeness as I am. She places her hands on my chest and moves her body—not just to the rhythm of the music, but brushes herself more desperately against my thigh.

I watch in complete awe as she closes her eyes, her lips parting in pleasure as she rides my leg in this crowded nightclub. Sure, nobody is watching or paying attention to us, but it's hard not to get lost—and so fucking turned on—as I watch her get off on the pressure and pleasure my body is providing her.

More than anything I wish I could slip my hand between us and feel the wetness I know has to be pooling there, but instead, I continue to guide my knee, letting her ride it out as my hand slides down the small of her back, over the curve of her ass, and finally brushes the bare skin of her thigh.

My hands yearn to explore every inch of her body, and it seems she wants the exact same thing, judging by the way her mouth falls open, her eyes shut tight, and her breath quickens. My hand grips the back of her thigh as I move my leg faster against her pussy, no longer caring to stay with the beat of the music. Instead, my only goal is to give her as much pleasure as I possibly can. It doesn't matter that my cock is pulsing with need or that she's the one getting the majority of the pleasure here. Watching her come undone is everything I could ever want or need at this moment.

With her hands still on my chest, I feel her fingernails dig in, as a sound barely audible above the loud music escapes her mouth. I just made her come, but instead of stopping, I let her ride it out until her damp forehead falls onto my chest.

"Fuck," she murmurs with a soft laugh, her tired, hooded eyes meeting mine.

Fuck is right. I just gave my little sister's best friend an orgasm—in the middle of a crowded club, and not only did I like it, but I want to make it happen again... and again. What the hell is wrong with me?

19

VERONICA

MY EYES FLUTTER OPEN, but the world feels too bright and too loud—even if the only noise in here is the buzzing going on in my head—forcing me to shut them once more. Last night me clearly had no respect for future me, forgetting to shut the blackout curtains as streams of light pour into my room. I usually welcome sunshine, but these rays feel like daggers, and my only course of action is to protect what's left of my throbbing, mushy brain.

Hell, that's putting it lightly. My head is pounding with a rhythmic throbbing. Someone tell me why the little drummer boy decided to start his session inside my skull so early, because that's exactly what this feels like. My lips part in a pained groan as I try to bury my head in the pillow, while my brain sifts through the fragmented pieces of my memories, doing its best to reconstruct what exactly happened last night.

I wish I could say feeling this horrible after a night of debauchery was a first, but unfortunately, that's not quite true. I'm well known for my reputation of letting loose and having fun, or at least I was before getting with Pete.

Being the significant other of Evergreen Grove's youngest town councilman was quite the constant balancing act. I was expected to uphold a squeaky-clean image, with him constantly reminding me not to drink too much or step out of line. And when I did, he made sure I knew about it.

The last time I had this much to drink, or anything close to this, was my bachelorette party. I should've been able to let loose and enjoy my last night as a single woman with my friends, but when Pete showed up at my apartment under the guise of 'checking in on me.' I was scolded and made to feel like I'd done something wrong.

Now, with the hazy memories of the night before flooding in, I sort of wish I hadn't indulged so much. Not only had I convinced Broody Bennett to let loose, but we'd gone all out on our night in Vegas. My mind tries to piece it all together, but it only seems to come back in fragments. There were the loud casinos, the constant clinking of the machines as we tried our hand at the slots, the smell of cheap booze in the air, and the pulsating beat of the dance floor, followed by the grand finale of a whirlwind ceremony in a seedy little chapel.

Holy Shit! Miles and I got fucking married last night.

My eyes snap open, jolted awake, and I push myself up, propping myself on my knees as I scan the room. The sudden movement makes my stomach lurch, but the nausea churning inside isn't from the hangover anymore. I can only recall hazy snippets of walking down the aisle toward Miles, with a cheesy Elvis impersonator crooning in the background, but here, in the flesh, is my new husband, lying face down in bed beside me, his breathing soft and steady.

Even now, I can't seem to tear my eyes away from his stunning form in nothing but a pair of black boxer briefs. His long, exposed back taunts me, tempting my fingers to trace the contours of his lightly-tanned skin. But no. He may be my husband, but that sort of thing is still off-limits. I want to believe there's still some dignity left in me—or at least I hope so.

Sure, he may have made me come in the middle of a crowded dance floor as we got lost in the moment and in each other, but I'm still ninety-nine percent sure we didn't consummate the marriage as husband and wife. Some memories from the night before are hazy or completely missing, but I can vaguely remember a lust-fueled make-out session as we undressed each other and made our way to the bed. After that, I'm certain it all came to a halt as the alcohol we consumed took its toll, and we passed out before it could go any further.

It's only when my eyes shift to Miles that I glance down at myself. I'm still wearing a pair of white, lacy panties, but that's it—my bare chest is completely exposed.

I gasp in horror, a silent *"Holy shit"* escaping my lips, as I frantically pull my arms up to shield my chest, praying the sudden movement doesn't wake him. He may have gotten an eye full last night, as well as a handful or two on the dance floor, but I highly doubt sober Miles is ready to see these babies on full display.

My eyes scan the room for something to change into as a new memory emerges—us booking an entirely different hotel room for the night after being offered some 'great deal' on a honeymoon suit to celebrate.

My head falls back, my bottom lip jutting out in a childish pout before letting out an annoyed puff of air. *Fuck me!* This means I have nothing to change into, which also means we both get to do the wonderful walk of shame, leaving the room in the same clothes we walked in with. Then again, this is Vegas, so at least I can take solace in the fact that we aren't the only ones in this predicament. Hell, we probably aren't even the only ones who were dumb enough to get drunkenly married.

Doing my best not to rouse my sleeping husband, I carefully slip out of bed. I reach for the first article of clothing I find, which just so happens to be Miles' white button up shirt. Slipping it over my shoulders, I button it up, at least high enough to cover the lady bits.

Feeling a little bit better now that I have some clothes on, I take stock of the mess we've created before my eyes finally land on my discarded dress by the front door. Oh God, of course drunk and slutty me would have wanted to strip out of it as soon as we walked in. Then again, if my memory serves me correctly, Miles had been just as eager to get that dress off me as I was.

My cheeks flush at the memory. I can still feel his piercing blue eyes drinking me in as if I were the sexiest thing he'd ever seen, and despite the shame, I can't help but remember how his adoration almost made me believe it might actually be true.

Careful not to make any noise, I tiptoe toward my dress. But my mission is thwarted when I notice a card, along with some paperwork sitting on the small entry table.

I pick up the card first.

"Mr. and Mrs. Bennett,

> Congratulations on your beautiful beginning! May your journey together be filled with love, laughter, and endless adventures. Wishing you a lifetime of happiness and cherished memories. Thank you for allowing us to be part of this special moment. Here's to your new forever!"

Setting the card back down, my gaze shifts to what appears to be a picture from the happy event. I lift it open and inspect. Right there is the proof in the flesh as Miles and I stand directly next to each other. If one didn't know better, they'd probably assume we were a happy, completely in-love couple, because those two certainly look it. My face is practically splitting with a proud, joyous grin, one arm raised high as I hold a bouquet of fake white roses. Miles is holding me close, one arm wrapped around my waist as he leans in to kiss my cheek.

I want to smile at the memory, and I wish I could enjoy this moment for the craziness that it is. Honestly, a Vegas-wedding is very on brand for me. But considering I just ran away from one wedding, only to end up married to my best friend's brother, it's not exactly a great look—even for me. This is definitely a new low, especially as I dragged Miles Bennett into this, of all people.

God, this man is truly going to hate me forever. Damn that stupid and delicious slushy! I'm positive it was the catalyst and the first of many bad decisions made last night.

Setting the picture down, I reach for the last paper, and likely the final piece of the puzzle. If I wasn't sure that last night was nothing more than a fever dream and a figment of my imagination, there's no denying it now. In my hands is a marriage certificate with both our names there in black ink. And yep, while maybe not as pretty as usual, that is certainly my signature. Miles and I truly did get married last night, and this is very, very real.

Looking back toward the bed, Miles is one lucky, oblivious bastard—at least for now—as he continues to sleep. This just isn't fair, since even now, he looks so fucking beautiful as a strand of hair falls over his closed eyes. I should let him sleep this off. Hell, he probably deserves to after the mess I've gotten us into, but there really is no running away from this.

Closing my eyes, I take one final deep breath and make my way toward him. As much as I want to shield him from the truth, he deserves to know what happened. More importantly, we need to figure out what the hell we're going to do about this.

20

MILES

"MILES, YOU NEED TO wake up," a voice calls to me, but I'm nowhere near ready to, nor do I want to open my eyes. There's already an unmistakable throb in my head, and a part of me already knows I'm not ready to face the repercussions of a long night of drinking and partying.

Instead, I keep my eyes closed and press my face into the soft comfort of my pillow, doing my best to block it all out. I should probably be worried—there's someone in my room after all. And not just anyone... Veronica Prescott, of all people. But right now, I'm desperate to delay the inevitable. The longer I sleep, the longer I can pretend nothing crazy happened last night.

If anything, the only major thought running through my head is the stark reminder of why I don't drink in the first place. Sure, I'll occasionally have a beer or two when I'm out with the guys from work, or at a bar, but that's about it. I refuse to become my father, and I'm pissed at myself for getting so out of control, because that's Bill Bennett's behavior right there, not mine.

I had only allowed myself to indulge to the point of blacking out once before, and that was all the way back in high school. That single night was enough to make me swear it would never happen again—and until last night, I had kept that promise.

Then again, I've also found myself saying yes to just about anything Veronica suggests. Hopefully, this will be the final straw that reminds me why I was never a fan of hers in the first place.

"Miles, I'm serious," she says, her voice demanding my attention as it rises in pitch. I try to ignore her, but she grabs my shoulder and pulls me to face her.

"Mmmm." I groan, still not daring to open my eyes.

"Miles. I swear to God, if you don't wake up," she threatens, her voice edged with panic. As much as I want to hide away, if only a few more minutes, I finally let my eyes peek open.

I suppose one thing to be thankful for is the fact that she looks just about as terrible as I feel. I may be a lightweight, but at least I'm not the only one affected by our rowdy night of recklessness. "You know, if you're really this insistent on waking me up, the least you could have done is have some water and pills on deck."

Okay, so obviously it's not her job, nor would I actually expect it, but given the way my brain seems to be slamming against my skull, it certainly would've been nice.

"You mean you didn't want to wake up to this instead?" she asks, her tone sarcastic as she holds up a sheet of paper in one hand and a picture in the other.

My vision is too blurry to make out what she's holding as I squint my eyes. "What is it?" I ask, still struggling to process what she's talking about or trying to show me.

"Our wedding license, babe. Apparently, I'm Mrs. Veronica Bennett. Don't you remember?" she asks, a fake sweetness in her tone as her words drip with sarcasm.

If I were a fully functioning adult at this moment, I probably would've shot upright and demanded answers, but my brain seems to be processing things at the speed of a snail, so I shake my head instead. "No, seriously. What is it?" I ask, slowly pushing myself into a sitting position, my achy muscles protesting with each movement.

"I'm serious, Miles. We got married last night. Even I wouldn't joke about this," she says, her voive grave as I register the frown on her face.

"No, we didn't," I scoff, snatching what has to be a fake certificate from her hand. There's no way I'd ever let myself do something that stupid. Sure, I was drunk, but even in that state, I'd hope I had enough sense not to make such a life-altering decision—I couldn't have been that dumb.

"Unfortunately, we did," she sighs.

"But this can't be real. This is just a stupid Vegas gimmick, right? Just some dumb souvenir we picked up to tease Blair with," I suggest. There is just no way in hell I'd ever be reckless enough to let myself get married in Vegas, especially not to Veronica Prescott.

She may have grown on me some this past week, but not enough to want to marry her. I also may have even made her come last night...

Fuck!

Thankfully, before I can ruminate on that for too long, she starts to speak again.

"I'm sorry to be the one to break it to you, but this is real. We're officially man and wife, oh dear husband of mine," she says, lifting her left ring finger to showcase a plain gold band.

With a jolt, I lift my hand to see a nearly identical one on my ring finger. "Fuck!" I curse again, but this time, out loud.

"Also, just so you know… We, uh, never…" She trails off as I raise a brow, waiting for her to continue, but she hesitates as her eyes find the floor.

"We never what?" I ask, my brows pinching together.

"Had sex… right?" she asks, her gaze finally brave enough to meet mine.

My eyes widen in surprise, as the thought hadn't even crossed my mind just yet. Then again, how could I be expected to remember anything that happened? Most of the night is a complete blur.

"I don't know," I admit, my voice a strained whisper as I struggle to make sense of this, my fingers clutching my chest as my heart pounds wildly against it. "What makes you think it's even a possibility?" I ask, even though I'm not so sure I'm ready to hear the answer.

She gestures with her eyes, and I notice she's wearing my shirt from the night before. I force myself not to dwell on how much I like seeing her in it. Now is definitely not the time for thoughts like those.

"I may be wearing this now, but when I first woke up, I was here, in bed, and I was completely topless," she carefully explains as I lift my hand to pinch the bridge of my nose. "I mean, I was still wearing my underwear, so that's a good sign, but I was actually sort of hoping you could confirm it completely."

I breathe a small breath of relief to know that at least she hadn't woken up completely nude. I suppose that doesn't mean nothing happened for certain, but I have to imagine it's as good of a sign as any that it didn't. I also will myself not to picture what exactly she looked like before she covered up with my shirt.

"To be honest, I don't remember much. The last thing I remember clearly is us dancing at the club," I say, and this time, it's her turn to blush, her cheeks turning a deep shade of crimson. Looks like I'm not the only one who remembers what happened on that dance floor. Though, maybe that's not necessarily a good thing. "I also remember us grabbing some more drinks and doing shots..." I stop, a blurry image of us doing body shots flashing through my mind, but I forcefully dismiss it, willing that thought to go right back to where it came from.

Her nose scrunches as she also seems to relive that same memory. "Yeah, I think after that, we went to another club before deciding that the only right way to celebrate being in Vegas was to do a totally Vegas thing and get hitched," she explains, a low, strained whine escaping her throat.

"Yeah, unfortunately I don't remember any of that," I admit, since that's the part where everything goes blank.

"That's probably for the best. It's not like it was a real wedding," she says, folding her arms across her chest, her fingers nervously twisting the fabric of my shirt. "I mean, obviously it was real, since we're actually married, but it's not like we're going to stay married," she rambles, throwing her arms into the air.

"Don't worry," I say, trying to swing my legs off the bed, but a groan escapes my lips as I'm instantly hit with a dizzy spell, fighting the urge to vomit. Honestly, I'm not even sure if it's the hangover or the news, but right now I'm absolutely sick to my stomach. "I'm with you on this. It was just a dumb drunken mistake. We'll get it taken care of," I assure her, closing my eyes as one hand falls to rest on my stomach.

With a soft exhale, she sinks onto the bed beside me. "I can't believe I ran away from one wedding only to end up married to someone who absolutely hates me," she whines, letting her face fall into her hands as she slumps over.

I shouldn't feel the need to comfort her, especially given my own worries, but I can't help it. My hand lands softly on her back, tracing soothing circles. "Come on, you have to know I don't hate you. If this past week has shown you anything, it should be that I only find you vaguely annoying." I try to joke in an effort to lighten the mood, which, honestly, isn't me. I should be yelling and screaming, since there's no way I was the one who suggested getting married on a drunken whim. This has Veronica written all over it, along with being some crazy idea that only she could come up with. But I'm not about to let her shoulder all the blame, even if, right now, it's tempting as hell.

"Oh, yes," she pouts, sitting up as I let my hand fall from her back. "Just what every new bride wants to hear: her husband only finds her vaguely annoying." She scoffs, though there's an amused lilt to her tone.

"Well, unfortunately for you, you may need to get used to it, because I've never claimed to be husband material. In fact, there's a good reason I've chosen to remain single for the majority of my life."

Sure, I've had a few occasional girlfriends, but there was a reason none of them ever worked out. The majority of those relationships ended with them breaking things off, not the other way around, making it easy to assume that I'm the obvious reason for the break-ups. Then again, what can they expect? I grew up with awful, shitty parents and grandparents as examples of what a relationship should be. While I've tried to live my life completely opposite of what I witnessed, I've also never been around anyone who's had a fully functioning and healthy relationship.

"I guess that's true. Drunk me really should have thought this through." She sighs, a self-deprecating laugh bubbling up from her chest before escalating into full-blown manic laughter.

There is nothing even remotely funny about what we're going through, and while I know this isn't a laughing matter, I can't help it—a grin somehow makes its way onto my face as I watch her lean forward, placing her hand on her stomach.

"I don't even know why I'm laughing," she admits through her giggles. "This isn't funny. I mean, the whole reason I ran away from Pete was because I knew it was destined to end in divorce, yet here I am. Married and bound for exactly what I just ran away from," she adds, her giggles dying down, but it doesn't take long to realize that something is wrong as she reaches up to wipe at a few stray tears, as the laughter turns into heart-wrenching sobs.

"Hey, come on now," I say, my protective instinct kicking in as I wrap an arm around her shoulder and pull her into me. She melts into my embrace, burying her face into my chest. "I know this wasn't something we wanted or planned for, but if you have to be married to someone only for it to end in divorce, at least it's with me, right?" I ask, though given the way she continues to cry, I'm not sure how comforting that actually is. "I know I'm not always the nicest or friendliest guy in the world, and I'm probably the last, or maybe second-to-last person you want to be married to right now, but until we figure this out, I promise to treat you the way a wife, no—*the way you*—deserve to be treated, okay?" My hand moves upward, my fingers gently threading through her short brown hair in what I hope is a much-needed gesture of reassurance.

The tears still flow, but I assume there's a sense of release in them, a way of letting go as she clutches me tightly as we sit together in the silence. While I know this isn't a real or a traditional marriage by any stretch of the imagination, I meant what I said. I doubt I'll ever truly be husband material, but I plan to take care of her. More than anything, I'll do whatever I can to take away the hurt and pain I know continues to plague her.

Maybe that's just a normal way for any man to feel about his wife, but given that she hadn't ever been my first choice, this feels a little different. As I continue to hold her, one hand continually running through her hair as the other traces the contours of her back, one thing I know for sure is that I never want to see her cry like this again. I'll do whatever I can to make sure that while she's in my care, she's always happy, even if it means stepping out of my comfort zone. Right now, I'm willing to do just about anything to see Veronica Prescott smile.

21

VERONICA

NOTHING RUINS A ROAD trip quite like accidentally getting married to your best friend's older brother. Or was it when I broke down and cried in his arms? At this point, it's probably fifty-fifty.

That's why, as soon as I pulled myself together and went back to my original hotel room, I sent him a text suggesting we make our way back home to Evergreen Grove. I'm not ready to see Pete or to deal with the vicious gossip I know is circulating, but you can only hide for so long—especially when you run into an even bigger problem along the way.

I'm no stranger to wild and often reckless ideas, but this feels like a new low, even for me. Thankfully, it's fixable—or at least I now know how, considering I spent the first hour of our drive home frantically Googling divorce and annulment options for a Vegas marriage. Despite my mortification, I found some comfort in knowing we weren't the only ones to make such a monumental mistake. Online forums overflowed with people dealing with the exact same issue, their stories offering minor solace in solidarity. Apparently, I'm not the only screw-up out there.

"So, what's the verdict?" Miles asks from the driver's seat, and I look up from my research.

"So, from what I'm seeing, if we want an annulment, the sooner we file the better, but we actually have up to two years."

"Two years? How long were you planning on staying married to me?" he asks, the corner of his mouth tilting into a smirk. "I may own my own business, but I promise I'm not rolling in cash if that's what has you so interested."

I give him a steely stare. "I liked it better when you were the grumpy one," I decide. While I can somewhat see the humor in our situation, the nerves of going back home have me on edge, especially given our newly married state.

It doesn't even matter that I know this is only temporary. I made a reckless, life-changing decision, and while I'm sure my loved ones back home will understand why I ran away from Pete, I'm not so sure they'll be as understanding about me randomly getting married in Vegas.

"Sorry," he says, trying—and failing—to wipe the smirk off his face. "I'll be sure to go back to my regularly scheduled programming of brooding stares and sarcastic remarks. I mean, come on, they don't call me Broody Bennett for nothing."

"Thank you, I'd appreciate it," I huff, an involuntary smile spreading across my face. "*Now*, back to what I was saying..." I trail off, giving him a quick, playful glare. "It really does seem like the sooner we get things moving, the better, because in Colorado, it still looks like it will take a couple of months before everything gets taken care of and our marriage becomes officially annulled."

"Really?" he asks, his smile finally disappearing as it fully registers that, while we both know this was never real to begin with, we're going to have to be married for at least a few months. "I always thought annulments were quick."

"Same." I sigh, the dull glow of the screen fading to black as I tuck my phone away.

"But at least it's not like we'll be getting divorced. That has to count for something, right?" he asks, his eyes flicking toward me for a moment before returning to the road ahead. "It will be like this never happened."

"I guess. It's better than nothing." I agree, doing my best to be as equally positive as he's trying to be, even if I know he's only doing it for my sake. Surprisingly, he's kind of good at this. Who knew?

Too bad my brain can't seem to let it go. The law might pretend it never happened, but with Evergreen Grove being such a small and gossipy town, it won't be long before everyone finds out about our crazy Vegas wedding. We'll forever be known as the fools who got married on a drunken whim. I thought being known as the runaway bride was bad, but now I get to add this to my résumé. *Yay me!*

"I'm sorry, Vee," he says, his fingers ghosting over my bare knee and giving it a gentle squeeze before returning his hand to the steering wheel.

"Don't apologize. It is what it is at this point. I just..." I sigh, trying to figure out how to put my thoughts into words. "I'm not sure I'm ready to face everyone back home just yet, and have them see how I've somehow turned into an even bigger disappointment than they already thought." I groan, my shoulders slumping in defeat.

"First off, we don't have to drive all the way back to Colorado tonight. We can stop somewhere if that's what you need" he reminds me, shooting me a quick glance. "Second, nobody in Evergreen could or would ever think badly of you. Honestly, it never made sense to me why everybody loved you, even with the craziness you seemed to put everyone through. But you're the town sweetheart, and I'm sure when everyone inevitably finds out what we did, it will somehow only endear you to them even more."

I roll my eyes. "Not everyone loves me. You should know that better than anyone. Then, when you add the fact that I left a jilted groom at the altar, only to come back home with a new husband, it's likely not going to be the best look. I mean, can you even imagine what Pete is going to have to say about this?"

"Fuck him. The guy is an asshole. Nobody cares what he thinks," Miles growls.

"Did you forget that he got voted into the city council? He's loved and adored by lots of people, and I'm pretty sure they're all going to have a lot of interesting opinions and things to say about what happened and what I've done since leaving him."

"Fuck them, and fuck what everyone in our small-minded town thinks."

"That may be easy for you to say, especially since you've always been good at brushing off what everyone thinks about you, but I'm not built that way. I was born with the gene that makes me desperately care about other's opinions," I admit, my voice laced with anxiety as my bottom lip pulls into a small frown. "Why do you think I tried so hard for so many years to get you to like me when you constantly made it obvious that you didn't?"

"And what did me not liking you actually do? Did it cause any actual pain?" he asks.

I shrug. "Maybe not actual physical pain, but that doesn't mean I enjoyed it, especially with you being someone who was so important to my favorite person in the entire world."

"And look, you finally did it. You got me to like you, so there's always hope," he adds, once again trying to be optimistic, which, coming from him, is kind of weird, yet oddly sweet. "Look, I'm not saying going home is going to be easy. I'm sure things will feel off for a bit, and people will be gossiping, but eventually it will all die down, and everyone will forget about all of this. They'll all eventually find something new to gossip about."

"Maybe." I give in, even if I'm not fully convinced. Sure, I might not always be the center of the gossip, but I have a feeling that after what happened these past few weeks, the labels of 'runaway bride' and 'Vegas wedding' will stick with me forever. It will always be a part of my story, whispered in hushed tones whenever my name is mentioned.

"So, what are we going to do? Do we want to spend the night driving all the way through to get home, or should we make one final pit stop and make this crazy adventure of ours last one more day?" he asks, leaving the decision up to me.

I tilt my head, weighing my options. Part of me wants to go home and start figuring out my new normal, but another part wants to delay the inevitable, even if it's just for one more day.

"Maybe we should stop," I finally decide.

"Thank God, because even though I said I'm good to drive and could handle it, this headache is coming back with a vengeance, and I'm ready for a break."

"Well, in that case, I'll start looking for somewhere for us to stay," I offer as I reach into my pocket and pull out my phone.

"The closer, the better," he adds, and I shoot him a sideways glance.

"You really need a break that badly? Why didn't you say something earlier?" I ask, returning my gaze to the open Google page.

He shrugs. "I know you're dealing with a lot, and the last thing I want to do is add to that by complaining about something I brought on myself. If you really wanted to get home, then I'd have done whatever was needed to make it happen."

"Miles," I admonish, turning in my seat to face him more fully. "Please don't do that. It's not like you aren't going through something too. Plus, we both know Blair forced you to come with me in the first place and it's not like you were planning on getting married anytime soon, least of all to me."

"That may be true, but I'm a Bennett. I'm used to being the town fuck-up, even if I've done nothing in my life to prove that to them. Maybe it was finally time for me to give them some ammo," he says with a casual shrug, his tone betraying a hint of bitterness.

My face drops. "I'm sorry," I apologize, my bottom lip trembling, as I feel the sting of tears burning the back of my eyes. I know Miles always blamed me for getting his sister into trouble when we were younger, and while I tried so hard to prove that he was wrong, now I've gone and done the same exact thing he always accused me of—this time, to him.

"Don't apologize. I'm a grown man, Vee. I made my own choices yesterday. You didn't force me to do any of that. I did it all willingly."

"Fine," I relent, since I highly doubt I'll be able to change his mind on the matter. He's stubborn, something I've known about him forever. "But please, next time tell me if you need a break or want to stop. This is our trip, not just mine, and I don't want you feeling like you have to do something just for my benefit."

"Deal," he says, his eyes not straying from the road. However, I'm not sure I believe him. His willingness to go above and beyond for me is truly admirable, but right now, I feel so unworthy—I don't deserve that level of kindness, especially not from him.

This road trip was supposed to be a chance for a fresh start, a way to clear my mind after Pete. But now, with each passing mile, I find myself haunted by Miles' old judgments of me from the past. Maybe I am nothing but a selfish brat, ruining the lives of others without a second thought or care for how my actions affect those around me. At this point, I probably deserve all the bad karma that's likely to come my way as we head home.

22

MILES

I MAY NOT KNOW Veronica as well as my sister does, but this week I've learned that she's a whirlwind of activity, constantly buzzing around and chattering away like the damn Energizer Bunny. Sitting quietly is not in her nature. Most of our trip has been her talking my ear off, and the only time I got a break was when she was listening to one of her murder podcasts or when she'd actually tired herself out enough to sleep.

However, ever since we decided to stop for one last night before our journey home tomorrow, an uncomfortable silence has settled between us.

Even when we ended up in a tiny diner for dinner, she was quiet, barely speaking. The only words exchanged were the ones I initiated—so clearly, not much.

"You sure you're okay?" I finally ask as we make the short walk back to our hotel, where thankfully, we were able to get separate rooms. We may be married, but that's in title only. Neither of us is ready to pretend there's more to this relationship than what it actually is.

"I'm fine," she says, sending me a tight-lipped smile as we cross the street.

"Yeah, that was convincing," I deadpan. I might have let her have her space in the car, and even at dinner, but I'm done playing pretend—even if that was what old Miles would have much preferred. In fact, the Miles from the start of this trip would have preferred we not talk to each other at all. Now, I unfortunately find that I care a little too much about her feelings—something I'm trying very hard not to read into.

"Sorry, I just have a lot on my mind," she admits, folding her arms across her chest as she somehow seems to sink even further into herself.

"I know I'm probably not your preferred audience, but I'm a pretty good listener, or at least that's what Blair tells me," I push, despite my better judgment.

"She is my usual go-to person for all my problems, and while you may somewhat look like her with your gorgeous baby blue eyes, I'm thinking you should just wait until tomorrow when I can actually chat with my usual Bennett sibling."

"Try me," I goad her. I should let this go, but I can't. I've always been a fixer. It's why I own and operate a mechanic shop. Sure, maybe the only person I usually care to fix problems for is Blair, but somehow, Veronica has weaseled her way in, and I'm desperate to see a smile on her face again.

"Okay, well, other than the obvious of having to return home with a husband, I realized that I'm also returning with no place to live." She sighs, the weight of her words causing her shoulders to physically slump.

"What do you mean?" I ask, my brows drawing together. "I get that you're no longer moving in with Pete, but you have your apartment, right? Can't you just renew your lease?"

"Nope," she says, the 'p' popping out of her mouth like a bubble. "Unfortunately, my landlord has already rented it out to his niece, so I'll only have a week after we get back to move my things out. I mean, I'm sure I'll be able to find somewhere to rent eventually, but until then, it looks like I'm going to be the twenty-eight-year-old loser who has to move back in with her parents."

I clench my jaw, trying to suppress the involuntary eye roll that wants to escape. "Oh, come on, things could be worse. In this economy, plenty of people live with their parents. Hell, some people would kill to have Mr. and Mrs. Prescott as their mom and dad. We both know they'd be happy to have you move back in."

She shoots me an apologetic glance. "Yeah, you're right. Sorry." She winces. Given how close she is to my sister, it's no surprise she knows all about our shitty parents, who could not have cared less about Blair or me, or what happened to us.

Hell, the only reason we weren't homeless or put into child protective services custody was because of our grandma, but even she made it pretty obvious that we were nothing but a burden and a responsibility she never wanted.

"I'm not trying to make you feel guilty or worse. If anything, I'm just trying to help you see that you have people. You have a support system when you get back. You have your family. You have Blair and Ford, and now you have me," I offer as casually as possible, even if the words feel strange on my tongue. Never in a million years could I have predicted that I'd consider her a friend, yet here we are.

"You?" she asks, a genuine smile finally gracing her lips. "We're friends now, huh?" she asks, bumping her hip into mine as we approach the entrance of our hotel.

"Don't make this into a big deal," I say, mimicking her stance as I fold my arms. "But it's true. You're not alone, and maybe," I start, realizing I'm actually about to suggest this. Finally giving in—despite my better judgement—I complete my sentence, "you could move in with me."

She freezes in her tracks, her eyes widening as she turns to face to face me. "With you? Okay, yeah. Sure. Be for real. There is no way you'd ever want me as your roommate," she says, sarcasm lacing her tone as she follows it up with a non-amused laugh.

I stop as well. "I said nothing about wanting you as my roommate, but I have the extra room, and it's not like it'd be forever. Just until you get on your feet and figure things out."

"What about Blair?" she asks, her eyebrows pinching together.

"What about her? If anything, she'd probably be all for this and is likely already planning to spend most of her time at Ford's. Plus, it's not like you two haven't shared a room or a bed before. Don't think I forgot about that night where you two drunkenly crashed at my place just a couple of weeks ago."

She catches her bottom lip between her teeth, barely suppressing an amused laugh. "You don't think it'd be weird? Plus, you know everyone is already going to be talking about us. Wouldn't this just add more fuel to the fire?"

I lift one shoulder. "I'm sure people are going to talk about us no matter what. Maybe this would actually give them something real to talk about this time."

I've never loved being the center of gossip and have made a conscious effort to keep my nose clean and stay out of their mouths, but I don't see why this should stop me from taking care of someone I've actually grown to care about.

"Maybe..." she trails off, her brow furrowing as she ponders my offer. "But if we did this, I'd have to pay you rent. I'm not looking to be some kind of charity case," she finally says, pointing a finger in my direction.

"That's fine with me." I shrug, even if I don't actually want to charge her anything. I can more than afford my own place, but if that's what it takes to get her to say yes, then I'll say whatever I have to.

I can't explain this feeling, this urge to make sure she's safe and taken care of, but it's strong, and it's something I can no longer ignore. I won't let her do this alone, not when I have the power to help.

"Are you sure about this?" she asks, the warmth of her smile evaporating as her brown eyes fix on mine. "I'm sure you think you can handle this after spending a week and a half with me, but we're talking about me moving in and being around twenty-four-seven. That's a lot of Veronica time."

"I wouldn't have offered if I didn't mean it," I assure her, doing my best to avoid the deeper conversation about the inexplicable pull I feel to make everything better for her. "Plus, I can't have my wife homeless, now can I? What kind of husband would that make me?" I joke, needing to add some humor to this, and not just for her sake, but mine as well.

"A pretty crappy one, but if you're not particularly fond of the woman you married, it's logical that you wouldn't want her to move in with you. After everything, I'd assume you'd want to see as little of me as possible."

"Just because I'm suggesting you move in for a little while doesn't mean we have to be best friends," I point out. "We both have jobs and different friend groups, so I'm sure we'll only see each other in passing. This isn't a big deal," I lie. This is an enormous deal and I know it, but once again, I can't help myself.

"Yeah, maybe you're right." She nods as a soft exhale passes through her lips, her shoulders slumping with a hint of defeat. "Are you really sure you're okay with this?"

"Yes. I'm sure. I wouldn't have offered it if I wasn't."

Deep down, a part of me knows I should question why I'm offering, but I'm still not ready to let my brain consider why that is.

"If you say so, but if at any time between now or even tomorrow when you've had time to thoroughly think this through and want to change your mind, that's fine. I won't hold it against you," she promises.

I shrug her words off as I walk back toward our hotel entrance. "Deal, but I can promise you, I won't change my mind," I say over my shoulder as she follows close behind.

Is asking her to move in with me the smartest decision I've ever made? Probably not. Especially since I tend to overthink everything and steer clear of situations that might backfire. But there's something about Veronica Prescott that pulls me in, something I can't shake. Maybe that should be my cue to keep my distance, to protect myself. But instead, I'm doing the exact opposite.

I like how she makes me feel—alive, untethered—and I'm not ready to give that up. Not now, and maybe not ever. For once, I want to live in the moment and do what feels right. I'll deal with the consequences later.

23

VERONICA

As WE ENTER THE Evergreen Grove city limits, the familiar scenery does little to ease the knot of anxiety tightening in my stomach. I love this place—it's home. However, for
the first time, I think I may now understand Blair's obsession
with running and leaving everything behind.

Sure, the people here are incredibly gossipy, but it never really
bothered me. My friends and I made a habit of being the center
of attention with our ridiculous and often childish antics, and
I barely gave it a second thought. But now? The mere idea of
talking to anyone besides Blair or Ford has my stomach churning with dread.

Even with how incredibly supportive my parents have always
been, that same anxiety lingers. The thought of seeing even a
flicker of disappointment in their eyes—especially after fleeing
one wedding only to show up with a brand-new husband—is
practically debilitating.

"Did you text Blair to let her know we're almost there?" Miles
asks, his deep timbre pulling me out of my thoughts.

"No, but I will," I say, reaching for my phone on the center console. "Although, I'm guessing she's been watching our location for a while now," I add, having sent her a pin when we left this morning. Given how excited and anxious she seemed, my guess is she's doing exactly what I'd be doing in this situation and religiously watching our pin get closer and closer to home.

"Probably," he agrees, keeping his eyes on the road. Looks like I'm not the only one dreading being back home, because even Miles, who usually seems emotionless, is practically vibrating with nervous energy, his knuckles white as he grips the steering wheel.

"So, it's still the plan to tell Blair?" I ask, needing the final confirmation. While we had discussed keeping this a secret from most people, we did both agree during the drive that we should at least tell Blair and Ford.

"Like you could keep it a secret from her anyway. I know you two. There's no way you could hide anything from her, even if you tried," he says, the corner of his lips tugging into a grin.

"I could if I really wanted to." I huff, even though I'm pretty sure he's right.

"Whatever you say," he says before silence settles over the car, broken only by the twang of a country song blaring from the radio. The music does little to soothe my nerves, especially as we roll through Main Street.

Yep. There's no denying we're back home now, especially as I spot some of Evergreen's residents walking around, all stopping to take in Miles' car, their eyes wide with curiosity.

In a town this small, everyone knows exactly who drives what—and Miles' cherry-red Ford Mustang might as well be a neon sign. I imagine it's not much of a secret that I sped off with him after ditching my wedding, so it's safe to assume the rumor mill has been working overtime. Now that we're back, I can already feel the weight of all the stares and whispers waiting for us.

"We really are back home, huh?" Miles asks, a quiet chuckle escaping despite the lack of genuine humor in his voice.

"I mean, were we really expecting a different kind of welcome?"

"Not really, but just wait, the real fun is going to be when we're forced to interact with them," he says, as I do my best not to shiver at the idea. The stares are bad enough, but I already know the questions will be even worse—loud, intrusive, and completely lacking in tact. It is the Evergreen way, after all.

Slowly, some of the worry dissipates as Miles pulls into his apartment complex parking lot, and just as I figured—or at least hoped—Blair and Ford are standing out front with Miles' bulldog Bubba on a leash.

"Blair!" I yell, waving my arms wildly. She smiles and waves back, handing Ford the dog's leash before jogging after the car as it pulls into a nearby parking spot.

"Ronnie!" she giggles, her voice filled with pure joy as she impatiently pulls open my door while I struggle with the buckle. Once free, I hop out and she envelops me in a warm bear hug. "I missed you so much."

"I've missed you too," I tell her, holding her close as she rocks us back and forth, the comfort of her embrace filling me with some much-needed relief.

"And what am I? Chopped liver?" Miles asks as he rounds the corner.

"Eh." Blair playfully shrugs as she pulls back from our hug. "I guess I missed you too."

"And hey, don't worry," Ford cuts in. "I know someone who certainly missed you," he says as we all look down at the white, chubby ball of fur jumping at Miles' legs.

"Hey, Bubs," Miles greets him, effortlessly scooping up the dog like he's nothing, even though the pup easily weighs 30 or 40 pounds. "Now you, I've definitely missed," he says, his voice taking on a softness you wouldn't expect from someone like him, and one you can't help but find incredibly endearing. I know it's just a dog, but did my ovaries just twitch?

Apparently, I'm not the only one who's noticed my strange reaction to this tender moment, as Blair nudges my arm, her eyebrows pinching together.

"Please tell me that look is only because this is a cute moment between a dog dad and his baby and that nothing else is going on here," she chides. While I assume this is all said in jest, I can't help it as my cheeks turn a deep shade of pink.

"Well, nothing like what you're insinuating is going on, but um, we do have some things to talk about."

Blair's eyes widen, clearly not expecting that sort of answer. "Wait, what?" she asks, her voice cracking with a newfound sense of worry as her eyes search mine.

"You don't need to stress out. It's nothing big, or at least nothing like what you're probably thinking." I attempt to assure her.

"Miles fucking Bennett, what did you do to my friend?" Blair practically interrupts, placing her hands on her hips, as both Miles and Ford look our way.

"Blair," I hiss as Miles' questioning eyes meet mine, before moving back to his sister.

"So she told you?" he asks.

Blair's icy blue eyes somehow widen even more. "No, not yet, but one of you better tell me what the fuck is going on," she says through gritted teeth, her eyes shifting between the two of us.

Miles' gaze locks with mine, his expression a mixture of reluctance and panic. It's clear he's not going to take charge here, so I guess it's up to me.

"Miles and I got married," I blurt, figuring there's really no way to sugarcoat it, so I may as well just put it out there.

Ford laughs, while Blair's eyes somehow grow even bigger as her mouth drops open.

"Oh, okay, I get it. You guys are just messing with me," she says, a disbelieving laugh escaping her lips. She doesn't seem to believe the bomb I just dropped, and honestly, I can't blame her. I've spent the past two days trying to find a way to make sense of it too.

"No, she's telling the truth. It was an accident, but we're taking care of it," Miles thankfully chimes in as he finally sets Bubba back on the ground. "We're getting this annulled as soon as we can, but things got a bit crazy when we ended up in Vegas and one thing led to another and we somehow got married," he casually explains, as if impulsively tying the knot in Vegas is no big deal.

Ford continues to laugh. "I'm sorry," he says as we all turn to glare in his direction, especially since the laughter bubbling up inside him makes it impossible to take his apology seriously. "That was just not what I was expecting you guys to say."

"Believe me, we didn't expect for this to happen either," I promise, my gaze once again landing on Blair. "Are you mad?" I tentatively ask, since her laughter has completely disappeared. Instead, her mouth is wide open in shock as she attempts to process our news.

"I wouldn't say mad is the emotion I'm feeling right about now," she manages as she breaks out of whatever trance she's in. "I guess I'm just surprised. How did this even happen? I mean, I know you said things got a little crazy, but what the hell? Getting married in Vegas? That's a bit much, even for you, Ronnie."

"No, I know. I get it. This is a lot to take in, but don't go reading into things, either. We haven't even kissed or anything," I try to assure her before my brows furrow as I realize that's not exactly true. "Or, I guess maybe we kissed when we got married, but we were drunk that night and haven't done anything like it since, or even before," I add, figuring she probably doesn't need to know about what happened earlier that drunken night or later on during our wedding night.

"It's really not a big deal," Miles cuts in as he casually moves to grab his bag from the back of the car. "It was just something crazy that happened, but it won't be for long, or at least not really."

"Not really? What does that even mean?" Blair asks, shaking her head in disbelief.

"Apparently, annulments take a bit longer to go through than most movies would have you believe. And well, because Vee is going to be moving in with me for a while," he casually explains, as if he didn't just drop yet another huge bomb on his sister.

"What!?" Blair shrieks again, her eyes darting from her brother back to me.

"Don't worry," I say, trying to calm her down as I place a hand on her arm. "It's nothing like that. It's just that my lease is ending next week, and since I'm not too keen on moving back in with my parents, your brother offered to let me stay until I get things figured out."

"He did, did he?" she asks, this time narrowing her eyes in Miles' direction.

"What?" he asks, slinging his bag over his shoulder as he leans against the back of the car. "You're the one always telling me I need to be nicer to your friend, and now that I'm doing it, you're giving me shit? Make up your damn mind."

Blair rolls her eyes. "I didn't mean to be nice, only so you could make your way into her pants."

"Okay," I interrupt, lifting my hands, palms out. "First off, nobody is getting inside these pants, and it's not like that between us. He's just being nice."

"Yeah, Blair. I'm just being nice." Miles smirks, a mischievous glint in his eyes as he seems to revel in his sister's outrage, while I, on the other hand, am panicking.

"You aren't helping," I growl, sending my own glare in his direction. "But seriously though," I continue, as I turn back toward his sister, "it's not a big deal. I promise. He doesn't see me like that. If anything, he only slightly tolerates me now."

"Uh huh," Blair says, not even the least bit convinced.

"Yep," Miles adds, reaching into the back to grab one of my bags as well. "And as much fun as this little reunion is, I'm going to head inside, but you all are welcome to stay out here and catch up for as long as you like," he says, shooting his sister another irritating smirk before giving me a reassuring nod.

I try not to look as nervous as I feel, especially as I watch Bubba happily trail after his dad.

"So, I guess this makes you two sisters now, huh?" Ford asks, still incredibly amused as he continues to fight the laughter that so obviously wants to come out.

"Yeah, I guess it does," Blair muses, turning toward me with an almost apologetic smile. "I'm sorry if I'm being weird. This is just... it's a lot to take in."

I shake my head. "No, don't worry about it. It's a lot for me to take in too," I admit, letting out a long, shaky breath. "Believe me, the last thing I ever expected was to leave Evergreen and one man behind, only to come back home married to a completely different one—one who can barely stand me at that."

Blair scrunches her lips to the side. "I'm not so sure I'd say he can barely stand you. He barely enjoys sharing his place with me when I visit. If he's offering to let you stay, that definitely says something."

"If you're worried there's something going on between me and your brother, let me put your mind at ease. It really was nothing more than a drunken mistake. There's nothing going on between us."

I see the doubt etched in Blair's eyes—and honestly, I get it. I'm not even sure I believe myself. Sure, I was somewhat truthful when I said nothing happened beyond the night we got married. But now? I'm starting to realize I might be falling for Miles Bennett. It's a terrifying thought, though only slightly easier to swallow because of how well I know him. This won't go any further than it already has. Maybe he tolerates me—maybe he even enjoys my company—but anything more than that feels impossible. In his mind, I'm likely always going to be nothing more than Blair's annoying and impulsive best friend.

"So what you're saying is, that I should just enjoy us being sisters for a short time before you get things taken care of?"

"Yes, that's exactly what I'm saying." I nervously chuckle, grateful that she now seems to have calmed down, and is embracing this for the crazy moment it was.

"Well, in that case, I want all the juicy details about your runaway bride road trip extravaganza," she says, drawing me in closer as she casually drapes her arm over my shoulder. "Babe, can you grab the rest of her things from the back?" Blair asks, shooting her new boyfriend her beautiful puppy-dog eyes as she bats her eyelashes at him.

"Of course. You two start catching up. I'll be up soon." He smiles like the lovesick man he so clearly is. "And Ronnie, welcome home. We missed you," he adds, turning his smile in my direction.

"I've missed you both too," I say, and I truly mean it. Sure, I needed to get away from Evergreen Grove, and a part of me is still uneasy about what coming home might bring. But right now, standing here with my favorite people? I'm exactly where I'm supposed to be.

24

MILES

"**Y**OU SURE YOU DON'T want to back out?" Veronica asks as I roll my eyes, working with Ford to carry the massive yellow couch out of the apartment. Unlike my place, which is on the second floor, hers is on the ground level, making it much easier to move things out as we load the moving truck.

The boxes pile up as Veronica and Blair sift through them, deciding what's coming to my place and what's going into storage. Meanwhile, Ford and I sweat it out, hauling the heavy stuff onto the truck.

"Don't tempt me," I struggle, my voice strained. While I appreciate the help with the heavy lifting, I'm not sure his skinny frame was made for this kind of work.

"Sorry, bro. I think it's too late to back out now, especially now that she's secured the bag and has that pretty little ring on her finger to prove it," Blair teases as I thankfully walk backward out the door, no longer having to listen or force a reply.

Ford, seemingly, knows better than to encourage her or say anything else as we struggle to finish this task, carefully setting it down in the truck, beads of sweat dripping down our foreheads.

Then again, judging by the way he's hunched over, breathing heavily with his hands on his knees, I'm not sure the guy even has the strength to say anything right now.

"Don't worry," I say, leaning forward and giving him a pat on the shoulder. "We're almost done with the heavy stuff. Just the bed and the dresser left."

He tries to speak, or at least I assume so, as his lips twitch, as if trying to form words, but all that comes out is a series of gasps for air, and instead he just nods.

"Maybe let's take a water break first," I suggest, more for his sake than mine. With the spring heat kicking in, the thought of water is tempting. But honestly, I'd rather just power through and get it done. Clearly, though, we're not built the same.

"Sounds good," he finally manages with a grateful smile.

I bite back a laugh and retreat inside, grabbing the water bottle I'd left on the counter.

"I think we're killing your boyfriend, Blair," I joke to my sister from her spot in the kitchen as she continues to wrap the glassware in newspaper and bubble wrap.

"Eh, he's tougher than he looks," she says, brushing me off nonchalantly.

"No, I think Miles is right. I might actually be dying. My arms feel like they're going to fall off," Ford says, his face pale and his voice shaky as he walks back inside the apartment.

"Aw, don't worry, babe. Tonight I'll hook you up with a nice massage."

"Oh, I like the sound of that," Ford grins, his voice carrying a suggestive lilt, a tone I don't exactly appreciate when it comes to my sister.

"Well, that only makes one of us, because I'd rather not know about these massages, or anything else you two choose to do behind closed doors," I say, my nose wrinkling in disgust.

My sister may be a grown adult, but in my eyes, she'll always be my little sister. As much as I appreciate Ford and the way he takes care of her, I'd rather not know about the inner workings of their relationship.

"Oh, come on. We're all adults here," Blair defends, stuffing a wrapped glass into a brown box.

"And I'm an adult who doesn't want to know about my sister's sex life," I say before shivering. Those are two words I never want to use in the same sentence ever again. "And on that note, I'm going to see if Vee needs any help in the bedroom," I say, more than ready to make my escape.

"Vee, huh?" Blair asks with a smirk and a wiggle of her eyebrows, but I choose to ignore her yet again.

Turning into the bedroom, I spot Veronica leaning over. I don't want to come off as a creep, but it's difficult to resist glancing at her perky, shapely ass, especially in the form-fitting hot-pink yoga pants she's got on.

Glancing over her shoulder, she sends me a quick smile, either too busy or too kind to acknowledge the fact that I just got caught checking her out. "Sorry, I promise I'm about done. I've almost cleared out all the dressers," she offers as she stands up and stretches her arms out in front of her.

"You're fine," I say, moving to take a seat on the stark white mattress that's been stripped of its comforter and sheets. "Just taking a little break for Ford's sake and wanted to see if you needed any help in here."

She lets out a knowing chuckle. "Let me guess, what you're really wanting a break from is the sugary-sweet, lovey-dovey duo?" she asks, shooting me a teasing grin before turning back to the box that's already half-full.

"Somewhat. It is a lot, huh?" I muse. Since the moment we got home, they've treated us to a front-row display of their constant touching and declarations of love. Though they've kept the overt PDA to a minimum, the lingering brushes of their hands and the longing glances leave little doubt that they're making up for lost time.

"A little," she admits, pulling open another drawer as she works on clearing that one out too. "Honestly, I love seeing them happy. It's a total win for the middle school me who predicted this happening. But after everything with Pete—and, well, us—it stings to know that I don't have that too. So yeah, it's a little tough to watch."

I stand up, reaching for the large tape gun and move to tape off the box she'd just finished packing. "Yeah, sorry about that. I hate that I've somehow gone and made things even more difficult for you."

She quickly shakes her head as she looks my way. "No, don't be. I know our situation is a bit messy," she admits with a scrunch of her nose, "but honestly, our friendship and knowing I have a place to stay are probably the only reasons I'm not completely losing it right now."

"I'm just glad I can help," I say, leaning against the dresser as I watch her continue to sort through the drawer, meticulously separating the contents into two distinct piles.

"You're a huge help, and I couldn't be more grateful for you and your sister," she adds, her dark eyes looking up to meet mine.

My stomach flips as I watch the corners of her lips curve into a smile, lighting up her entire face. I've always known is Veronica was a beautiful woman, but damn! When did she get to be this gorgeous? Or have I just always chosen to be this oblivious?

I do my best to smile back, making sure not to reveal the true effect she's having on me. Thankfully, she doesn't seem to notice as she returns to sorting through the drawer, until she freezes, her eyes locking onto its nearly empty contents.

My brows furrow. "What? Is everything okay?" I ask, my back straightening.

"I completely forgot that this is where I put it," she says, lifting the giant rock of a wedding ring. I had known she'd done something with it, since I noticed she'd come back into the car without it the day she ran away, and we left on our trip, but beyond that, I hadn't given it much thought.

"Fuck. That puts the one I gave you to shame," I lamely offer, hoping to get her to smile, since clearly seeing that ring again has stirred up a bunch of old emotions.

A forced chuckle escapes her lips, but her eyes remain fixed on the ring as she idly spins it between her fingers. "Yeah, well, it seems like this ring meant about as much as yours does, so a lot of good that did me, huh?" she frowns, her shoulders drooping as she moves to sit on the bed I vacated just moments ago.

"You're not regretting running away, though, right?" I ask cautiously as I take a seat beside her.

"No." She sighs, shaking her head. "I just... I can't believe I let it get that far. I feel so stupid."

"Hey," I say, scooting closer as I drape my arm across her shoulders. I'm not usually this touchy-feely, but I find myself willing to do whatever I can to shield her from the pain. "Listen to me, he's the idiot here, not you. He's the one who treated you like shit and let someone as amazing as you slip through his fingers. You did nothing wrong, and you weren't stupid. He led you to believe he was someone else. Nobody can fault you for wanting to see the best in someone you loved. In my book, that doesn't make you foolish—it makes you brave. You opened yourself up to someone, and that takes guts. If you ask me, it only proves even more how truly amazing you are. He's the only idiot here, and we both know he never actually deserved you. So please, don't blame yourself."

"But I do blame myself," she says, releasing a shaky breath as the ring falls into her palm and she closes her fist around it. "I should've known better. I ignored all the signs, and I let him change me. I let him have control, and—"

I interrupt. "Vee, you have to forgive yourself. Should things have gotten that far? Probably not, but you were in love and giving someone you cared about the benefit of the doubt. He's the one who took advantage of you and the situation. This isn't on you. This is all on him," I continue, my hand gliding softly up and down her arm.

"Do you really expect anyone to see it that way?" she asks, tilting her head up to look at me, her sad, brown eyes meeting mine.

"Honestly? Probably not, at least not in this town. But do you want to know my official motto that gets me through all the bullshit this town puts me through?"

"Hmm?" she hums softly, a questioning tilt to her head.

"Fuck 'em."

I thankfully earn a smile as the corners of her lips lift. "That's really your motto?"

"Yes, and it hasn't steered me wrong yet. If I let everyone's thoughts and opinions of me affect me, I'd have gone crazy years ago. The only opinion I care about is Blair's, and even that is iffy." I shrug as her smile only grows. "As long as I know my truth and am proud of myself, and stand by the decisions I make, that's all that really matters."

She nods, looking down at her closed palm. "Well, unfortunately, I'm not so sure I'm proud of any of my recent decisions. Not only did I wait too long and run away, costing all of us thousands of dollars, but I married my best friend's older brother on a drunken whim. Pretty sure those aren't decisions anyone should be proud of."

I place a hand over my heart as if her words hit me right where it hurts. "Ouch!"

She lets out a playful huff and nestles her head into the space between my shoulder and chest.

"What?" I innocently ask. "I mean, you did just say that you weren't proud of our marriage. I mean, come on. Way to cut a guy down."

"Oh, okay," she starts, clearly not buying what I'm selling. "So, what you're saying is that you're happy we got married and have absolutely no regrets?"

"Not exactly, but there are worse people I could have ended up married to."

"Bullshit!" She laughs, a sound that actually sounds rather magical right about now. "There's no way Miles from two weeks ago would ever say that there's possibly someone else he could be married to who's worse than me."

My hand drops from around her shoulders and I push myself off the bed. "Well, I'm no longer the same Miles I was two weeks ago," I admit. "And I have to believe that you aren't the same person you were back then, either. We've both learned from our mistakes, and maybe we've also learned that maybe we were wrong and that certain people aren't always who we think they are or expect them to be."

Maybe it's a little different given our two situations. She had to learn her fiancé wasn't who she wanted him to be, whereas I learned the complete opposite—that Veronica Prescott isn't who I assumed her to be, either—she's so much better.

"Don't tell me you might actually like me now," she teases, pushing herself off the bed and closing the space between us.

In the past I probably would have taken a step back, wanting distance, but instead, I find myself stepping toward her, our bodies almost touching.

"And what if I do?" I ask, my eyes searching hers before they involuntarily fall to her perfectly plump pink lips. Plump, pink, and entirely kissable.

"Pretty sure I should be the one asking you that question right?" she says, her voice lowering to an almost whisper.

"So, are we ready to move this dresser now, or what?" Ford's annoyingly deep voice cuts in, breaking the moment as I leap back.

"Oh, uh," I ramble, scratching the back of my neck. "I guess that depends on Vee, here," I say, my eyes falling back to the small, dark-haired woman whose charm has me completely under her spell.

"Almost ready," she says, scurrying back toward the dresser as she continues to sort through one of the drawers. "But, uh, the bed is ready to move if you want to get that out of here," she suggests over her shoulder.

"Yeah, we can do that," I say, letting out a strangled sound before turning toward a seemingly oblivious Ford, who adjusts his glasses and nods.

"Alright, sounds good," he agrees, moving toward the other side of the bed.

While a part of me has been dreading carrying the rest of the heavy stuff out, especially since I seem to be doing the majority of the heavy lifting, another part of me is relieved. If there's one thing I could use right now, it's a distraction and a release, since I should definitely not be thinking about Veronica Prescott's lips, especially how good I know they'd feel against mine.

Yes, some physical exertion and maybe a cold shower later are exactly what I need.

25

VERONICA

"PIZZA'S HERE!" MILES YELLS from the other room, the delicious smell of pepperoni and cheese drifting through the air.

"I'll be out in a second!" I yell back as I hang up the last shirt in my closet.

It still feels surreal that I'm moving into Miles' place, but at the same time, it feels... right. Strangely enough, this feels much more natural than all those times I imagined myself in Pete's fancy custom-built home—the one he commissioned, furnished, and decorated entirely on his own. Many might have looked at it and seen a dream home, but not me. Maybe if he'd ever let me have a say, things would've been different, but I was shut out of the process entirely.

Here though, I've been given free rein to decorate my room however I want. Miles even offered to let me bring in some of my own furniture and put his stuff in storage until I move out, but I wasn't about to create more work for anyone, especially after seeing how exhausted the guys looked after moving everything into storage The last thing I'd want is to force them to carry out

Miles' stuff and bring my heavy furniture up an entire flight of stairs.

Taking one last look around the room, I breathe a sigh of relief. There's still plenty to do—unpacking, settling in, and making it feel like home—but the most important thing in all of this is that I officially have a space to call my own while I figure out my next steps.

With the tempting smell of Bob's Quick and Tasty pizza wafting through the air and into my room, I happily make my way toward the living room.

"Oh, good. You showered," I tease, noticing his still-wet, freshly showered hair as I try to ignore the fact that he's once again wearing my favorite manly uniform: a tight-fitting white T-shirt and pair of gray sweatpants.

"Did I really smell that bad?" he asks, lifting a slice of pizza onto his plate before reaching into the cupboard to pull out another plate for me.

"Only a little," I tease, shrugging as I join him at the counter. "But don't worry, it sort of worked for you. The majority of the women I know love that whole sexy, sweaty, manly look you had going on."

"Oh, yeah?" he asks, adding one more slice on his plate before moving to lean against the opposite cabinet. "And are you one of these women?"

"I think I could be," I say as I slip a slice of pepperoni onto my plate before turning back to face him. "I've always been the opposite of your sister when it comes to our taste in men. She always liked the tall, lanky, and super nerdy or artsy types, while

I've always preferred mine to be more muscular and rugged," I explain before taking a much-needed bite.

"I don't think I believe that. Pete was definitely not the muscular, rugged type," he challenges with a small chuckle as he lifts his slice to his lips.

"Just because he was who I ended up with doesn't mean he was my type," I say with a casual lift of my shoulder once I swallow.

"Hmm," he says, not looking like he believes me, but it doesn't matter because he's wrong. I'm actually starting to think that hot, muscly, grumpy blonds might be exactly my type, especially as my eyes roam his body. Yep, definitely my type.

"So," I begin once more, crossing one leg over the other, "now that you know mine, I have to ask, what exactly is Broody Bennett's type?"

"I don't know," he answers, looking down at his plate. "I'm not sure I have one."

"I suppose I could maybe see that being true for you, given I've never seen you with a woman, let alone a girlfriend. But come on—you have to have a type. Everyone does."

He raises an eyebrow. "I didn't realize you were paying such close attention."

I lift my slice and let it hover in the air in front of my mouth. "Well, we live in Evergreen Grove. What else is there to do? It's all about people-watching—seeing who's with who and talking about exactly what they're doing behind those closed doors."

He lets out an annoyed huff. "You and the rest of this ridiculous town need to get a life. But fine. If you really must know—I like brunettes," he confesses.

My lips curve into a wide grin. "Is that so?" I ask, a little too excitedly. But when you get Miles Bennett to open up about something, especially something so personal, it's hard not to get a little excited.

"Maybe, but honestly, I really don't think I'm all that picky."

"I don't know about that. I have a feeling you're a lot pickier than you're letting on. I wasn't lying when I said I've never really seen you with anyone, so clearly, you must have some pretty high expectations."

"Alright, then, fine. If you want more, I like brunettes who aren't from Evergreen. When I go out, it's usually with women from as far away from this crazy-ass town as possible."

I nod, the movement slow and deliberate, before tilting my head back and forth from side to side. "Okay, well, I can't say I don't understand. The dating pool is pretty small here," I admit, especially since, as of right now, I'm pretty sure I've gone on dates with all the eligible bachelors in our town. Given that my most recent relationship ended with me running away at the altar, I can't exactly see myself being a hot commodity anymore, either.

"Way too small," he agrees as he lifts a slice to his lips, just as Bubba comes to my side and paws at my leg.

"Hey there, Bubs," I say, bending down to rub the spot behind his ears.

"He's just trying to get you to feed him some crust," Miles says knowingly, nodding down at the sturdy bulldog planted in front of my feet.

"That, or he just loves me. Huh, Bubs? We're besties," I say, smiling as I continue to rub the spot I know he loves. H tilts his head to the side and gives my hand a few affectionate licks. It could be exactly what Miles is saying, and he's just trying to get a taste of the yummy garlicky goodness, but I want to believe it's more than that. In fact, he's spent the majority of the time since I arrived at this apartment following me around.

"Besties, huh?" Miles asks, eyeing the two of us, and it's obvious he's not quite sold on the idea.

"Yep, and I fully plan to make myself his favorite person during my stay here," I decide, intent on riling Miles up since clearly his dog is his soft spot.

"You can try, but I've been with him since he was just a pup. I'll always be his favorite."

"Challenge accepted." I grin, tapping my chin deviously with my free hand. "In fact, I'm going to make myself your new favorite person, too. I can already tell I've chipped away at some of your walls, but by the time I move out, you'll be so hooked, you'll be sending me daily texts begging me to come back."

He chuckles, shaking his head. "Oh, that's cute. But spoiler alert, it's not happening. Best of luck though, because I'm sure you're going to need it."

"I don't need luck. In fact, I'm positive that I can do it. I am quite lovable, you know?"

"I've heard some rumblings about that, but given that I usually only hear that sort of thing from Blair and Ford, I'm not sure I'm fully inclined to believe it. Especially considering I'm not sure I trust either of their judgment."

"Well, I mean, I did get you to marry me in Vegas, as well as got you to do a few other things, so I think even you might find me a bit more lovable than you're willing to let on," I playfully challenge, setting my plate to the side before crossing my arms in front of me.

His cheeks redden, and I know I've got him right where I want him. "Well, as we both know, I was pretty hammered when that happened," he says, rubbing the back of his neck. "So, I'm not sure anything I did that night counts," he adds, clearing his throat and seemingly doing his best to regain his composure.

"And what about now? You're not drunk tonight are you?" I ask, pushing myself off the counter as I slowly inch toward him.

He straightens, setting his plate to the side. "No…" he trails off, clearly waiting to see where I'm going with this, and honestly, so am I.

This is likely the last thing I should be doing, especially since he's doing me such a huge favor by letting me stay. The last thing I need to do is complicate things, but I can't help myself, especially given the ways his eyes have darkened and are currently following my every movement as I make my way across the small kitchen.

"Well, in that case," I say, stepping closer until my bare feet nearly brush against his, our chests only inches apart. I tilt my head and bite my lower lip, watching as his gaze follows the movement, just as I'd hoped. "What do you think of me now?"

"Fine," he gives in, his voice taking on a deep, velvety tone. "Maybe you're a little more likable now, but I wouldn't go as far as saying lovable. If I had to categorize it, I'd say what you look like is undeniably fuckable."

I take an inhale of breath, definitely not expecting that answer from him, but it's not one I hate either. If anything, it only makes me want to push the boundary even further, especially as my mind drifts back to the night we got married, when only a few hours earlier he made me come in the middle of a crowded dance floor. If he could make me feel that good with just his leg, I have to wonder how much better he can make me feel with a different body part.

"And are you going to act on that?" I ask, my voice barely above a whisper.

"I'm not sure it'd be a good idea," he counters, raising one hand and using the back of his fingers to run a tantalizingly slow line down my bare arm.

Goosebumps prickle along my skin, following the movement as a mounting pressure builds between my thighs. I know it's nothing but a simple touch to the arm, but it's definitely doing things to my body.

"Probably not, but when have I ever been known to make good choices?" I ask, pulling my bottom lip between my teeth.

He drops his hand. "Well, it's a good thing I am," he says, sliding to the side and breaking all contact between us. "You're my sister's best friend, and I'm your new roommate. We can't complicate things."

Just like that, it feels as though a bucket of cold water has been dumped over me, and I let out a visible breath. He's right, I know he is, but that doesn't mean I like it. If he had let it happen, I easily would've let things go way too far. I would have let him do whatever he wanted to me—no questions asked.

"Yeah, no, you're right." I sigh, nodding as I close my eyes, willing my heart to return to a normal pace.

"I'm going to, uh," he says, pointing over his shoulder with his thumb, "head into my room, but let me know if you need anything, and feel free to make yourself at home."

I'm honestly not sure what to say to that. I place my hands on my hips and nod, watching as he calls Bubba to follow him.

Once his door shuts, I cover my face with my hands and slowly drag them down. I really need to pull myself together because if I can't control these raging hormones, I'm screwed. I know I can always land back at my parents' house if it comes to that, but that's the last place I want to end up.

Plus, how hard can it really be to not flirt with Miles Bennett?

26

MILES

I PLACE MY PHONE face down on the desk and let my head fall into my hands, my fingers digging into my temples as I scrub at my face. Even though I've made an appointment with a lawyer in the next town over to try to keep things under wraps, it's still hard to believe I got myself into this mess in the first place.

Not only am I way behind on all my book keeping duties here at work, but I actually let myself contemplate having sex with Veronica Prescott last night. There's even a small part of me that *still* wants to say it's fine—she *is* my wife, after all, and it wouldn't have to mean anything. But I can't do that. I have to be smart about this, even if my dick keeps trying to convince me otherwise.

It took a second shower last night to get my body under control, even if it ended with me fucking my hand to rid myself not just of the tension, but the temptation as well. Too bad it didn't work, since it was her face in my mind that I ultimately came to.

I just need to stay strong. Eventually, she'll move out, and our marriage will be annulled, but the tension between us will still linger. With my sister back in Evergreen for good, there's no avoiding the fact that Veronica and I will run into each other more often than not. We're just one big mistake waiting to happen, and I refuse to let us walk into yet another one.

"Knock, knock," a voice I know all too well calls out, as they rap a few times on my office door.

"Come in," I yell to Blair as she opens the door and makes herself comfortable, setting her bag on my desk, and sits in the chair directly across from me.

"I brought lunch," she says, holding up a white paper bag before also setting it down between us.

I raise an eyebrow. "Why do I feel like this is going to cost me something?"

She lets out a soft gasp, covering her heart with her palm. "Miles! Why would you ever think that?" She plays along, doing her best to look offended, though a smile peeks through. "Can't a girl just bring her big brother lunch without any expectations?"

"With a normal sister, yes, but I know you. So, what's up? What do you need now?" I ask, reaching forward to pull out the sandwich she must have picked up from Simon's Deli.

At least she knows me well enough to know my order, I think to myself as I carefully unwrap my Italian sandwich.

"Okay, so you know how I just purchased the old building on Main Street?" she asks, and I nod for her to continue.

Most of our reunion after arriving home had centered around the trip and the whirlwind events that led to our wedding. But Veronica and I did our best to steer the conversation back to Blair and Ford. That's when they officially announced they were together—and Blair shared even more exciting news. She'd been working with Mary-Beth, the town's realtor, to purchase the old model train store and turn it into her very own photography studio.

"I've officially gotten the keys and the green light to get started, and could really use some extra hands. Any chance you'd be willing to be one of them?" she asks, linking her fingers pleadingly and holding them under her chin.

"And by 'helping hand,' what exactly would that entail?" I ask before lifting the sandwich to my lips and taking a bite. Obviously, I'll help her with whatever is needed, but I want to know exactly what I'm getting myself into before I formally agree.

"Well, I'm not sure if you've seen the place recently, but the inside is pretty gross and filled with tons of old shelves and tables. So, first, I'll probably need your and Ford's help to get all that moved out."

I try to resist rolling my eyes, knowing exactly what comes with working with Ford, but I keep my mouth shut as she goes on.

"And then after that, I plan to do some painting, but Ronnie has already agreed to help with that side of things..." She casually waves her hand.

"So, what you're saying is that you need me for all the dirty work, and you and Vee get to do all the fun, easy stuff?"

She smiles, subtly lifting one shoulder. "Maybe a little, and Vee, huh?" she asks, making note, for the second time, of the nickname I've come up with for her best friend.

"Yeah, and what about it?" I ask, doing my best not to make a big deal out of it as I shove another bite of sandwich into my mouth.

"I don't know, I guess I just find it sort of interesting that you have your own little nickname for her, that's all," she states, lifting a brow in my direction as she crosses one leg over the other.

"I know what you're doing," I say, speaking through a mouthful of sandwich. "And there's nothing to read into here. It's just a nickname—nothing more, nothing less."

"I don't know. You've known Ronnie for as long as I have, and it's always felt like you refused to follow the rest of the crowd and call her Ronnie. But now, after spending less than two weeks with her, you have your own little nickname. It's just a little suspicious, is all I'm saying, especially when you came home married to her to top it all off."

"And don't forget that it was a drunken mistake, and that I've already called a lawyer and have plans set in motion for us to get this thing taken care of. Believe me, there's nothing weird or nefarious going on here."

She tosses her hands up, palms facing me. "Hey, you're the one making this into a big deal."

"Don't even," I say, letting the rest of my uneaten sub fall onto the wrapping. "Don't act like I'm the only one making things weird."

"Okay, fine. I may be making things a little weird, but can you really blame me? You've hated my best friend for as long as I can remember, and now all of the sudden the two of you are besties, with her living in your apartment. And let's not forget that she's now your wife. You have to admit, that's pretty fucking weird, Miles."

I let out a small chuckle, because, honestly, she has a point.

"Okay, yes. I never liked her all that much—" I start, but she interrupts.

"Oh, it was more than just you not liking her. You made that crystal clear," she says, her eyes narrowing, not about to let me off the hook on this one.

"Okay, fine. I more than disliked her, but I can admit that maybe I was wrong and she's actually not as bad as I thought," I confess, even if it stings a little.

"Normally, I'd be ecstatic to hear that, but I'm going to be honest, I'm kind of worried."

My brows furrow. "Why?"

She rolls her eyes. "Because she's my best friend and you're my brother. I'm pretty sure that makes me legally obligated to kick either of your asses if either of you hurts the other, and I'm not looking to do that."

I laugh once more. "Okay, I can promise you she's not going to be breaking my heart."

"And what about you breaking hers?" she challenges, tilting her head to the side.

"I'm pretty sure, to do that, she'd have to be into me like that, and I can assure you, nothing like that is going on," I lie, because last night was proof that maybe things are a little more complicated than I care to admit.

She doesn't believe me either, as her head falls forward. "I know you like to think that I'm blind and that I'm still nothing more than your silly and naïve little sister, but that couldn't be further from the truth. I can see that something's changed, and that something is going on between the two of you. I know you two better than I know the back of my own hand, and at this point, it's pretty fucking obvious."

A sigh escapes my lips as I shake my head and look away. "Look, Blair," I offer, daring a glance back in her direction. "Yes, I may now somewhat enjoy her company, and I get that I misjudged her before, and that's on me. But I need you to understand something: nothing is going to happen between us. You're my top priority; always have been. I would never risk our relationship—or yours with her—over something that I know could never truly work. Veronica's important to you, and, somehow, she's also become important to me, too. Hurting either of you isn't an option. Trust me on that, okay?"

Her lips form a straight line as she lets my words settle before she finally nods. "Okay, good. I believe you."

"Thank you. Now tell me more about what all I'm expected to do to help get your business going," I say, more than ready to change the subject—and thankfully, she seems just as ready and willing.

For now, and more than ever, I'd rather focus on the fact that my sister is finally settling down in our little hometown. It's a much-needed and welcome distraction, one my brain so desperately needs. I'd do just about anything—and I mean anything—to keep the thoughts of Veronica at bay. The more I think about her, the harder it gets to remind myself that she's someone I can never have, especially after this talk with Blair.

27

Veronica

Normally, lunchtime is my favorite time of day, especially since it gives me a chance to decompress and gossip with my teacher friends, but today is different. For once, I desperately need the distraction of teaching so I can think about anything other than Miles Bennett.

Ever since last night, and, well okay, maybe even a few days before that, he's all I can think about. It doesn't help that I had yet another sex dream about him—a continuation of our interaction in the kitchen but instead of him ending things and walking off, it was him eating me out on the kitchen counter, as if I were his favorite meal, before he carried me to his bedroom and we finished up in there.

Just thinking about the dream makes my skin prickle with heat, and I can feel my cheeks burning, but I play it cool as I set my lunch bag on the table and sit across from Ford.

"How's the first day back?" he asks as he rips open a bag of Cool Ranch Doritos.

"You know, it hasn't been too bad," I admit.

As expected, everyone in town knows that I ran away from the altar, leaving the beloved town councilman a mess. So yes, I fully expected comments to be made, and these high school students did not disappoint. Then again, as many of their parents are notorious for being the town's biggest gossips, it's no wonder their kids have picked up similar habits.

As I walked into my classroom this morning and spotted a photoshopped picture of Julia Roberts in a wedding dress and sneakers—with my face photoshopped onto hers—I was too impressed by the creativity to be upset. If you're going to roast me, at least do it with style, and they definitely did.

First off, what an honor to be compared to the beautiful Julia. Second, I did exactly what they all say I did, so why try to act like the victim in this? Okay, so obviously they don't know the full story of why I felt the need to get as far away from Pete as possible, and they don't need to. I have no plans to slander his good name, even if part of me thinks he deserves it. I just have to hope that eventually everyone in town sees through him the same way I finally did.

He doesn't look convinced. I can see the compassion and worry hovering over his features. "Really?"

"I mean, there have been some rough patches, and I wish I could have taken more time off to process everything that's happened these past two weeks, but I can't exactly ask people not to wonder or be curious. As much as I hate the gossip train that exists here, in this case, I'd be wondering what the hell happened, too."

"I guess. I suppose I should feel lucky that I'm one of the select few who actually gets to know the behind-the-scenes tea," he admits with a sheepish grin.

"Tea, huh? Are you finally going to fill us in on what happened?" Gemma asks as she takes a seat at our usual table, with Maeve sitting across from her in her usual seat as well.

Gemma and Maeve, other than Ford, of course, are two of my favorite people at this school and were also two of my bridesmaids. However, while I filled in Blair and Ford before I made my escape, I left my other two friends in the dark that day.

"You mean Ford didn't fill you in already?" I ask, somewhat surprised as I unzip my floral lunch bag and slip out the contents.

He coyly shrugs. "I didn't know if I was allowed."

I roll my eyes. "It's Gemma and Maeve, you doofus," I tease, reaching out to smack his arm. "Of course, you could have told them."

Okay, so maybe with Gemma, who has a flair for the dramatics given her position as the actual drama teacher here at Evergreen Grove High, there's a chance she could have gossiped about it, but Maeve, I know without a doubt, wouldn't have told anyone.

"Okay, good. Because I've been dying to know what happened. One second you were asking to be left alone, and the next, Ford and Blair were announcing to everyone that the wedding was off," Gemma explains, excitedly linking her fingers in front of her face as she leans her elbows on the table.

I wince. "Yeah, sorry about that. I just really needed to get out of there."

"Don't worry about it, sweetheart. We understand. You did what you needed to do, and that's all that matters," Maeve adds, placing a comforting hand on my shoulder and giving it a gentle squeeze. "The details don't really matter, and if you don't feel comfortable sharing, you don't have to. We can wait until you're ready."

"Maeve, shhh!" Gemma playfully chastises as she places a finger in front of her lips and shushes the school counselor.

I let out a small laugh. "No, it's fine. I trust you two to keep this between us," I say, sending a grateful smile toward Maeve before looking back at Gemma.

"Well..." Gemma coaxes, spinning her hand in a small circle as if beckoning me to continue.

"I think, deep down, I knew for a while that Pete wasn't the right guy for me. Thankfully, Blair coming back to town helped me see it more clearly, and Ford here..." I pause, smiling in his direction, "reminded me of the type of relationship I really want. Walking down that aisle would've been a mistake. I'm sure Pete's going to be pissed—probably for a long time—but someday, he'll realize it too. We aren't right for each other, and ending it now was the right move for both of us."

"Well, as I'm sure you've heard from Ford, and from my experience as well, divorce is never fun, so I'm proud of you for realizing it before it got to that point," Maeve says, which, coming from her, I definitely appreciate.

While Maeve grew up in Evergreen Grove, she moved away at eighteen to attend college with her high school sweetheart, whom she ultimately ended up marrying. However, three kids later, he turned out to be a cheating asshole, which sent her running back home with her children to Evergreen to live with her parents. While I'm so glad I get to have her here as a friend, I know it hasn't been the easiest of transitions.

"Yeah, I'm definitely thankful I get to avoid that side of things, even if there are also some other aspects of being known as the town's runaway bride that I'm not exactly looking forward to," I admit with a sigh, reaching down to open the Tupperware of mixed berries that I packed the night before.

"Eh," Gemma says, waving it off. "Before long, someone here will do something stupid and you'll be old news. Just give it time."

"Then again," Ford starts, a playful smirk on his lips, "Ronnie is usually the go-to for causing town drama, so she may be out of luck in that department."

"Oh," Maeve says, lifting a finger. "Maybe you just need to do one of your other crazy Ronnie shenanigans, surprise the heck out of everyone, and give them something new and exciting to talk about."

I really wish I were better at hiding my expressions because, as I bite my bottom lip and wrinkle my nose, it's clear that Maeve and Gemma have already picked up on the fact that I might have done exactly that.

"Wait, what are we missing?" Maeve asks, her eyes darting between me and Ford, who is just as horrible as I am at this, as his eyes zone down to the bag of chips in his hand.

"I may have already done something stupid, and perhaps way worse than running away from the altar," I whine, pushing my food forward before letting my forehead fall to the now-empty space.

"Worse than running away from your own wedding?" Gemma asks, clearly intrigued, and I don't blame her.

"Okay, now this is something you *really* can't talk about or spread around," I say, lifting my chin as I look up at the two of them.

"We won't. Promise," Maeve says, and Gemma nods in agreement.

"Well, you know how Blair's older brother, Miles, was the one who drove the getaway car?" I ask, glancing between the two women.

"The really hot and grumpy mechanic? Oh, we know him," Gemma says, wiggling her brows.

I let out another breath before I sit up and lean in toward them, lowering my voice. "Well, I may have drunkenly married him in Vegas."

Both of their mouths drop open in shock, while Ford, who already knows, leans back, slightly shaking his head.

"Holy shit!" Gemma exclaims, a bit too loudly for my liking, as a few teachers glance in our direction. Thankfully, from what I can see, nobody is really paying all that much attention. "Sorry," she apologizes, crinkling her nose. "But, wow, I definitely didn't expect you to say that."

"Yep," I say, drawing out the 'p' and nodding my head slowly.

"Well, so much for not having to deal with getting a divorce," Maeve offers in solidarity, sending me a regretful frown as she runs a comforting hand along my back.

"Yeah, well, this one I'm at least not too worried about. We both realized it was a stupid mistake, and Miles is already working on getting the whole thing taken care of, so at least I have that going for me."

"You know, as far as random husbands go, I'd say you hit the jackpot. Miles Bennett is a fucking babe," Gemma chimes in appreciatively.

For the first time, I get why those comments used to drive Blair up the wall. Sure, I may have been guilty of saying something similar once or twice, but at least I always followed it up with, '*Too bad he's such an asshole*,' or something equally disparaging.

I get it. Miles is an incredibly good-looking man, and I can understand why people would notice. But honestly, I don't want to hear anyone else say it. I know it's ridiculous, since he's not *actually* mine, but still... Sure, he's my husband—for now—but like I've already told them, it won't be for long. Yet for some annoying reason, the thought of him being with someone else bothers me more than it should.

Hell, I could even see him being into someone like Gemma, looks-wise at least. She's a couple of years younger than me, which means she's a good five to six years younger than Miles, and he did say his type was a brunette. Gemma is exactly that, with her long brown locks.

Not only is Gemma the drama teacher here, but she also teaches dance and has the long, lean body of a dancer to match. Hell, if I were into women like that, I know I'd be all over her. She's gorgeous and has a fun personality to match. Then again, she's a bit loud and dramatic, so maybe I can at least be at ease over the fact that those traits would likely disqualify her from being his true match.

"He is pretty good-looking," I agree, releasing a loud breath of air.

"Well, at least you have that going for you," Maeve tries to offer. Unfortunately, as nice as it is to know that someone as smoking hot as him would marry me, that excitement can only go so far.

"But I really mean it, guys. I can't have this get out. I promised Miles we would keep this under wraps," I explain as they both nod their heads in understanding.

"Don't worry. We'll keep your secret safe," Maeve promises.

"Thanks, ladies," I say, reaching down for a blueberry and popping it into my mouth. "So, besides me running away, what else happened around here while I was gone?" I ask, changing the subject. While I can understand the excitement and the craziness of my news, I really need a break from this, especially since my goal was to think about Miles as little as possible.

Then again, I'm pretty sure I'm failing miserably, because as I continue to pop berries into my mouth and listen to them rattle on about everything I've missed, all my mind can think about is my husband, and how fucking sexy he looked last night in those gray sweatpants of his.

28

MILES

WALKING THROUGH THE DOOR, my eyes go straight to the brunette who has tucked herself in on my couch. She looks right at home, snuggled under a large, fluffy pink blanket, her legs slipped beneath her, with Bubba nestled in close.

She glances over her shoulder, her smile a soft curve that steals the air straight from my lungs. "Do you always get home this late, or are you purposely avoiding me?" she asks, trying to keep her voice light and teasing, yet it's obvious there's a hint of worry there too.

"I promise, I wasn't avoiding you," I say, setting my keys on the black entry table. "I'm just a little behind, is all. Just doing what I can to catch up."

She sends an apologetic smile my way. "Sorry. I'm guessing that's my fault."

I dismiss her worries with a wave and move further into the apartment, leaning behind the couch to give my dog a few affectionate pets and scratches behind his ear. A sweet smell of vanilla and strawberries wafts from Veronica, as I do my best to ignore it. "It's really no problem. I haven't taken a break in what feels like forever, and honestly? Every single one of my employees stopped to tell me how glad they were that I finally took some time for myself. Apparently, this was long overdue."

"You're sure it's okay? I'm starting to worry that I've gone and derailed your entire life," she says with a frown, tilting her head toward mine. "I mean, I stole you away, tricked you into marrying me, moved into your house, and to top it off, you're also behind on your work."

"Seriously, it's not a big deal. By tomorrow, I'll be all caught up," I insist, and just as I look up, a gruesome, bloody scene catches my eye on the television screen. "What the hell are you watching?" I ask, my face contorting in disgust.

"It's *Criminal Minds*," she says as her eyes casually drift to the screen as well.

"You and your murder shit," I say, shaking my head and giving Bubs one final pat before pushing myself off the back of the couch.

"You should really give it more of a chance. It's actually pretty fascinating, and as an added bonus, I'm now an expert on how *not* to get murdered."

"That, or now you know how to commit a murder and get away with it," I counter as I head toward the kitchen, reach into the fridge, and pull out a bottle of water.

"You know," she says, turning to face me, "statistically, they say that 40% of murders are committed by a spouse or intimate partner, so maybe *you* do need to worry."

I twist the cap off the bottle with a pop. "I'm starting to think *you could* pull off a murder and get away with it. You've got that sweet, innocent face, and somehow, you've been getting away with crazy shit for years. Honestly, the fact that you're still one of the most beloved people in this town is either a miracle or proof that you've mastered some kind of witchy voodoo magic and have us all under your spell."

"Exactly," she says with a sugary-sweet smile. "You think pushing everyone away with your whole 'Broody Bennett' routine is keeping you safe, but let's be real—if a murder went down around us, everyone would totally be side-eyeing you. Meanwhile, I'd be the innocent victim in all of this."

"You're diabolical." I chuckle before bringing the bottle to my lips and taking a sip as she returns her smug grin toward the television.

"Have you had dinner yet?" I finally ask, my stomach releasing a soft growl as I realize I haven't had a moment to grab a bite or have any sort of snack since Blair stopped by my shop earlier this afternoon.

"Kind of. I've mostly just been grazing and snacking on crackers, cheese, and grapes—you know, the whole 'girl dinner' thing," she admits, her eyes remaining fixed on her creepy-ass show.

"That's it? Sorry, princess, but that doesn't count. I'm going to make you a proper dinner."

"No, it's fine. You're already hooking me up with a place to live. You don't need to make me food, too."

"Why not?" I ask, reaching into the cupboard as I pull out a pan. "I'm already making something for myself, and adding an extra serving isn't going to create any additional work."

"Are you sure?" she asks, clearly conflicted. "I don't want to put you out."

"I wouldn't have offered if I felt put out or didn't want to do it," I promise, turning to grab some ingredients out of the fridge.

Veronica shrugs off the blanket and strolls toward the kitchen, casually leaning against the doorframe. "Anything I can do to help? And fair warning: I'm a disaster in the kitchen, but I am willing to try."

"How are you at chopping vegetables?" I ask, assuming it's an easy enough job that's usually pretty hard to mess up. Well, other than the possibility of uneven cuts or cutting herself, but I'm not overly concerned about that. She is a grown woman, after all. How bad could she truly be?

"I'm okay at it," she says, brushing a piece of her chestnut-colored hair behind her ear before moving toward the sink to wash her hands.

"Well, then, there we go." I nod, setting her up with a small station of a cutting board, a knife, and the various vegetables that need chopping.

"I can only half-guarantee, though, that I won't end up cutting myself."

"Well, as long as you don't bleed on the veggies, we're good," I joke, keeping my tone light. Beyond my humor, though, I can tell she's worried. She's strangely tense—shoulders stiff, jaw set—and the last thing I want is for her to feel on edge. We're just making dinner. It's not like we're performing brain surgery here.

"Well, how about this? If I do cut myself and bleed, I promise not to get any on your precious vegetables," she offers, the workings of a smile playing on her lips, some of her nerves thankfully seeming to evaporate.

"Perfect. That's all I ask," I chuckle as she gets into place and starts cutting while I work on seasoning the chicken.

"Yeah, unfortunately, my work in the kitchen was one of Pete's least favorite things about me. He always said it wasn't very 'wifey' of me, since whenever I tried to cook, it usually ended up undercooked, over-seasoned, or burnt to a crisp. I'm kind of a disaster in the kitchen."

My hands involuntarily clench into fists, my body visibly tensing. What a fucking asshole. "Not very wifey?" I ask, repeating her line. "What was he looking for, a wife or a maid?"

She lets out a less-than-amused laugh. "To be honest, I'm not quite sure," she admits as she continues to chop. "All I know is that I never measured up, no matter how hard I tried."

"Well, Pete is a fucking idiot, so who cares what he wanted? He's someone else's problem now," I say, trying to remind myself of this as well, since right now I'd love nothing more than to give that asshole a piece of my mind.

"I suppose so," she muses, clearly lost in thought as I glance over at her.

My eyes go wide, and it suddenly makes perfect sense why she had mentioned being hopeless in the kitchen. Not only are her chops incredibly uneven, but she looks like she's about to slice off a finger.

"Shit, Vee," I say, rushing over and pulling the knife out of her hand.

"What?" she asks, stunned by the sudden movement as she tilts her head to look up at me.

"Hold on, one second," I say, carrying the knife over with me and setting it in the sink before washing my hands to avoid cross-contaminating. Once that's done, I grab a new knife and move to join her. "Let me show you the proper way to cut so you don't actually cut off your finger and bleed all over the food."

"You know, I really was trying to be careful," she pouts, but I shake my head.

"I'm sure you were, but I also didn't realize how serious you were about the probability of cutting yourself."

"You really that worried I'm going to ruin our dinner?" she asks, a playful grin tugging at the corners of her mouth as she tilts her head to look at me.

"No, I'm worried that you're seriously going to injure yourself and I'll have to take you to the hospital for stitches," I explain, nodding for her to move over and make room. "Now, let me show you the proper way to hold a knife."

"I did warn you earlier that I was pretty hopeless in the kitchen," she reminds me with a soft whine.

"You're not hopeless. Honestly, I couldn't care less if you ever learn to cook a real meal. But knowing how to properly handle a knife? That matters. For my sanity, if nothing else—because the last thing I want is to worry about you getting hurt."

"If you say so," she says, nodding for me to continue.

Holding the knife up, I make sure she takes notice of where my hands and fingers are situated. "Now," I begin, "don't just pay attention to how I'm holding the knife, but watch how I'm holding the zucchini as well," I say, since, honestly, in watching her, that had been my biggest concern.

After making a few slices and finishing up the vegetable, I pull out a new one and hand it over. "Your turn," I nod, stepping aside so she can once again take her place.

With a new, confident grip on the knife, she steps in and begins to chop as I move in close, proudly nodding my head at her now perfect technique. The kitchen should smell like the seasoned chicken I've been preparing or the fresh vegetables she's slicing, but my senses are overwhelmed by the intoxicating scent of vanilla and berries. I should focus on her cutting, but my gaze shifts to the delicate sliver of skin exposed on her neck. A sudden, intense urge washes over me. It would be so easy to reach out, trace my fingers along her soft, pale skin... and worse, make an entirely new trail with my lips.

My mind continues to wander, drifting back to the moment when the two of us were pressed up against this very counter. I could've easily taken control then and done exactly what I'd so desperately wanted—lifting her onto the counter and pressing my lips against hers—if only I'd been man enough. That same temptation takes over even now, my dick twitching in my pants as I quickly take a step back. "Well, looks like you've got it," I say before she can realize what's happening as I scurry back toward the stove to turn up the heat.

"Well, you're an excellent teacher," she says, her smile warm and genuine as she turns back to her work. The rhythmic sound of her knife hitting the board is a counterpoint to the racing thoughts in my head, which thankfully, she seems too focused on to notice.

"Well, you're a mediocre student," I tease, reaching for the oil and dropping some into the heating pan.

"You know, I'm actually surprised by how much you seem to know about cooking. Blair always seemed a lot like me, since we preferred to going out to eat, and I guess I just figured it was the same for you," she says, continuing to chop.

"That's because I did all the cooking growing up, and she never had to worry about it."

"I guess that makes sense, but who taught you how to do it?" she asks, curiously glancing over her shoulder.

"Nobody," I admit, not really in the mood to discuss it, but I'm also not about to brush it off, since I'm sure she's going to press it either way.

"What?" she asks, her eyes widening. "Then how did you learn?"

"It was all self-taught I guess." I say, reaching for the chicken and dumping it in the pan as a loud sizzle fills the air. "The adults in our lives were never going to do it, so if there was ever going to be a proper meal for me and Blair, it was up to me. I really had no other choice."

Sure, my dad and grandma may have been around, but they certainly didn't care whether we had a fresh or hot meal on the table. They may not have cared about that sort of thing, but I certainly did, especially as a protective older brother. My sister deserved so much better than what we got.

"Oh, wow," she quietly offers, her chops pausing. "I guess I never realized it was that bad. I mean, I know you and Blair were left to your own devices and had to look out for yourselves in many ways, but I guess with that sort of thing, I never put much thought into it."

"I don't think Blair did either," I admit, flipping the chicken over in the pan and making sure to give each side a good sear. "And that's exactly how I wanted it to be. Our childhood was shitty enough, and if there was anything I could do to make her life easier, I'd do it—even if it meant taking on more of the responsibility myself."

"Wow," she says barely above a whisper. "Blair was really lucky to have you. Hell, she still is."

"It's not a big deal," I mutter, keeping my eyes on the chicken, not daring to look in her direction. I already know what I'd see—pity. That's the last way I'd ever want anyone looking at me—especially Veronica. I'd even take the judgy-ass stares of those who still see me as trash over someone looking at me and seeing nothing more than a sad, pathetic loser with a tragic backstory.

"It is a big deal, but if you don't want to talk about it, we don't have to. I know Blair hasn't always wanted to open up about things either, but if you ever need someone to talk to or even vent to, just know that I'm here," she says, reaching over and giving my arm a small squeeze.

"Thanks, Vee. I appreciate it, but you're right. It's not something I want to talk about," I insist, trying to keep my voice even. "If you want to finish up with the veggies and take a break, I can handle the rest from here," I offer, needing to create some space. Not only is her lingering scent still throwing me off, but now I can't stop thinking about how she might see me differently, as though I'm nothing more than some kind of pathetic charity case.

"Will do," she says before finishing up, and I thankfully get a moment to decompress as she leaves me alone in the kitchen to complete our meal.

A small comfort in all of this is that, at least now, I don't have to worry about anything happening between us. There's no way someone with a life as perfect and full as hers would ever be interested in someone as broken and pathetic as me.

29

VERONICA

"I CAN'T BELIEVE YOU got me to wake up this early on a weekend," I whine as I fall into a metal chair, closing my eyes.

"Oh, come on," Blair says, coming up behind me and squeezing my shoulders. "It's not *that* early."

I disagree with a large exaggerated puff of air. "Speak for yourself. Eight is way too early for a Saturday morning."

"Hey, at least she didn't make you come in at six to get things ready," Ford hollers from the other side of the room as he continues to move out the old shelves in Blair's new photography studio. On second thought, maybe "new" isn't the right word for this place.

Given that it's one of the many buildings along Historic Main Street here in Evergreen, this place has been around for a while, and since the old model train store that used to occupy this space has been gone for a good five years now, this place has definitely seen better days.

I suppose that's what we're all here for, since we've been recruited not only to tidy the place up, but also give it a fresh paint job to spruce it up. I really shouldn't complain. Blair having this studio is one of the main things keeping her here and excited about Evergreen—other than us, obviously—and for me, that's a win.

"It's still way too early," I groan. Meanwhile, Blair gets back to work on the wall in front of us, grabbing one of the set-aside paint brushes and dipping it into the large gallon bucket.

"How about this?" Blair says, stopping mid-stroke as she looks at me over her shoulder. "We all take a quick break, and Ford and I can go grab some coffee and muffins from The Steamy Bean."

I sway my head from side to side before sighing dramatically. "I suppose that could work."

I still feel like it's way too early, but from my experience there is very little that coffee—and especially one of those special white chocolate raspberry muffins—can't cure. Maybe that's all I need to give me the extra push to get going today.

"Hey, Ford," Blair calls out, setting the brush back down. "I promised Ronnie here some breakfast and coffee from The Steamy Bean. So congratulations! You've officially been chosen as my special helper to pick it up and bring it back."

"You don't have to ask me twice," he says, clearly exhausted and ready for a break as beads of sweat form along his forehead.

"And what exactly are we supposed to do in the meantime?" Miles asks, walking toward us with his arms folded. My eyes instinctively drop to his biceps, where the fabric of his shirt pulls tight against his muscles. Unlike Ford, he's completely unbothered by the manual labor, and it's not hard to see why, given the way his body practically exudes strength and pure masculinity.

"Just relax and we'll pick it all up again after we get some food and liquid energy in us," Blair suggests as Ford walks her way, pulling her hand into his.

"Works for me," I say, more than willing to keep my ass planted in this chair. I've never been an early riser and have always been one of those people you shouldn't talk to or bother until they've had their morning cup of joe.

If I'd actually thought things through, I would've stopped for coffee before heading over. But after my first week back from my much-needed vacation, my body is running on empty. I spent the entire morning hitting snooze on my alarm, barely dragging myself out of bed with only minutes to spare before meeting Blair and Ford.

Luckily, one doesn't actually need to dress up to work and paint, especially since I'm in an oversized, well-worn Evergreen Grove High School T-shirt and leggings. Even my hair is a mess, loosely tied back with a purple scrunchie, with far too many strands breaking free, but I'm too exhausted to care.

"Figured," Blair says with a knowing smile before nodding for Ford to head out the door, leaving me and Miles behind.

While I'm more than happy to stay relaxed for as long as possible, he grabs Blair's discarded brush and picks up right where she left off.

"Really?" I ask, my shoulders drooping. "We're supposed to be taking a break. You're going to make me look bad."

"I'm pretty sure you're making yourself look bad," he states, his tone lacking the usual venom and carrying a more playful edge instead.

While golden retriever boyfriends seem to be all the rage right now, I'm thinking I might prefer the german shepherd type. There's something strangely appealing about a man who's tough and grumpy on the outside but fiercely loyal and protective when it counts. Sure, it's less fun when he keeps his walls up, but I'm finding it incredibly rewarding as he finally starts to trust and let me in.

"You're probably right, but it's so much more comfortable to sit and be lazy," I argue, settling back in my chair even more.

"You might also have a point, but the sooner we get this taken care of, the sooner we can get out of here and have our weekend back. Maybe get you home in time for a nap, or maybe for another one of those creepy shows you like to watch."

A loud whine escapes my lips. "Ugh, why do you always have to be so right?" I grumble, as I regretfully push myself out of the chair I've made myself *way* too comfortable in.

"I wouldn't say I'm *always* right, but what I am, is eager to get out of here at a decent hour."

"Why?" I ask, reaching for the brush that Blair set out specifically for me, which, unfortunately, is free of paint, but not for long as I finally sink it into the large bucket. "You got a hot date tonight?"

His face scrunches up, his mouth pulled into a tight line as he sends me an incredulous stare. "You really think I'd be dating someone else while married?"

A delightful warmth spreads through me at his words, even if I get how illogical it is.

"Yeah, but it's not like we're married for real, or at least not in the way it counts. If you really wanted to, you'd be free to date whomever you want," I remind him, even if saying so makes those warm and fuzzy feelings evaporate just as quickly as they came.

"Who would I even go on a date with in this town?" he asks, turning his attention back to the wall as he makes wide strokes.

I let out a small chuckle as I start painting as well. "There are plenty of interesting women in Evergreen."

"Name one," he challenges.

"Gemma," I state without thinking. "In fact, she may have mentioned the other day that she thinks you're pretty smoking hot."

"Hmmm," is all he mumbles in return as I sneak a glance his way.

"Hmmm? What does that even mean?" I ask, finding myself annoyingly curious. I'd like to think I wouldn't stand in the way if there was an actual connection between my friend and him, but the green-eyed monster is definitely making its appearance, since it's not something I want to see or even think about—even if I'd been the one who brought it up in the first place.

"It doesn't mean anything. I don't even know Gemma, other than that she was one of your bridesmaids."

"So you don't find her attractive?" I ask, trying to look non-plussed as I continue to move my brush up and down the wall.

"I didn't say that."

I stop mid-stroke. "So you are interested, then?"

"Well, I definitely didn't say that either," he says, stopping his painting as he turns to look at me. "Why do you even care? You really want me out there dating that badly? I mean, come on. You aren't seriously trying to set me up with one of your friends, are you?"

"I mean, no, not really." I mutter, doing my best to avoid his gaze.

"Well, then what do you want out of this?" he asks, turning his body to fully face mine, forcing me to look at him as his eyes search mine. Suddenly the air in here feels way too thick with tension.

"I want..." I start, my gaze locked on his, but I can't let myself fall into this trap again, especially not after he turned me down the other day. "What I want..." I finally continue, using a husky tone as I take a step toward him, "is for you to stop being a goody-two shoes who makes me look bad."

His brows furrow, clearly not expecting that response, nor the swipe of my brush across his cheek, leaving a big white mark behind.

His mouth drops open. "You did not just do that," he says, his eyes growing dark as he takes a step toward me, while I have the good sense to match his movement and take a large step back as well.

"I mean, I sort of did," I say, triumphantly smiling, the corners of my mouth twitching with laughter that's desperate to escape.

Before I can react, his arm swings out, and with a swift motion, his paintbrush makes a bold swipe across my cheek. I try to turn my head in time to block some of the damage, but I'm not quick enough.

"Hmm, well, I guess I sort of just did that right back."

"I can't believe you, Broody Bennett. This is so not becoming of you," I playfully chastise, the giggles I'd been trying to push back finally making an appearance. I'm not sure how I was expecting him to react, especially since he's usually the put-together type, the one who hardly ever acts on impulse, and despite the fact my entire left cheek is covered in paint, I fucking love it.

"So I'm guessing this is unbecoming as well?" he asks, a warning in his tone as he comes at me again. Luckily, I dodge, darting to the side and ducking with a loud, girlish squeal.

"Did I just create a monster?" I ask, quickly dunking my brush back into the white gallon bucket before lifting it in front of me like a sword, or maybe a shield. At this point, I'm not quite sure.

"You realize you're the one who started this, right?" he asks, holding his brush out in front of him as well. "All I wanted to do was paint so we could get out of here."

"Okay, fine. We can call a truce. Plus, I'm pretty sure Blair isn't going to be too happy if we waste all her paint on each other instead of the walls."

"A truce? You really think I'd trust that coming from you?" he asks, still keeping his brush up and ready to go.

My mouth drops open and I place my free hand over my heart. "Ouch, Miles. I'm a woman of my word. How could you ever think that?" I ask, and this time I raise both my free hand

and the one with my brush up into the air, as if to surrender before ultimately bending down to place it on the ground.

He gives a slow nod, his lips curling into a mischievous grin. "Wrong move, princess." Before I can even process his words, he's already darted toward me. I let out a shriek as I scramble to run, but it's no use—he catches me effortlessly, lifting me up and throwing me over his shoulder like I'm nothing more than a sack of potatoes. "I'm putting you in time-out," he announces with a smirk.

"A time-out? Really?" I ask, attempting to look up at him over my shoulder.

"Well, what would you prefer instead? A spanking?" he asks.

"I mean, if you're offering," I cheekily reply, as he just shakes his head.

"Okay, well, that's enough from you," he says, slowly lowering me to the ground. "But you better be on your best behavior."

"And what if I'm not? Am I going to go back in time-out, or will I actually be lucky enough to get one of those spankings you just offered?" I tease, liking the way his cheeks flush a bright pink.

"Don't tempt me," he says, doing his best to recover as his eyes darken.

I take my bottom lip with my teeth, my gaze meeting his. "But what if I like tempting you? If anything, it should be you who stops tempting me, especially if you aren't actually going to man up and act on it," I challenge, since it certainly wasn't me who stopped things the other night.

"I don't think you fully grasp what you're asking for here or what the negative repercussions of all this could be," he says, his voice a low, husky growl. Ignoring the warning, I step closer, the air between us somehow charging even more.

"Believe me, I know exactly what I'm asking for," I say, meeting his gaze with confidence. "And I'm not worried, and I don't think you should be either." Maybe I should be taking this more seriously—even with the paint smeared across his cheek—but in this moment, nothing has ever made me want Miles more than I want him right now.

A bell chimes from the front door, and while I stand my ground, Miles takes a step back, scratching at his neck with his free hand. "Took you all long enough," he says, trying to act casual and not like we were just caught in the middle of an important conversation.

Blair's eyes scan her new studio, her gaze taking an extra moment to assess the both of us and the trouble we'd caused. "Really, guys?" she asks, making her way inside as she hands over my usual white chocolate mocha iced coffee.

"What?" I innocently ask before bringing the cup to my lips and taking a sip.

"Don't 'what' me," she says, jutting out her hip as she places her now free hand atop it.

"Don't worry. We didn't make a mess," Miles cuts in, thankfully taking some of the heat off me as he walks toward Ford and grabs his own coffee.

"Yeah, and you're lucky because—" Blair starts, but Miles interrupts.

"And you're lucky that we're here on our day off helping, so you get what you get," Miles responds, his happy-go-lucky attitude from just moments ago completely gone.

"Okay, so," Ford cuts in, his usual peacemaker self making an appearance, "now that we all have our coffee and caffeine for the day, what do you need us to do next?" he asks, as Blair takes a moment to recenter herself and lets out a calming breath.

"You two finish with the shelves, and now that the grouchy princess has had her coffee, maybe she can finally help me with the painting," she says, tilting her head toward me, a small smile tugging at her lips—the kind of smile that feels like a peace offering after the earlier tension.

"I think that can be arranged." I return her smile, and while the coffee helps, my mind is buzzing, especially after everything that just went down with Miles. I'm wide awake now. My only regret? We never got to finish that conversation. But after the way he looked at me and how his walls seem to be coming down, brick by brick, I have no intention of letting this be the last of it.

30

MILES

HAVE I BEEN AVOIDING leaving my room because of a short little brunette with siren brown eyes? Yes. Does that make me a coward? Probably, but I prefer to think of it as self-preservation. I'm not scared of much, but there is something about her that absolutely terrifies me. It's not just the way she looks at me, like she knows she has the power to bring me to my knees, but the fact that she's got me thinking about her at all hours of the day like some lovesick teenager.

A part of me has always known she was trouble, especially watching her charm my sister into one mess after another. Despite all the warnings I gave Blair, I never quite grasped just how good she is at burrowing under your skin and saying all the right things. But now I get it. I should know better, I really should—but damn, she's too fucking irresistible.

I know I can only hide out here for so long without looking like a complete loser, especially with my stomach growling loud enough to be heard from the other room. It's clear I need to go out there, if only to grab a quick bite.

With a frustrated sigh, I toss my phone aside, push myself up, and head for the door. With my hand on the knob, I stop, take a centering breath, and open it. How in the world have I let a 5 foot nothing someone turn my life so upside down?

Apparently, I was worried for nothing, as not only is the kitchen empty, but so is the living room. Do I chance it and actually make myself a decent dinner, or do I hurry while I can and make myself a less nutritious snack plate, like the ones I usually give her crap for? Okay, so maybe I now get the appeal of her so-called "girl dinner."

As I open the fridge and scan my options, the sound of Veronica's door creaking open signals the end of my brief moment of peace. I should've known it wouldn't last.

"Wow, the snack goblin makes an appearance," she teases with a playful lilt as she follows me into the kitchen.

"A snack goblin? Really?" I ask, turning to glance over my shoulder, which turns out to be a monumental mistake.

Not only is she wearing a grey low-cut crop top that shows off a decent portion of her stomach, but she's also sporting a pair of equally short shorts—if they can even be called that. She has to be doing this on purpose.

I do my best not to show how affected I am by her presence, but I'm sure I fail as I avert my eyes back to the fridge. I need to get out of here, and fast.

Snack plate it is.

"Well, what else do you call someone who locks themselves away in their room all day and only seems to make an appearance to grab something quick to eat?" she asks, leaning against the counter.

"Someone who's been busy," I lie, even though I've spent my day wasting away, doom-scrolling through social media.

"Oh yeah? Doing what?" she challenges innocently, clearly seeing right through my bullshit.

"Does it really matter?" I ask, reaching for the ham, mustard, and a few other ingredients to throw together a sandwich.

"When it's obvious you're trying to avoid me, then yeah, it does," she says, pushing herself onto the counter before crossing one leg over the other. For someone so short, she somehow has legs for days. I do my best not to let my eyes trace every inch of her bare skin as I set my ingredients down on the counter as far away from her as possible.

"Why would I be avoiding you?" I ask, trying to sound as innocent as she does while reaching into the cupboard for a loaf of bread.

"You tell me," she challenges, a knowing grin spreading across her face.

"I already told you I wasn't," I lie through my teeth. That's exactly what I was doing, and what I plan to do for the rest of the night. Hell, maybe even forever if I don't get these thoughts of mine under control.

"Well, sorry if I don't believe you, but you're making a sandwich instead of one of those elaborate dinners you're famous for. *Clearly*, something is up."

"Maybe I just want something simple," I state, the double meaning clear, especially when everything with Veronica seems so incredibly complicated.

"I don't know. I think after being around you for a while and getting a small taste of things, I want the opposite. Simple is boring. I mean seriously, who wants mediocrity when you can have something much more fun and exciting?"

"Well, maybe not everyone is meant for fun and constant excitement. Maybe some people do much better with a simple and boring existence," I suggest, reaching for the drawer near her legs and opening it, doing everything in my power not to notice how incredibly tempting her smooth, silky legs look.

"I suppose you're doing a good job of proving that to be true, but I don't think that's actually what you want," she insists, as I chance a look up at her, just as my hand closes around a butter knife from the drawer.

"And what makes you think it's not what I want?"

"Well, the way you've been doing everything in your power not to look at me until now, almost as if it's causing you actual physical pain to look in my direction."

If only she knew, because the truth is, it's the complete opposite. Looking at her sends waves of pleasure through me, a warmth that radiates from my chest to my toes. It's the avoidance that's painful, especially when all I want to do is let my eyes explore every inch of her body. It doesn't help that it's so obvious that's exactly what she wants from me, too.

"I'm looking at you now," I offer, but soon force myself to look away as I do my best to create space between us, pulling out two slices of bread and getting to work on building my sandwich.

"You call that looking?" she asks, clearly amused.

"Was it not?" I challenge, sneaking a glance in her direction. God, everything about her is so fucking tempting, especially as she leans back on the heels of her palms, propping herself up in a way that makes my eyes want to travel every inch of exposed skin—especially the parts that are still clothed, as I can't help but imagine what they look like underneath.

"Not really. Do you not like what you see?" she asks, tilting her head to the side and lifting an eyebrow.

I love everything about what I see, but I can't say that, not aloud. "You know you look good," is what I say instead.

"Maybe, but I think I'd still much rather hear you say it aloud."

I close my eyes and let out a frustrated puff of air. "You look good," I say, finally turning to truly look at her. "Was that good enough for you?"

The corner of her mouth lifts into a smile. "It was good, but I think it'd be a lot more fun if you actually showed me what you think about me too," she adds casually, as if what she's suggesting isn't some big deal that could turn both of our lives completely upside down.

"I can't do that."

"Why not?" she presses, pushing off her palms as she leans forward, my eyes straying toward the cleavage peeking through, perfectly on display.

With every ounce of self-control I have left, I force my eyes to meet hers. "Because what I want to do with you isn't something a person should ever do to their little sister's best friend."

"What about to their *wife*?"

I let out a huff. "You're only going to be my wife for a short time."

This answer seems to satisfy her, as her smile widens. "Then take advantage of what little time you have, especially when that wife is so incredibly willing and desperate to let her husband do whatever he wants to her," she says, uncrossing her legs before letting them spread apart.

"*Fuck*," I inwardly curse, my resolve weakening as I carefully set the butter knife down on the counter and turn to face her. "This is something you really want?" I ask, needing to hear her say the words out loud.

I'm not an idiot. I know when a woman wants to be fucked, but this with Veronica feels different and so much more complicated. There are so many this could go wrong, and while I'd love to tear off her clothes and take advantage of her in every way she's begging me to, I can't rush into this. I have to be logical.

"It's what I want, and I know you want it too. Just do it, Miles. Take what you want from me," she all but whispers, as my eyes fall to her beautiful, plump lips.

"This is only a one-time thing. You know that's all this can be, right?" I clarify.

"If that's what you need to tell yourself, then sure."

"Vee," I say, needing her to take this seriously because I sure as hell am.

"I don't know what you want me to say, because I think I'm going to need more than one round to get you out of my system. But I will say this: we can make this a short-term thing, and only until our annulment goes through, because why shouldn't we? We're two willing and consenting adults. Why can't we take advantage of what's right in front of us?"

There are still so many reasons running through my head as to why this is such a fucking horrible idea, but I'm tired of fighting it—especially when I seem to be the only one left doing so.

"Fuck it," I say, fully giving in as I take a step toward her. My hand lands on the back of her neck, my thumb cradling her jaw as my mouth finally crashes into hers. A guy can only handle so much temptation—especially when it looks and sounds exactly like the woman who's been consuming my every last thought for the past two weeks.

31

VERONICA

M Y BODY IGNITES THE moment Miles's lips crash against mine, an all-consuming fire I couldn't extinguish even if I wanted to. But why would I? I'm done denying that this isn't something I want.

I've kissed my fair share of men, even one I thought was my forever. But this? This is different. It's more than just a kiss—it's raw, desperate, and overwhelmingly intense, almost as if he needs to claim every inch of me before all of this disappears. But I can promise I'm no Cinderella, and there's no clock striking midnight to scare me away. I want this—I want him—every heated, breathtaking second of it.

It's intoxicating, or rather *he's* intoxicating. His passion isn't just something I feel; it's something being seared into my soul, leaving a mark I know I'll never shake. This moment will be a part of me forever, and I'm completely okay with that.

With one hand cradling my neck, his other lands on my waist as he pulls me into him. Needing to center myself, I let my arms drape over his shoulders, my fingers immediately tightening in the soft hair at the nape of his neck.

His tongue traces the seam of my lips, silently begging for entry, which I happily oblige, savoring every inch and touch that he offers me, especially given how hard I've had to work for this.

Maybe getting someone to kiss you shouldn't be a battle, and under normal circumstances, I'd wholeheartedly agree. But right now? With his lips devouring mine as though he's been equally starved for this moment, and the electric pull radiating through every inch of my body, I couldn't care less about what I should or shouldn't allow. All that matters is how this man makes me feel, and how I'll do whatever it takes to uncover more of him. If this is how he kisses, I just know he knows how to fuck.

Wrapping my legs around his middle, I pull him into me, needing to feel pressure on my aching center. He complies, moving even closer, as the hand by my cheek dips lower, gliding over my clothed chest before palming me through the thin fabric of my top. I press myself into his touch, moaning into his mouth.

His hand sinks even lower as his lips leave mine, peppering a trail of kisses along my neck and jawline. I'm not even sure which sensation to focus on. I'm obsessed with the way his lips feel as they work their magic, but it's hard to ignore the sensation of his hand sliding under my shirt before moving back up. I'm sure I deserve to be tortured, considering how I came in here openly teasing him, but it's clear this man knows exactly what he's doing as his hand moves achingly slow toward my breast.

No one can say I didn't come prepared, as I purposely chose to go braless. It might not have been fair to use my body like this, but I'm desperate for him, and that desperation is likely obvious as I unconsciously whimper, my head tipping back as his lips continue their trail upward as his hand cups my breast. I strain, arching my back into it.

I don't have the time to be embarrassed. I'm way too engrossed in the way his hand moves over my sensitive skin before he runs his fingers over my pebbled nipple, simultaneously nibbling on my ear lobe before pulling back.

My body wants to cry at the loss of contact. While a part of me spirals into panic, fearing he might be having second thoughts, he instead reaches down, gently lifting my top over my head. I willingly oblige, raising my arms.

I'm ready for him to get back to business, but instead, his eyes take me in as he runs his tongue across his bottom lip. "So damn perfect," he compliments. Maybe with anyone else, I'd feel shy and self-conscious, but not with him. If anything, I can't help but feel pride in the fact that Miles fucking Bennett thinks I'm perfect. Leaning forward, he presses his lips to my now freed nipple, running his tongue over it before giving it a light nip, his free hand palming the other.

I lean back on the counter, pressing myself toward his mouth, savoring the way his tongue works so expertly on my nipple. My legs cling to his middle even tighter before he switches sides, giving the other breast equal attention. The possibility of me coming from this alone feels incredibly real, but I'm not given enough time to test the theory as his mouth moves down my body, taking his time as he peppers kisses along my skin.

Despite my desire to completely immerse myself in the moment, I find myself unable to resist the urge to open my eyes and meet his captivating icy-blue gaze as he reaches the top of my shorts.

"Miles," I whine, my lower half unconsciously writhing, needing him to go lower, and I don't even care if he hears the distress in my voice. I need him, and I need him now.

One of his rare smiles crosses his lips as he slips his fingers into the sides of my shorts, lowering them down my legs, until I'm completely bare to him. He carelessly tosses them onto the kitchen floor.

"Fuck, Veronica. Who knew my wife had such a perfect, and pretty little pussy? And it's soaking wet just for me," he murmurs appreciatively, taking me in before lowering his head between my thighs. Instead of giving me what I want right away, he takes his time, lavishing attention on the sensitive skin of my thighs before thankfully getting dangerously close to my aching center, which is all but begging for attention.

"Please, Miles," I cry out once more, desperate for relief.

"Oh, don't worry. I fully intend to satisfy my wife tonight, but first, I need you to tell me what you want me to do," he commands.

I'm more impatient than ever, but I'm also willing to give him what he wants, as long as he's just as willing to give me what I want in return. Luckily, he doesn't fully keep me waiting. His lips trail up my thigh, inching closer to where I need him most, his eyes never leaving mine.

"I want you to lick my pussy. I want you to make me come with that perfect mouth of yours." I give in, not caring how pathetically desperate I sound, even to my own ears, because it's the truth. It's exactly what I want—no, what I *need* him to do.

"Your wish is my command," he murmurs, delivering on that promise as he flattens his tongue and runs it along my achingly wet seam. My body reacts instantly, far too eager as I involuntarily thrust toward his face.

"So greedy." He chuckles, his voice deep and velvety smooth. "But I like a greedy woman who knows what she wants. And I fully intend to be the one to give it to her. Hell, while you're mine, I'm going to make sure I ruin you forever, so if anyone else so much as *thinks* they can make you feel this good, you'll always think of me." Then his mouth is on me, taking my clit between his lips, and my body arches off the counter as a loud moan escapes past my lips.

I'm not surprised that he knows exactly how to use that mouth and tongue of his, sucking and twirling it against the sensitive bud. Maybe it was just something hot to say to get me even more riled up, but I'm pretty sure he's doing exactly what he promised—ruining me. No one has ever made me come this undone, and I don't know how anyone else ever will.

I may be greedy in my desire as he continues to fuck me with his mouth and tongue, but luckily, he seems just as needy. His hands grip my bare ass, pulling me even closer. I tangle one hand in his soft, thick hair while using the other to steady myself against the counter, my hips bucking in time with his hungry, demanding mouth.

"Fuck, Vee," he whispers into my lips. "You taste so sweet and so much better than I even imagined." Before I can respond his tongue moves down to my core. This time, he dips it inside me while one hand slides forward, his thumb creating a perfect rhythm against my throbbing clit.

I wish I had the ability to say something smart or sexy, but all I can manage is another loud, satisfied moan as he continues his work. This time, he switches it up. While his lips once again capture my small nub, his fingers trail along my drenched slit before shoving one finger inside.

"Oh, God, Miles," I swear, but instead of sounding like a curse, it comes out as pure adoration. I was right—this man *knows* what he's doing.

He seems to appreciate the encouragement, rewarding me by sucking harder and adding another finger. Then with effortless precision he curls his fingers toward my stomach and a feeling I've never quite experienced before erupts inside me. Never in my life has a man made me feel this good, and Miles has done it both quickly and effortlessly. A part of me wishes I could hold on longer, if only to make this moment last forever, but I can't take it anymore. I give in, surrendering completely, my hips thrusting toward his mouth and touch.

Sounds I'm not sure I've ever made before escape, mixed with a few choice curse words and his name, as I ride out the most intense orgasm of my entire life. Instead of taking this as his cue to stop, he keeps going, pumping his fingers in and out of me while his mouth continues its relentless assault, thankfully not slowing down or letting up.

I finally make it over the edge, coming down from the highest of highs, my body turning into jelly. He may have done the majority of the work, but I still find myself needing to recover as my heart pounds against my chest.

Yet even after a job well done, he doesn't pull away. He stays, carefully licking up every last drop of what I've given him, savoring the taste of me.

"Hopefully that met your standards," he says, his hands drifting slowly up from my backside. One hand steadies me at the waist, while the other supports my neck, his thumb once again brushing soft circles against my cheek. "Can't have my wife thinking her husband doesn't know how to satisfy her."

I'm sure the smirk on his lips means he's only teasing, but the way he says *wife* sends another spark straight to my core. There's something about that word—coming from him, attached to me—that ignites something I can't ignore. It feels possessive in the best way, even if it's not something I should take to heart. Yes, I'm his wife, but for how long?

"You more than met my standards. No complaints here," I assure him, as I gather the energy to lean forward, pressing my lips to his, tasting the salty sweetness of myself on his mouth. "Now, hopefully, I can show my gratitude by making you feel just as good," I whisper against him, my hands sliding to the bottom of his T-shirt before lifting it.

I've seen him shirtless many times before, especially during our beach trips, but the thought of being able to touch and explore him with my lips and fingers brings a new level of excitement as I fully admire his muscular upper body.

I waste no time placing a hand on top of his pec while hungrily pressing my lips into his once again. I part his mouth with mine as my tongue slips into his. I take full advantage of where we're at as I run my hand over his defined six-pack, appreciating the individuality of each separate muscle, while my other hand moves to the back of his neck, entwining my fingers into the hair at the nape.

He seems just as happy to let this happen as he moves in closer, allowing my hand to continue its journey south as I feel those sexy-ass V-shaped muscles, almost like a beacon, guiding me toward where I know we both want me to explore.

Or at least I assume it's what he wants since he doesn't stop me as my hand slips beneath his pair of gray sweatpants and boxer briefs. Unsurprisingly, his cock is stiff and completely ready for me.

"Fuck," he curses into my mouth before pulling away, his head falling back in pure ecstasy. I take this moment to let my lips explore the scratchy, unshaven part of his neck while my hand continues its exploration. I grip him in my hands, taking in both his girth and length.

"We need a condom," he finally says, since it's clear we're both on the same page with our wants and needs. "Come here," he impatiently urges, wrapping his arms tightly around my back as I release my grip on his cock and encircle his neck with both arms, and my legs around his waist.

With ease, and his hands supporting my ass, he carries me toward his bedroom. We may be close, my bare skin pressed against his, but I need more as I press my lips against his before once again trailing them down his jawline and planting heated kisses at the hollow of his neck.

Thankfully, his apartment isn't large, so the short distance from the kitchen to his bedroom feels almost effortless. Even with one hand on the knob, he easily hauls me inside, as if nothing could stop him from carrying out this mission. While I would be fine being tossed around, he doesn't drop me. Instead, he carefully lowers me onto the soft mattress.

I'm more than ready to let him ravage my body, but takes things much slower as he pulls back, his eyes reverently taking me in as his gaze wanders across each and every curve. It soon becomes my turn to marvel as I prop myself up on my elbows while he finally reaches down to lower his sweats and boxers, his gorgeous cock springing free, and I involuntarily run my tongue along my lip.

I want to taste him and let him fuck my mouth, but it seems he has other plans as he crawls over me, pressing more heated kisses to my lips before once again pulling back. Seemingly no longer in the mood to torture me or make me wait, he reaches into his bedside dresser and pulls out a condom. He clearly knows what he's doing, ripping it open with his teeth, and sheathing himself in record time.

"Tell me you want this, because once I start, I don't think I can stop," he says, as he hovers over me, his eyes searching mine.

"I want this. Take me, Miles. Make me yours. Ruin me forever," I say, fully giving in, not caring if that's exactly what will happen. All that matters is us, here and now.

My words don't seem to scare him off as his eyes darken and he presses his lips against mine. Needing to feel the closeness I desperately crave, I wrap my legs around his back as he lines himself up against my entrance.

"Miles," I beg, my voice coming out way more whiny than I'd like, but I mean it. I need him—now.

Finally, he pushes himself inside me with a loud groan and I match his movement with a thrust of my hips and a loud cry. I can feel him stretching my walls as he fills every last inch of me.

We both seem to be filled with a similar desperation as I meet each of his thrusts, rolling my hips into his. It makes sense, after how long the two of us have tried to fight and deny the fact that this is something we've both needed for a while, and clearly for good reason.

As cheesy as it sounds, my body feels as though it was made for him, filled with unrelenting pleasure as he continues to thrust in and out of me, my nails digging into his shoulder blades.

"Miles," I cry out over and over. Normally, it's not necessarily my style to be so loud and vocal, but damn, this man knows how to work my body, especially as he pulls back just enough to sink one of his hands between us, his thumb brushing against my clit.

"Oh my God," I moan loudly.

"No God here, just me." He proudly smirks, which, coming from him, is incredible, especially given his usual serious demeanor. "That's it, beautiful. Keep taking my cock so fucking well, like it was made just for you," he pants, thrusting again and again.

I want to tell him that he's right, but I don't have it in me. I can only reply with another loud moan, somehow encouraging his movements even more. I want to drag this out longer, especially after already receiving one amazing orgasm from him, but my body certainly appreciates his as I feel myself getting close again. As my back lifts off the bed, my nails claw perfect little moon-shaped dents deep into his back, while my other hand digs into the sheets.

I cry out his name once more as a powerful orgasm consumes my body, intense wave after wave rippling through me, culminating until he gives one last thrust and releases himself with a satisfied groan.

It seems to take us both a few extra moments to recover as we come back down to earth. While I half-expect him to roll off, his gaze drops to mine, his blue eyes softening as he leans down, his lips brushing my forehead with a feather-light touch before he finally rolls over.

"Well, fuck," he curses, the words heavy with exhaustion as he lets himself fall onto the mattress beside me.

"No regrets though, right?" I ask, my hand falling to my chest, where my heart plays a frantic rhythm against my ribs.

"How could I ever regret something that felt like *that*?" he asks, turning his head to look at me, and God, he's gorgeous.

I reach over with my free hand and brush a piece of his sweat-soaked hair away from his eyes. "Just making sure I didn't freak you out or anything."

"It's gonna take a lot more than that to freak me out. Plus, maybe you were right. If something can feel this good, why fight it? It's only temporary, right?"

The joy I'd been riding just moments ago slips away, deflating like a balloon with a slow leak. I do my best to keep the ache from showing on my face—it's not like this isn't what I'd just agreed to.

"Yep. It's only temporary," I agree, my voice heavy with heartbreak, as I lie back on the bed and stare at his popcorn ceiling.

As he rolls out of bed to deal with the condom, I sink back into the pillows, shaking my head as I scold myself. *This is only temporary*, I try to remind my foolish heart, repeating the words over and over like a much-needed mantra. But even as I do, the weight of them feels like a lie. If I'm not careful, I'll break the promise I made to Blair—and to myself—and actually fall for Miles Bennett.

Unfortunately it's becoming obvious that maybe it's already happened, as that newfound realization hits me like a tidal wave, knocking the air from my lungs. Somewhere along the way, I let my guard down, and the impossible happened. I've fallen for my best friend's brother, and it's only a matter of time before that hard truth leaves me with yet another broken heart.

32

MILES

I'M AN ASSHOLE. I know I should be taking advantage of the situation I'm in and the fact that I have a gorgeous and willing woman to hook up with, especially when our chemistry is off the charts, but I can't do it. I know I said I was fine with things being temporary, and a part of me knows I should be making the most of the connection I have with Veronica while it's still an option, but honestly? It's just not that simple.

As much as I'd like to say Veronica is nothing more to me than being Blair's quirky and impulsive best friend, that's just not the truth anymore. She's *way more* than that. Not only has she become my friend as well, but she's weaseled her way in and become one of the most important people in my life.

Every time I see her, my day feels a little brighter, and each smile she sends my way feels like the warm hug I never knew I needed. She's changed my life completely, and as much as I hate to admit it, it's been for the better.

Not that she would know that as I've actively been going out of my way to avoid her. I get it. I'm a piece of shit. She deserves way more than a man who chooses to sleep with her only to ignore her the next day, but I don't physically have it in me to act like this is normal or like it's something I can handle.

I like to think of myself as a tough guy, someone who isn't afraid of getting hurt, but the last people I truly let in were my parents. When they both showed their true colors and left me broken, I swore I'd never let anyone else get close enough to have that power. Yet, here's Veronica, inching dangerously close to breaking down all those carefully built walls. As much as I want to let her in, I can't. Not when we both know this situation isn't built to last. It's temporary, and I can't afford to forget that.

Eventually, our sham of a marriage will be annulled, and she'll move back out. She'll once again become nothing more than Blair's best friend and I think it's time we both stop acting like reality isn't breathing down our necks.

Unfortunately, one thing I've learned is that the constant proximity in our tiny, cramped apartment makes avoiding her nearly impossible.

That's precisely why I've spent the past few days at work, putting in overtime, or at least attempting to make it look like I am. There really is only so much you can do before you run out of real work.

Sure, the folks of Evergreen are probably thrilled their vehicles are being serviced in record time, but it's not like we were ever drowning in work to begin with. Then again, maybe that's a blessing in disguise because these twelve-hour workdays are starting to catch up with me. Case in point: after someone dropped off their truck for an oil change, I was forced to retreat to my office for a breather, my body all but shutting down on me.

Every joint in my body feels like it's filled with molten lead as I sink into my desk chair, my face falling into my hands.

When the bell rings at the front of my shop, I let out a new groan, for an entirely different reason. I know I want and need the work to avoid a particularly perky little brunette, but I'm not sure I have it in me right now to put on a fake-ass grin and help someone new. I'm running on fumes as it is.

"I'm coming," I croak, my voice raspy and weak as I struggle to push myself up from the chair, but before I can fully stand Veronica walks into my office. "What are you doing here?" I ask, worry creasing my brow. "Is everything okay?"

"No, things aren't okay," she says, her hands landing on her hips. "And I think it's me who should be asking you that question. You haven't been home in days. Or, I don't know, you must have come home at some point since Bubba's food and water bowl always seem to be filled, but apparently, it's only when I'm not around. So what the hell is going on? Did my vagina really scare you away?"

I sigh. "Vee—" I start, lifting a hand, but she interrupts before I can say more.

"Don't '*Vee*' me. I know what you're doing, but what I really want to know is, why?"

I close my eyes, trying to gather my thoughts, not wanting to make this worse, but it's as if my brain has flipped the switch to 'off,' refusing to put together a clear sentence. "I just... I don't want things to be weird between us."

She rolls her eyes. "Too late for that. Things are already weird between us, but what you're doing is only making it weirder. Yes, I know I was the one who pushed for this," she says, pointing at me before back at herself, "but I wouldn't have suggested we do anything if I knew this was how it would end up. If this is any indicator of how it's going to be from here on out, I'd rather just move out now and salvage what I can."

"No, that's not what I want. I don't want you to leave or move out," I argue weakly, taking a step toward her as she stays where she is, her hands firmly planted on her hips.

"Why? Clearly, you're avoiding going home, and I know it's because of me. I'm not okay with that, and neither is Bubba. He misses you. Hell, *I* miss you," she pleads, her eyes softening.

"I miss you too," I admit. I probably shouldn't be saying that out loud, especially when I'm still so terrified of becoming even more attached, but in my current state of exhaustion, it's too hard to lie or say anything else. "I just..." I try again, but my foggy brain continues to work against me. Instead, I shake my head and let out a much-needed, centering breath.

"What's wrong?" she asks, her brows furrowing as she drops her hands and takes a step forward.

"I'm just tired." I mumble, not wanting her to worry.

"I'm not surprised. Have you even gotten any sleep these past few days?" she asks, her tone pointed yet concerned. And she's not wrong—she knows I've been sneaking in long after she's gone to bed and heading out before she wakes up. If I were smart, I would've set up a cot in my office given the amount of time I've been spending here.

"I've gotten a few hours each night," I offer, attempting to find some relief as I lean back and put most of my weight against my desk.

This doesn't stop her from worrying, as her eyes take me in appraisingly before she finally steps forward and reaches out to touch my forehead.

"What are you doing?" I snap, swatting at her hand, but given how weak I feel, the effort is wasted.

"Miles Bennett," she curses, not stopping her movement as she dodges my swat and places her hand on my forehead. "You're burning up!"

I move my head away from her touch, even though the movement is dizzying. "I'm fine. I think I've just overworked myself. All I need is a good night's sleep, and I'll be as good as new."

"This is more than just overworking yourself. You have a fever," she insists, her hand falling to rest on my cheek. "You're sick. So what's happening now is that you're going home and getting straight into bed."

With what little energy I can muster, I raise an eyebrow. "You really think that's going to work and that I'm going to listen to you?"

She tilts her head upward and lets out a small huff. "As a matter of fact, I do."

"Okay, and what if I decide I'm not going to listen?" I challenge.

"I'm not even going to answer that, because I'm not taking no for an answer. It's already been decided—you're coming home with me right now. End of story."

I wish I could say I had some fight left in me, if only to tease her, but I just don't. On top of that, lying down sounds heavenly.

"Fine, I'll head home soon, but I have one more job to finish before I can close up," I explain, trying not to let the mere idea of working overwhelm me.

She shakes her head. "No, sorry. That's not happening. I'll call Sam, have him finish the job, and he'll close up. As for you, you're done for the night, and maybe even for the next day or two as well."

I attempt to raise an eyebrow. "I'm not sure who you think you are—" I start to say, but she doesn't let me get very far.

"I know exactly who I am. I'm your wife, and your wife says you're going home and getting into bed, and that's final."

I'm not one to give up easily. I'm usually all about fighting the good fight. But damn, hearing her say those words does something to me. I know I shouldn't let her get under my skin, especially since, deep down I'm fully aware it's not real, at least not really. Still, no matter how hard I try to keep my guard up, she keeps finding new ways to get in.

What's more, Sam would kill for the extra hours and only left earlier because we didn't have any work for him to complete after how much overtime I've been putting in.

"Alright, fine. Let me just grab my keys, and we'll go," I relent.

"You don't need your keys. I'm driving you," she insists, and I'm not sure what to think about her demanding demeanor, especially when I've never been all that good at letting other people tell me what to do. Worse yet, I think it's kind of turning me on. I like bossy Veronica. "And before you worry or argue about it, I'll have Ford and Blair bring your car home later, because I can assure you, you're in for a world of disappointment if you think for even one second I'm about to let you drive home in your condition."

"I have a fever; I'm not dying," I deadpan.

"Yeah, for now, but we're not taking any chances. I know you get off on being a grumpy and stubborn asshole who doesn't like to listen to anybody, but we're done here. The sooner you get that through your thick skull, the better."

I sigh, shaking my head. "Fine."

It's clear she doesn't believe me when I insist I'm not dying and can walk by myself as she links her arm through mine as if she's the one carrying me to the car, but I'm definitely not that far gone. I may feel like crap, but I'm still standing. Yet, I can't deny how good it feels to have her close and to know that someone genuinely cares enough to be here. It may be a small, simple thing, but damn, it makes all the difference.

Fuck. I thought being around her before was overwhelming, but this is so much worse. An odd, comforting warmth spreads through me, and I'm all too aware it has nothing to do with the fever and everything to do with the woman walking beside me. And that is truly fucking terrifying.

33

VERONICA

"THANK YOU SO MUCH for bringing it," I say, reaching across the doorway to give Blair a grateful hug.

"Of course. Plus, we all know Miles would freak out and throw a little temper tantrum if his car wasn't home by the time he started feeling better," she jokes. "The man is a drama queen when it comes to his babies."

"And here's the soup," Ford tacks on, handing over the giant to-go carton from The Starlight Diner, filled with the chicken noodle soup I requested.

"So he's currently getting some much-needed rest, but I'm sure he'd be okay if you wanted to check on him," I offer as I take a step back and motion toward his bedroom.

Blair wrinkles her nose. "Nah, I'd rather let him sleep. Plus, if I'm being honest, I'm not looking to catch whatever germs he has going on, so just send him my love instead."

"Will do," I say, leaning forward one more time and giving them each one last quick hug goodbye.

After waving them off, I set the soup down in the kitchen and tiptoe toward Miles's room, easing the door open to peek inside. Bubba lifts his head from where he's curled up beside his owner, giving me a look that feels as relieved as I am that Miles has finally found his way back home. Not that I gave him much of a choice in the matter.

I had already marched into his office with a plan, but after walking in and realizing how sick he was, there was no way I was going to let him continue whatever annoying game he was playing.

I lean against the doorway, watching him sleep. With his mouth ajar and his messy blond locks falling haphazardly into his face, he looks a little silly, but somehow, even like this, he's still one of the most jaw-droppingly gorgeous men I've ever laid eyes on.

I was never blind. Miles has always been attractive, and even from a young age, I recognized that my best friend's older brother was a smoke show. But I never once thought about doing anything about my attraction to the older male.

Then again, with the way he's been actively avoiding me, maybe it would've been smarter to stay away. But I suppose knowing something and acting on that knowledge are two separate issues. I know my reputation precedes me and that I'm well-known for my horrible decision-making, but even with things the way they are now, I'm not ready to be done with him or us.

I get that spending more time around him is only going to make my feelings grow, and that eventually, my heart is going to end up even more shattered and broken, but I can't help myself. I'm the moth, and he's my flame, and right now, I'm more than willing to let this attraction kill me.

He begins to stir, a soft exhale leaving his lips as his eyes flutter open. He flips the hair out of his eyes before they land on me. I should be embarrassed that he caught me watching him sleep, but as he shoots me one of those elusive smiles, I have no fucks to give.

"How are you feeling?" I ask, giving myself permission to enter as I move to sit on the edge of his bed.

With another soft groan, he attempts to sit up. "Better, I think," he grumbles, but given his tired, exhausted eyes, and how much effort it took him to make that small bit of movement, I'm not entirely convinced.

"Let me see."

Despite being sick, he still manages enough willpower to roll his eyes. "I'm fine, Vee. Don't worry about it."

I refuse to listen. Scooting closer, I lift the back of my hand and hold it to his forehead. He isn't thrilled, but at least he's no longer fighting me on it.

"You're still a bit warmer than I'd prefer," I mull it over, tilting my lips to the side as I figure out our next move.

"Veronica." He huffs, saying my full name in what I can only assume is his attempt to show just how serious he is, but I ignore it. "I'm fine. I've been taking care of myself for 31 years. I can deal with a little fever all on my own."

I frown, fully aware of the history he and Blair share—absent parents and a grandmother who couldn't be bothered. Yet another unfortunate moment where I'm forced to confront just how profoundly different his childhood was from mine.

Growing up, whenever I got sick, my parents went above and beyond to make sure I was as comfortable as possible. While they couldn't take away the pain or discomfort, they more than made up for it with their love and attention. Whether it was cuddling with me in bed or playing my favorite Disney movies on repeat, they had a way of turning even the worst days into something that felt safe, and like everything was going to be okay.

"I'm aware that you can take care of yourself, but why should you have to? Please, just let me do this," I practically beg.

He shakes his head. "I've never let anyone take care of me—not even Blair."

"Yeah, I've noticed," I grumble with a less-than-amused chuckle. "But I'm sure you've also noticed that I'm not someone who takes no for an answer, so you might as well just get used to it," I add. What we have going on may not be permanent, but while I'm here, he's just going to have to deal with a boundary-crossing wife.

"Yeah, I think I'm starting to realize that." He sighs with another shake of his head. "But I really don't see the point. It's a fever. I'm not sure there's much more you can really do."

"Oh, believe me, there is plenty more I can do, starting with a cool shower, some soup, and settling in while we watch your favorite movie," I say with a decisive nod.

"Soup? I thought you hated cooking."

"I do, which is why I asked Blair and Ford to stop at the Starlight Diner and grab some soup while also picking up your car," I casually explain, a proud smile lighting up my face.

"Really?"

"Really." I nod, my head tilting to the side, not really sure why he seems so confused.

"You got all that taken care of while I was sleeping?" he asks, his eyes softening.

"Sure did. I even checked in with Sam, and just like I knew he would, not only did he finish up with the last car, but he also took care of closing up for the day. He also agreed to work the next two shifts so you can take the next few days off to recover without having to worry or stress about it."

I can tell he doesn't look all that pleased to know that I'm shutting him out of his own business, but despite trying to hide it, I can also see a noticeable sense of relief.

"Oh, well, thank you, I guess," he manages.

I let out a small laugh. "That took a lot out of you to say, huh?"

"It really did. I've never been all that good at letting go of control."

"Believe me, I've been besties with Blair since we were five. I get how you Bennetts are, but just like I often have to tell her, I'm here, so stop acting like you have to do it all by yourself. And speaking of not doing everything by yourself, let's get you in that shower."

"I don't need a shower. I'm not even sure I have the energy to take one," he protests.

Even from my sitting position, I place my hands on my hips. "What did I just tell you? I'm here, and I'm going to help. But I promise, it will feel good and will hopefully be what finally breaks that fever of yours."

A sound halfway between a laugh and a scoff escape his lips. "I'm not a child. I don't need help getting in the shower."

"Maybe you don't, but I'm going to help either way, so you might as well just give in now."

It's obvious he isn't pleased to still have me bossing him around, but I think it's finally sinking in that I'm not backing down as he lets out a defeated sigh.

"Just give me a few minutes, and I'll have your shower ready," I say, standing and heading toward the ensuite bathroom. I turn on the water, carefully adjusting the temperature—warm enough to be comfortable, but not so hot that it won't help bring down the fever.

Once everything is ready, I head back to the room, helping him up as I lead him toward the bathroom. I reach for his shirt, and he once again tries to swat my hand away, but I swat his hand right back.

"Vee," he warns, his tone serious.

"Miles," I say, my tone just as stern.

"I can undress myself."

"We've already established that you can do lots of things by yourself, but today, I'm taking care of you, so I think it's time you stop fighting and just let go once and for all."

His lips form a tight, straight line, but the fight seems to vanish as he lifts his arms above his head.

"Good boy," I tease, my fingers reaching for the bottom of his T-shirt as I lift it over his head, doing my best not to get distracted by the abs that are still as toned and sexy as ever.

"You're ridiculous," he says, the newly formed smile betraying his act of annoyance.

"And you're stubborn as hell. We both have our issues, but since I put up with you, it looks like it's your turn to put up with me."

Thankfully, that seems to shut him up, at least for now, as I bend down to take care of his gym shorts and boxers. Of course, my horny-ass brain needs to take a moment to appreciate how good he looks as my mind also drifts back to the other night, but I shove those thoughts aside as I remind myself why I'm here and what I'm supposed to be doing.

He's just about to take a step toward the shower when I reach down and lift my shirt over my head.

His mouth drops open. "Whoa, wait. What are you doing?" he says, his eyes blinking rapidly, his gaze falling to my bralette-covered chest before his eyes find mine.

"I'm showering with you."

He seems to stutter for a moment as he does his best to put together a complete sentence. "I-I don't understand," he finally manages.

"This way, you can just relax and stand under the water, and I can take care of all the rest."

He tilts his head to the side, but I shake my head, knowing exactly what he's going to do—tell me he doesn't need my help. But once again, I don't care.

"Just get in. You already know I'm going to do this anyway, so stop using what little energy you have trying to fight me on this."

His lips form another tight line, but finally, he releases a large exhale before moving to stand under the water.

I take this as my sign to finish undressing before he can stop me and climb in after him.

The water is cooler than I'd like, but I can tell it feels amazing on his overheated skin as he closes his eyes, doing exactly what I wanted him to do as he finally lets go and relaxes.

I use this as an opportunity to grab his bar of soap, working it into a foamy lather in my hands before running them down his arms.

He opens his eyes as he watches my movements, our gazes meeting for a moment before I finally avert mine. I can't get distracted. As good as it feels to run my fingers across his slick skin, and as much as my body has a completely normal reaction to this intimate act, I don't let it stop me from completing my mission.

A soft moan of appreciation crosses his lips as he closes his eyes. Glancing down, I can see his body is also reacting, and as much as I'd like to fuck him with either my hand or my mouth, I know now isn't the time. That will be for when I get him back to his healthy self, but right now, making him feel better in a different way is my mission.

I already feel like we've crossed off a major milestone here. Letting someone else take care of him doesn't come easy, but feeling his body relax under my touch tells me I'm making a difference. The real challenge, though, will be seeing if he allows this to continue. Sure, I expect him to push back—he's Miles Bennett, after all—but I'm determined not to let that stop me. I'm fully committed to nursing him back to full health, even if it takes everything I've got. Because the truth is, just like with his sister, I'm realizing I'd do just about anything for this man.

34

MILES

"Y OU REALLY DIDN'T HAVE to do this," I tell Veronica for what feels like the millionth time as she carefully hands me a steaming bowl of chicken noodle soup.

"Of course I did," she says, brushing me off before walking around to the other side of the bed and climbing in.

I'm not entirely sure what I did to deserve the kind of care she's giving me. Honestly, it's taken every ounce of self-restraint not to tell her off, kick her out of my room, or even out of the apartment altogether. But if I'm being honest, I can't deny that it's been... well, nice. I've never had someone take care of me like this, and while letting go of so much control has been hard, I can't say I hate it either.

"I'm not sure I agree, especially since I'm pretty sure most people don't get showered by someone else," I counter, considering no one has ever done that for me, nor is it something I'd have ever thought about doing for someone else.

"Just because it's not something that happens often, doesn't mean it's something that shouldn't happen at all."

I try not to roll my eyes, especially since I'm not sure I even have the energy. Veronica may have been right about the shower breaking my fever, but that doesn't mean it didn't tire me out, even with her doing the majority of the work.

I suppose one thing I can be grateful for is that I no longer feel like I'm teetering on the edge of death. I might have downplayed how sick I actually was when I told Veronica I was feeling better, but the truth is, I was completely wrecked. Without her stepping in—forcing me to rest, take medicine, and actually relax—I'd probably still be fighting off the worst of it.

"Well, don't go thinking this is going to be some recurring thing," I warn her as I dip my spoon into the bowl and take a bite, the warmth of the broth spreading through me. Damn. Yet another thing she gets to be right about. If this were like any other time and I'd gotten sick, I probably wouldn't be feeding myself or constantly drinking my liquids like she's been forcing me to.

"Eh, I don't know. We'll see." She casually shrugs while reaching over me to grab the remote off my bed as she flips on the television. "So, what are we watching?" she asks, changing the subject, which is likely for the best. I'm not sure I have it in me to keep arguing about this.

"We?" I ask, glancing over at her as I pause my spoon mid-bite. "I'm not even sure you should be hanging around me. This is probably contagious, and the last thing we need is you ending up sick too."

"I work in a high school with snot-ridden kids who never wash their hands. Believe me, I've built a stronger immunity than a cockroach at a nuclear testing site."

I lift a skeptical brow, resisting the urge to smile at her dumb joke.

"Seriously, when I first started, I caught every cold, flu, and plague imaginable—especially at the start of the year. But now? My body's basically the Terminator. If I can survive a horde of germ-infested teenagers coughing directly in my face, I can handle being around you."

"If you say so." I sigh, finding it not worth getting into. "I still don't think it's a smart idea..."

"If you're worried about me making you return the favor and take care of me if I get sick, don't. I'm not going into this with any expectations. You've already helped me more than I could ever help you. We can just consider this my weak attempt at paying you back for everything you've done for me."

My brows furrow. "You don't owe me anything, and if that's why—"

She interrupts, holding up her hand. "That's not why I'm doing this. I'm doing this because I want to, and because I believe everyone deserves a little help now and then—even a grumpy smart-ass like yourself."

"Well, I still don't think it's fair that you're in here putting yourself at risk, even if you do have the immune system of a cockroach."

"Miles," she whines, tilting her head back and letting it fall against the headboard. "Just let me do this, okay?"

"Fine, but let's get one thing straight—I don't do debts. You can act like I don't owe you anything in return, and that's your choice, but I'm keeping tabs. And believe me, I owe you. Big time."

"I still don't think that's how any of this should work, but if that's what helps you sleep better at night, then fine. You'll owe me one," she says with an exaggerated roll of her eyes. "So, back to my earlier question, what are we watching?"

"Whatever you want," I reply, dipping my spoon back into the soup.

"I'm not sure you're understanding how this works. You're the sick one, so you get to pick. Now pick. I mean it too," she says, waving a stern finger in my direction. "Because if not, I'm going to choose *Criminal Minds* or a Disney movie, both of which I know aren't your favorite, so you better just give in and choose something before I do."

Normally, the idea of watching either of those would have me battling her for the remote. But this time, I can't muster the energy to care—or maybe it's not just the exhaustion. Or maybe it's something else entirely that's making me strangely okay with letting her take the lead.

I may not enjoy admitting it out loud, but her being here, especially when she doesn't have to be, and despite risking her own health, means more than I'll ever care to admit. Sure, I can count on Blair, who seems to have already done her part with the soup and my car, but even back in the day, when we were kids, we never went this far for each other.

Back then, we'd help with medicine or bring water to the other if they needed it, but let's be real—we mostly avoided getting close so we would't catch whatever the other one had. That was especially true with our grandma, who, despite doing absolutely nothing to help, always acted like we were inconveniencing her just by existing.

"Just pick something." I nod toward the television before setting the half-eaten soup onto my bedside table. As good as it feels to eat something, that's all I can handle for now. The fight my body has been putting itself through to ward off the germs has more than taken its toll as my eyelids grow heavy with exhaustion. "I'm probably going to nod off as soon as it starts anyway."

She purses her lips, tilting them to the side for a moment before finally giving in.

I shift, adjusting myself until I'm lying down as she takes over, signing into her Disney+ account and selecting *Big Hero 6*. I can't say I've seen it before, and considering how quickly I plan to pass out, I'm pretty sure I'll be asleep before it gets good anyway. Part of me wants to tell her she can leave and that I'll be fine on my own, but knowing her, I'm fairly certain she'd shut me down before I could even finish the offer.

Instead of keeping her distance, like a smart person should, she makes herself more comfortable, moving in closer and settling directly next to me.

"You're crazy, you know that, right?" I ask, because at this point it feels like she's continually choosing to tempt fate.

"I've been told that before." She proudly smiles, taking it as a compliment.

I know I should keep fighting her on this, but instead, I lift an arm, beckoning her in closer as she fully curls into my side, resting her head on my chest.

Earlier, the added warmth would've made me uncomfortable, but now, I soak it in and savor the comfort her body offers.

In fact, I don't think I've ever felt safer or more at peace than I do in this moment.

Even with the movie playing in the background, I quickly drift off. Everything feels almost too perfect, and despite my illness and the knowledge that this is temporary, all I can do is savor the moment. I don't want to think about what's coming next. Right now, all I want is to be here, in this moment, lying next to the most perfect woman I've ever known.

35

VERONICA

"I STILL DON'T GET how you got Miles to agree to Karaoke night." Blair laughs, her voice rising above the version of Sabrina Carpenter's "Espresso" being attempted by the Sampson sisters, two of the regulars at the Timberline Tavern's Tuesday Sing-Out Karaoke Extravaganza.

While Evergreen Grove may be small, the Timberline Tavern is anything but boring. The bar keeps things lively by offering a variety of themed nights to keep the crowd entertained, from karaoke nights (like tonight) to The Timberline Trivia Showdown, Bingo, and even themed dance parties. Personally, I'm a sucker for the '80s dance nights—they always bring the best vibes. I mean, who doesn't love dressing up in neon?

Maybe our track record isn't flawless—after all, the last time we were all here was just before my wedding, which ended with Miles telling Pete off for fat-shaming me. But perhaps that's exactly why we need to come back.

While a lot of places in town are tainted with the memories I shared with Pete—some good, some bad—my only course of action is to move on and keep ignoring the gossip and stares.

Thankfully, after having been home for a few weeks now, most of the chatter has died down, and those brave enough to say anything to my face have already done so.

"Apparently, he owes me," I answer Blair, leaning against the bar while we wait for the drinks we ordered for our table. Across the room, Ford and Miles sit, clearly uncomfortable. They mostly get along, but Ford has never been the type to feel at ease around Miles. The way he's sitting now, tense, with a forced smile, is a perfect reminder that while some things have changed, there are still certain things you can always count on.

"You say that, but I'm pretty sure after all these years, Miles owes me plenty of favors, yet I've *never* gotten him to agree to karaoke night. Hell, I thought it was a miracle the night I got him to join us for Trivia."

Glancing back at the guys, Miles also looks uncomfortable, but I believe for him, it's for an entirely different reason. He's definitely an introvert, and large crowds aren't his thing. That's precisely why I can't help the flutter in my belly at the knowledge that, despite all that, he's still here—for me.

"I mean, if anything, I'm the one who technically hooked him up with the soup, so I'm pretty sure it's me he owes this big favor to," Blair jokes, lightly nudging her elbow into my arm.

"Well, that sounds like a brother-sister type problem and something for the two of you to figure out," I tease, just as the song ends. The crowd erupts into applause, everyone clapping and cheering. Blair and I join in, cupping our hands around our mouths to amplify the sound. We have to keep the tradition alive with the two of us still being the loudest ones in any room.

"I don't know," Blair picks up where we left off as the applause dies down and the next singer is called up.

"You don't know what?" I ask, my brows knitting together.

"About this being a brother-sister type thing. It's starting to sound more like a husband-and-wife type of thing. Is there anything you need to start sharing or get off your chest?" she presses, and this time, it's her eyebrows that rise.

"Blair!" I shriek, reaching over and giving her a light shove. "Of course not. We're just roommates," I insist, trying to make it sound like less than it is.

"Yeah, roommates who are married and can't seem to keep their eyes off each other."

"Oh my God, no. That's not how it is. at all" I nervously giggle, shaking my head, even though I can feel the color rising to my cheeks at the accusation.

"Not how it is? He's looking over here right now," she counters, as I turn my head and glance back toward our table. Just like she said, he's staring directly at me. He sends an acknowledging nod my way before glancing back toward the small stage as the music for NYSNC's "Bye Bye Bye" starts up and the performer begins their rendition—completely off-key, might I add. "So, what was that you were saying about it not being how it is?"

"I think you're just reading into things," I lie, my posture straightening as I attempt to look anywhere but at Blair or her way-too-good-looking older sibling.

"Ronnie, we've been best friends since kindergarten. I know you. What's more, Miles is my brother, who I've known my entire life. You really think I don't see what's going on here?"

I scrunch my nose, crossing my arms with a dramatic sigh. "Alright, fine. You got me," I say, shooting her a mock glare. "I might be *ever so slightly* developing feelings for your brother. Happy now?"

"I fucking knew it!" she proclaims, though I can't quite tell if this is happy news for her or not. "I kept telling Ford after you guys helped me at my studio that something was up, but he kept insisting I was just reading into things."

"No." I sigh, my shoulders drooping, finding no use in lying to her, or really even to myself. "There is definitely something going on, at least on my end."

"Oh, I wouldn't stress about that. Like I said, I know Miles, and trust me, it's written all over his face every time he thinks he's sneakily stealing another glance at you. Believe me, it's mutual. And let's not ignore the fact that he willingly showed up to karaoke night. *Karaoke night*! For Miles, that's like scaling Mount Everest just to impress you. If that's not a neon sign screaming *'I've got it bad,'* then I don't know what is."

"Well... what do you think about it? Are you okay with this?" I ask, nervously nibbling my ruby-red, painted lower lip.

She lifts a shoulder in surrender. "What other choice do I have but to be okay with it? Do I wish things were different? Maybe, but that's only because I'm terrified of either of you getting hurt and it somehow straining my relationships with both of you. At the same time, it's kind of exciting. You being with my brother and getting to be my sister for real? That's a dream come true," she explains, a genuine smile crossing her face as she reaches for my hand, giving it a light squeeze.

"Well, don't get too ahead of yourself here. There may be feelings being explored, but this is far from being an actual relationship. I mean, come on. You know your brother. He's so hard to read, and half the time I think he's only tolerating me because I'm your friend, and then other times..." I trail off, my gaze shifting back to steal another small peek at the man who's been causing all this confusion.

She waves her hand to cut me off. "I get it. You're my best friend, and I'm happy for you, but I'm sure there are certain parts of this whole '*thing*' that I don't need to hear," she says, visibly shuddering. "But I will say this: I've never seen him act like this or look at any other woman the same way he's looking at you. That speaks volumes, and I hope you know just how special you must be to him."

Hearing her words, a familiar warmth spreads through me, making my stomach flutter. Before I can stop myself, a soft, almost involuntary smile tugs at my lips. My gaze instinctively drifts back toward him, and for a moment, everything and everyone in this loud, crowded bar fades away.

"Okay, wow. You really do have it bad, huh?" she asks, as I do my best to stop being a space cadet and return to our present reality. "I mean, I was pretty sure I sensed it earlier, but now that I know for sure, it's so obvious. Hell, I've never even seen *you* look at anybody else like that before—not even Pete."

I wrinkle my nose at the mention of my ex-fiancé's name. In the grand scheme of things, it really hasn't been all that long since I called off the wedding, but even this short time apart has given me the clarity I need. I still can't understand how I ever convinced myself he was "the one," especially when a man like Miles Bennett exists.

"Can we please not say his name out loud? What if he's like Beetlejuice and just saying his name summons him here?" I joke, if only to lighten the situation. I'm having way too much fun to let myself spiral and go down that rabbit hole tonight.

"Good call. I mean, I'm sure we'll eventually have to run into him at some point, but the longer we can push it off, the better," she agrees. "I'm not sure I'd ever look at my brother and call him a catch, but even I'll admit he's a much better option than Pete West."

I wrinkle my nose and send her '*the look*.' "You said his name again. One more time and you're going to screw us over," I warn. "And come on. Your brother isn't that bad."

She sends me an apologetic look before miming the zipping of her lips. "And, no, he's really not. I know he can come off rough around the edges, but when it comes to those he cares about, he's all in and will never let anything bad happen to them. At least I know that if you two do end up together, your heart will always be safe. Just..." she trails off, looking back toward her brother. "Don't break his heart. I know he seems tough, but deep down, all he's ever needed is for someone to love him unconditionally."

My gaze follows hers as I take in the gorgeous male. "I have no plans to hurt him, but who knows, this might not even go anywhere. As far as I know, as soon as the annulment is taken care of, he plans to be done with all of this," I explain, pointing between him and me.

"Hmm," she hums thoughtfully. "I'll believe that when I see it," she decides, shrugging one shoulder, just as our drinks arrive, along with an order of their amazing donuts with the chocolate dunking sauce.

With the drinks and donuts in hand, we make our way back toward our table and set everything down. Blair, with her hands now free, places them on Ford's shoulders as she leans over him. He turns his head, and their lips meet in a sweet and tender kiss.

"Ugh, can you please not do that right next to me?" Miles begs, his face contorting into one of disgust.

"Nope. Sorry. You're just going to have to deal with it," Blair proudly states, as I slide back into my chair between Miles and Blair. At least Ford looks a little embarrassed as his cheeks turn a bright shade of red. "You're just jealous."

Miles scoffs. "Jealous?"

"Yep. If only you could be so lucky to have someone to kiss whenever you wanted," Blair teases as I close my eyes and shake my head.

Miles folds his arms and sits up straighter. "Sorry to disappoint, but kissing in public isn't my thing and never will be," he says, reaching for his beer and taking a long swig.

I know exactly what Blair was trying to do, but it's clear it didn't land the way she'd hoped. Even worse, a sinking feeling settles in my stomach. It's not like I was expecting him to confess anything, and I certainly wasn't expecting him to kiss me in front of everyone—yet somehow, it still leaves me wondering if Blair is wrong about her brother's feelings toward me. Maybe my worries are justified, and I'm not as important to him as he is to me.

Soon, the music and singing come to an end, and the crowd once again responds with claps and cheers before the next performer is called up.

"Hey, aren't we after Buddy?" Ford asks as Buddy, the local barista, takes the microphone and begins a dramatic rendition of "Don't Stop Believin'" by Journey.

"Yeah, I'm pretty sure we are. So, what song are you going to grace us with tonight, Ronnie?" Blair asks, since, like usual, I was the one from our group to volunteer to go first.

"I haven't fully decided yet. Should I go for shock value or keep it simple tonight?" I ask, tilting my head in thought. The majority of the rumors about me have finally started to die down, and while I probably shouldn't add any more fuel to the fire, taking the easy way out has never been my style.

"I think that depends," Ford begins, his usual rational side emerging. "What kind of shock value are we talking about here?"

"Nothing too crazy." I casually shrug, lifting my hand as I pretend to carefully examine my nails, which definitely need some help after not having had a manicure since right before my wedding, or at least the wedding that was supposed to take place between me and Pete.

"Define '*not too crazy*,'" Miles finally speaks up as he turns his smoldering gaze in my direction.

"I guess you'll just have to wait and see," I say, a devious smirk lighting up my face as I drop my hand, and reach for the fruity concoction I'd ordered, and bring it to my lips for a sip.

I wouldn't say I planned this, but a sense of pride fills me as Miles' gaze follows my lips as they wrap around the straw.

"Ugh," Blair cuts in. "And you give us crap?" she asks as I try not to cough and choke on the red liquid I'd just consumed.

"What?" Miles asks, doing his best to act like he hadn't just gotten caught by everyone at the table. "I have no idea what you're talking about," he says, folding his arms and leaning back in his chair.

"And next up, we have Ronnie Prescott," the owner calls into the microphone once Buddy finishes up.

I know I should probably pick a song that lets me blend into the crowd, but that's not who I am. I was made to stand out. With Pete gone, no longer dimming my shine or making me second-guess myself, I'm ready to own that stage.

Let them talk. Let the whispers start up again. Hell, I'll bask in every second of it. Plus, the only attention and eyes I really care about being on me are Miles's. And judging by the way he's watching me walk up toward the stage, maybe Blair was right—I might already have exactly what I want.

36

MILES

"**S**HOULD WE BE NERVOUS?" I ask, my fingers raking through my hair as I push a few stray strands away from my eyes.

"It's Ronnie. Of course we should be nervous," Ford chimes in.

"Oh, come on," Blair shushes us. "It's karaoke. It's not like she can do anything all that crazy or shocking. It's not like this is amateur night at the strip club or anything wild like that."

"Why does it sound like that's something the two of you have done before? Actually," I say, holding up a hand, "I don't want to know."

"I think I'd be interested to know," Ford says, his eyes lighting up before I send a glare in his direction, causing him to shrink back into his chair. "But, uh, not really. That'd be weird. That's gross," he adds, clearly backpedaling as he shakes his head and wrinkles his nose.

"Let me hear you, Evergreen Grove!" Veronica calls into the microphone as she walks across the platform, her stage presence taking over as if this is her concert and we all showed up just for her and everyone that performed before were the opening acts. The way the audience hangs on her every word, hooting and hollering as they cheer, is truly something. It's clear she has them wrapped around her finger and I'd be lying if I said I wasn't right there with them, utterly transfixed. She has my full attention—every last bit of it.

"My name is Ronnie Prescott, and this is 'Bed Chem,' by Sabrina Carpenter," she says into the microphone before pointing and nodding toward the man in charge of the music.

I can't say I know this song, since old-school rock and the occasional country tune are more my thing, but it's hard not to bob my head to the beat, especially as I focus on the lyrics coming out of her pretty little mouth.

It's not just her confidence—it's the way she owns the stage, strutting effortlessly in her short pink plaid dress paired with a matching off-the-shoulder sweater that teases just the right amount of skin. Since when did a bare shoulder have the power to be this damn sexy?

It's not even about how beautiful she looks, but the way she all but commands the attention of everyone in the room as she moves her body. What I wouldn't give for this to be a private show just for me, especially since many of the moves she's doing are similar to the ones she did when we were in Vegas on our wedding night, her hands gliding suggestively across her body, the memory stirring a familiar warmth that goes straight to my groin.

She turns her back toward the crowd, tossing her short brown locks as she bends and looks at us over her shoulder while shaking her ass. Sitting up straight, I attempt to adjust myself.

This is karaoke night, for God's sake. I shouldn't be this turned on—but then again, everything she does is sexy as hell. How did I miss this all before? She's not only mesmerizing me with her body and looks, but she's also just so damn unexpectedly charming, cute, funny, and downright adorable—qualities I've never wanted to associate with Veronica Prescott until now.

It certainly isn't helping that she keeps looking in my direction, something I doubt is going unnoticed by the nosy-ass crowd, especially as she sends a playful wink in my direction.

While her performance is a thousand times better than anyone else's who has been on stage, a part of me is relieved as the music comes to an end and the applause rings out. It's not surprising that it's the loudest ovation that anyone has gotten all night, especially with Ford and Blair standing up and cheering extra loud.

"That's my girl!" Blair yells, pointing a finger at her best friend as Ronnie blows her a kiss in return.

I try not to let myself get jealous over the gesture. As much as I'd love to have all her attention focused solely on me, I know it's for the best that she isn't blowing kisses my way with so many watchful and judgmental eyes. The wink she gave was more than enough—or at least, it should be. However, when it comes to Veronica, I'm not sure anything will ever feel like quite enough. I'm always going to selfishly want more.

Veronica takes in the applause till the last possible second. Giving one final bow, she grabs the end of her dress and offers a small curtsy before handing off the microphone to the emcee for the evening as he announces Blair's name next.

"Looks like I'm up," Blair declares with an excited smile, pushing up from her spot before Ford sends her off with a kiss. I feel like I'm intruding on something private as they let the moment linger a little too long.

Not wanting to feel like some creep, I let my eyes sweep the room in search of Veronica. Finally, I see her standing just to the side of the small stage where someone seems to have stopped her.

I try not to overthink it, though it's hard when that familiar sting of jealousy creeps in, burning just a little hotter this time. She's easily the most gorgeous woman in this bar. Of course, other men would want her attention, but just because they want it doesn't mean I'm okay with them having it. Over my dead body—or theirs. Either works.

My shoulders stiffen as I tilt my neck from side to side, trying to loosen the building tension. I should give her privacy, but my eyes have other plans as they roam back toward where the man still has her cornered. My eyes narrow as I finally realize what's happening, unsure how I completely misread the situation. That isn't just some random nobody talking to her—it's her ex.

"No fucking way," I growl, alerting Blair and Ford that something is amiss, and they steer their attention toward Ronnie and Pete.

"Oh, *hell* no!" Blair says as the three of us push our way through the crowd.

"What do you think you're doing?" I say, shoving Pete to the side, paying little attention to how roughly I do it. This man deserves none of my care or respect.

"I should be asking you the same question," Pete spits back as I move to stand between the exes.

"I'm only going to ask this one more time: What the *hell* do you think you are doing?" I ask more sternly, making sure to enunciate my words.

"I'm talking to my fiancée. I'm pretty sure that's allowed," Pete calmly answers as he stands taller, folding his arms across his pathetically scrawny chest.

"Ex-fiancée," Blair cuts in as she moves to stand next to Veronica, who, unsurprisingly, has shrunk behind me, making herself as small as possible.

"Whatever. I still think I'm allowed to get some answers, especially after seeing her prance around the stage like the little slut I always knew she was," Pete snarls, attempting to look around me so he can meet Veronica's eyes as he says it.

With no hesitation, I ram my forearm into his neck and pin him against the wall.

"That's my *wife* you're talking about," I snap, the words leaving my mouth before I even fully register what I'm confessing. But it doesn't matter. No one disrespects the people I care about—especially not her. She is my wife after all, and I'll always have her back, no matter what.

"Your what?" Pete chokes out, seeming more worried about my word choice than the fact that I'm only seconds away from pummeling that pathetic rat-like face of his.

"You heard me, and nobody disrespects my wife like that, so you better think long and hard about what you intend to say next," I warn, my eyes boring into his horrified face as I keep him pinned, only loosening the tension a tiny bit.

"So, what? You're not only a whore, but a cheating whore?" Pete asks, clearly disregarding my threat.

Fire and rage roar within me, every muscle coiled with the intent of making him pay. But as I raise my fist, Blair and Veronica reach for me, pulling me back. Their touch is the only thing that pierces through the haze of anger—the only thing keeping him safe from the pain I'm ready to unleash.

"He's not worth it, Miles," Veronica says, her voice pleading.

"No, he's not, but he shouldn't get to go around spewing hateful shit from that disgusting mouth of his," I say, my grip tightening on the neck of his shirt. "He doesn't deserve to be in your presence, let alone to ever be able to say your name aloud."

"This is just priceless," Pete laughs, though there's no shred of humor in his voice. It's laced with something unhinged, almost manic, as he swats at my hand. Only for Veronica's sake, I let go. He straightens, brushing himself off with exaggerated disdain. "Honestly, I think I dodged a bullet. I already felt like I was settling when I proposed, but if her idea of moving on is hooking up with the town reject, well... I guess I wasn't wrong. Go ahead, Veronica," he says, his voice dripping with venom as his eyes dart toward her. "If trash is what you're into, don't let me stop you."

His words mean nothing to me. I've heard that same thing, as well as all the other variations of it, since I was a kid. But clearly, Veronica has taken it to heart as her eyes harden and she raises her hand into the air as if to smack him.

Luckily, there seems to be just enough time to step in as I wrap my arms around her middle and pull her back into me. "He's not worth it, remember? Who cares what this fucker thinks?" I whisper into her ear, doing my best to remind her of what she just told me. Yes, I get it. I hadn't liked what he said about *her* either, but I certainly don't need her fighting my battles or having any regrets on my account.

"I'll be with whomever the hell I want, Pete," Veronica finally fires back, her voice sharp as her eyes burn with anger. Despite my earlier suggestion to let it slide, I can't help the surge of pride at the fiery determination pouring out of her. "And let me tell you something—anyone, and I mean anyone, would be a step up from you, you miserable excuse for a human. Oh, and for the record, Miles is more of a man than you could ever dream of being. So why don't you save us all the misery, take the real trash out of here, and walk your sorry ass out of this bar."

A few claps ring out, starting with Blair and Ford, but in this nosy town, it's no surprise that everyone else in this room has stopped to watch the inevitable train wreck. It isn't long before the entire bar joins in.

Pete's eyes narrow, and as he opens his mouth to say more, I release my grip on Veronica's waist and take a step toward him. "I *highly* suggest you do what the lady says."

"Whatever," he grumbles, running a hand through his hair, trying to hold on to the incredibly small scrap of dignity he has left as he waves his hand dismissively and turns to leave, a few of his buddies following behind him.

"Good luck with that political career of yours," Blair calls after him, a smug grin on her face. I'm pretty sure he lost a lot of respect from the people of Evergreen tonight. Everyone knows that Veronica Prescott is the town's sweetheart, and if you mess with her, you're messing with everyone else.

My eyes follow Pete, making sure he actually leaves the building before turning back toward the woman of the hour. "You okay?" I ask, my eyes searching her face. While there seems to be a smile there, it looks forced, and her body trembles in response.

"Yeah, I think so." She nods before letting out a breath as her eyes sink toward the floor, the weight of what just happened fully consuming her.

"Should we get some air?" I ask, reaching for her hand, not caring who watches. We're already going to be a huge topic of conversation, so why not give them something real to talk about?

"Yeah, I think I could use some," she agrees, lifting her gaze to mine.

"You guys keep having fun. We're going to go out back for a few minutes," I tell Blair and Ford, and my sister raises an eyebrow. I'm sure it's normal for her to be the one comforting her best friend in times like these, but there's no way I'm leaving her side tonight, especially not after everything that just happened.

"Alright, well, just let me know if you guys need anything," Blair says, her eyes moving between the two of us as we uniformly nod. The crowd parts for us as we make our way down the hallway, past the restrooms, and out the back door leading to the empty alley.

She has every right to feel hurt and overwhelmed by what just happened and what I revealed in front of everyone, but I can only hope that none of the pain she's feeling is because of something I did or said. Either way, I have every intention of making it up to her. Whatever it takes to see a smile on that perfect face of hers, I'll do it—no questions asked.

37

VERONICA

WALKING INTO THE CRISP spring air, I take a minute to fill my lungs and take in a much-needed breath to steady my racing heart.

"You sure you're okay?" Miles asks as the large metal door slams behind us, giving us the privacy I crave. Normally, I'm all for the extra attention my usual antics bring on, but right now, I need to be away from prying eyes as I pull myself together.

"I think so. Who knows, maybe this was all for the best. Running into Pete was going to happen at some point, so why not have it happen in front of the entire town?" I cringe, pushing my bottom lip out into a pout.

"I know the timing wasn't ideal, but at least now everyone has seen past the act he's been putting on. The mask finally slipped, and the truth came out for everyone to see."

"I hope you're right." I sigh, letting my back fall against the red-brick wall. "He was pretty good at hiding his true colors, though, wasn't he?" I muse, mostly to myself. Not only had I fallen for all of it, but I also let our relationship get way more serious than it ever should've. The fact that I let us even reach the point of a wedding day is beyond embarrassing. How could I have been so naive?

"Normally, I'd take the time to brag and say that I always knew that guy was a piece of shit, even all the way back in high school, but I'm sure that's the last thing we need to talk about," he says, sliding in next to me and leaning one foot against the wall as he crosses his arms.

"No, not exactly," I agree, my head tilting to rest on his shoulder.

"You aren't mad at me, are you?" he asks as I glance up at him.

"Why would I be mad at you? You had my back in there. That was huge and meant everything to me."

He shrugs his opposite shoulder as he looks down at the ground. "Well, I did just out our marriage to the entire town. Pretty sure that within the next hour, everyone in Evergreen is going to know about us."

I let out a soft, breathy chuckle. "Honestly, that's the least of my worries right now. Plus, maybe it should be out there. I'm horrible at keeping secrets, and it's not like this is something that will probably shock a lot of people. I'm kind of known for my crazy antics."

"That may be true, but the fact that you ended up with me, of all people, is likely pretty shocking. Even I don't fully understand it."

"That makes two of us, but I have no regrets. There are worse people I could be married to," I casually add, tilting my chin on his shoulder to gaze up at him, knowing this little fact all too well.

"Yeah?" he asks, a pleased grin slowly finding its way onto his face.

"Yeah," I whisper, turning my body so I can stand directly in front of him. Not wanting to waste any more time, I lean up and press my grateful lips to his.

His hands snake around my middle as he kisses me back. "Well, that makes two of us," he whispers against my lips before spreading them open with his tongue.

I let myself go completely and melt into him and our kiss as my hands, which had landed on his chest, move upward. One hand cups his cheek, and the other slides up the back of his neck and into his hair.

Instead of deepening the kiss, his lips leave mine and make an exploratory trail down my collarbone until he's kissing my shoulder. "You are so damn sexy, Veronica Prescott," he mumbles into my skin as I tilt my body towards his lips, craving more.

"The feeling is mutual, Bennett," I assure him, letting my head dip backward to give him better access as his lips continue exploring. Maybe being in the back of some alley where anyone could walk out for a smoke break isn't the ideal place to be having this sort of moment, but that doesn't stop us, especially as his lips sink lower, until his mouth reaches the swell of my breasts.

He seems to be feeling the same way I do, nowhere near ready to stop as one of his hands slides down under my dress until he's caressing the back of my thigh until he lifts my leg up, as I hook it around his body. He pulls me in tighter, his hardness pressing into me as I let out a soft, contented moan.

"You are a god damn fucking queen, and that man never deserved you," he mumbles against my flesh, leaving a trail of nips and kisses in his wake as his lips once again travel upward. "In fact, I don't think I've ever been more turned on than when you put him in his place."

I let out a soft hum as his lips return to my neck.

"However," he starts again, his grip loosening as he lets me fall softly to the ground, my feet gently hitting the pavement. "I don't want to talk about him anymore. I'm going to make you forget all about that pathetic asshole. And then," he continues as he lowers his body toward the ground, his hands leaving a trail down my ribs, stomach, and thighs before he ends up on one knee. "When I'm finished with you, I can promise you, I'll be the only man you think about ever again."

"I don't know, that sounds like a pretty high bar to set," I tease, looking down at him as I place a hand on his shoulder, the other swiping at one of the stray strands of hair that's fallen in front of his gorgeous baby blues.

"I'm not worried about it." He confidently reaches for my leg and sets it on his thigh, his hand slowly trailing up the bare skin as it slides up the back of my thigh.

Neither am I, but I don't plan on telling him that. I'm already addicted, and I'm sure anything he does to me tonight will only add to that addiction. While I should be worried, it's the opposite. I want to experience this with him. Hell, I'll take anything he's willing to offer.

His hands don't stop as they move up the skirt of my dress, circling around to the front. Unlike my ex, it's clear this man has worked hard, as I feel the roughness of his calloused hands moving across the skin of my stomach before going higher, until he takes my bra-covered breast in his hand.

A soft sigh leaves my lips as I let my head fall back against the wall once more, closing my eyes.

"Eyes on me," Miles demands, and while I'd love to tease him, I instead give him my full attention as I glance down. "I want you to see how a real man takes care of his wife."

My body shivers at the use of the word '*wife*.' It no longer matters that I know our marriage is temporary. In so many ways it's not even the use of the word 'wife' that does it for me. It's the use of the words 'his' and 'my.' I love knowing that I'm his, and most importantly, that for now, he's mine, too.

Following directions, I watch as his hands reach for my panties and pull them down my legs, lifting each one to make it easier for him. Instead of tossing them aside, he tucks them into his pocket with a playful wink.

I would laugh, but I'm too caught up in everything else as his hands start at my ankles and trail back up my legs at a tantalizingly slow pace. He takes his sweet time as his rough palms and fingers move across my skin, leaving a trail of goosebumps in their wake sending a delicious tingle throughout my entire body.

His hands don't stop at my thighs; instead, they continue their slow and seductive ascent as his hands slide up my now bare ass, lifting the skirt of my dress. He looks up, our eyes meeting briefly, but he soon averts his gaze as he leans forward, kissing the smooth skin of my left thigh before giving the same attention to the other.

Needing to hold on to something, my hand finds support as my fingers tangle in his hair. This only seems to fuel his hunger as his mouth finally goes to where I need it, his tongue sliding along my slit. "Fuck, Vee. Your tight little cunt is dripping wet." He sighs against my warm center, his hot breath against my aching core only intensifying my need.

"Please, Miles," I beg, pleading for him to continue, as my fingers tighten around his hair.

"Only because you asked so nicely," he replies before wrapping his lips around my throbbing clit, a loud gasp escaping me in response.

Thankfully, he does exactly what I need him to do as he sucks, licks, and nips all the right places, and I buck myself toward his ready mouth.

"So needy," he chuckles, but it in no way dissuades him as his mouth moves lower. He once again runs his tongue along my slit, gathering as much of me as he can before he starts to fuck me with his tongue, while one of his hands slides up and around to squeeze my breast.

I'm a mess for him, and the sounds coming out of me are completely indecent. My panting and moans grow louder as I try to hush them, biting down hard on my bottom lip.

"Don't you dare. I want to hear you," he tells me as he pulls his lips away, but thankfully only enough to place a soft kiss on my thigh before he latches back onto my clit, working the magic that I've only ever been able to experience with him.

"But..." I pant, trying to share my thoughts but struggle, as another loud moan leaves my lips as I buck my hips into his talented mouth. "What if..." I trail off once more.

"Fuck everyone else. The only ones that matter here are me and you," he tells me as he drops the hand that had been palming my breast, bringing it down and immediately inserting a finger inside of me.

"Miles," I cry, feeling myself getting so close to reaching that pinnacle high. "I'm almost there."

"Just let go, baby. Be a good wife and come for me, Mrs. Bennett," he commands before inserting another finger inside of me, curving it just right toward my belly as his teeth lightly latch down onto my sensitive, throbbing nub.

I cry out as my body experiences the most intense orgasm I've ever had, my head falling back against the wall. He doesn't stop, though, as he continues to coax out every last drop of passion, fucking me both with his fingers and tongue.

I come down from my high as he continues to lick, taking in everything I've just given.

Once finished, he carefully removes my foot from his leg, smoothing down my skirt in the process and even taking a moment to fix my top before wrapping his arms around my middle.

I should be more than satisfied, and I am, but I still can't help myself as I hungrily claim his lips once more, another new sound leaving my lips, especially as his teeth latch onto my bottom lip.

"You taste how fucking sweet you are?" he asks, my gaze meeting his as he finally pulls away enough for me to look at him.

"I did, but it's you I want to taste now," I proudly admit, a dangerous smirk pulling at his features.

"And you will, but first I'm taking you back home. As much as I want everyone to know that you're mine, it's probably best nobody sees the indecent things I have planned for you, because I'm not looking to get interrupted."

"Oh, yeah?" I ask, intrigued, rubbing my thighs together as I can already feel a new ache burning for him.

"Yep, now let's get out of here," he tells me, pressing his lips to mine once more as his hand falls into mine.

The polite thing to do would be to go back inside and tell Ford and Blair that we're leaving, but I imagine they'd understand. Then again, they'd probably assume I needed to leave because of my run-in with Pete, though they couldn't be more wrong.

In fact, Pete is the past and already forgotten. The only man on my mind right now is Miles. While that should worry me, as long as I get to keep experiencing this with him, that's all that matters.

38

MILES

I'M NOT THE TYPE of guy who completely loses himself because of a woman, but Veronica Prescott has completely flipped my entire world upside down in only two months. Strangely, I don't hate it. My life seems to be a hell of a lot brighter and more colorful, and only half of that is because my home has slowly been taken over by Veronica and her things.

It's not a surprise to anyone to learn that my favorite color is black. Just open my closet, and you'll see that seventy-five percent of it is dark, along with my decor. Slowly, though, more and more of Veronica's things have appeared around the apartment. If this had been anyone else's shit, I'd say something and put a stop to it—but with her, I can't—or really, I won't. What she wants, she gets. Hell, I'd give her the entire fucking world if that were an option.

The truth of the matter is, I'd do just about anything to see her smile, even if it means letting her bright and colorful clothes, blankets, plants, and decor take over the living room. Hell, even the outfits that I once rolled my eyes at for being absolutely ridiculous are now something I love seeing, especially when they're randomly tossed or scattered across my bedroom floor.

Even coming home is something I look forward to more each and every day. Bubba had always seemed to be all I needed, but there's something different about walking through the front door only to find Veronica sitting on the couch, her face lighting up just as much at the sight of me.

Plus, my dog is equally smitten. I can see it even now as I stand in the kitchen, finishing up the last of the dinner dishes, while the two of them snuggle on the couch and some ridiculous crime documentary plays in the background.

I glance at the sink, knowing I should tidy up a bit more, but the selfish pull to be near her is impossible to ignore. Shutting off the water, I dry my hands, my heart picking up the pace as I stride toward the couch.

Between Veronica, with her legs draped across the entire thing, and Bubba, with his head in her lap as she writes in some large notepad, there isn't much room, but I make do as I lift her feet, with her pink and yellow painted toes, and take a seat, letting them fall into my lap.

"You want me to move?" she asks, looking up from whatever she's been working on.

"Nope. I'm fine just like this," I assure her as I take one of her feet in my hands and begin a light massage.

She raises an eyebrow, not fully convinced, but she doesn't press it, lifting one shoulder instead. "If you say so," she says, seemingly distracted.

Her eyes move back down toward her pad, which I soon realize is a sketchpad. Normally, after dinner, she works on grading art projects and doing schoolwork while I clean up, but that pad clearly means something else. I tilt my head to the side as I watch her sketch, and my mouth tilts into a smile as her tongue lightly darts out to the side in concentration, before her eyes lift and they meet mine.

Her cheeks turn a light shade of pink, almost as if I've somehow caught her doing something *she* considers suspicious.

My brows knit together. "What?" I ask, a soft chuckle leaving my lips as my hands switch to working on her other foot.

"Nothing," she says, closing the pad and tucking it aside.

"This doesn't feel like nothing. What are you drawing over there?" I ask, assuming that's what she must have been up to. Plus, it's not like I hadn't seen her sketching and drawing like that plenty of times during our road trip.

"Who says I'm drawing something?" she asks, innocently fluttering her lashes.

I tilt my head to the side. "What else would you be doing with a pencil and a sketchpad? Now, come on," I say with a suggestive nod. "Spill it, so I'm not forced to drag it out of you."

She lets out a scoff. "And how exactly would you do that?"

"I have my ways," I say, a boyish grin tugging at my lips, a look that seemingly only she has the power to bring out of me.

"Prove it," she challenges, and with that, I tug on her foot, pulling her body toward me as I reach out to tickle her side. The gamble pays off as girlish laughter erupts, uncontrollable and infectious, filling the room with a melody of gorgeous giggles that makes my chest swell.

"Miles, no, stop," she begs through her laughter.

"Only if you show me what you were doing over there," I demand, my hands continuing their movements as my fingers get dangerously close to her armpits, which I'm assuming, like most people, is her most ticklish spot.

"Okay, fine, stop. Stop. I'll show you." She gives in, letting out a small chorus of giggles as I remove my hands, holding them in the air to surrender.

"Good to know I've cracked the code on exactly how to get what I want," I smirk.

"You know, there are *other*, much funner ways you could have gotten it out of me," she challenges as she reaches for the sketchpad, still holding it tightly against her chest.

"I don't know, that was pretty fun," I admit with an arrogant grin, draping my arm across the back of the couch.

"I was thinking more along the lines of sexual favors, but if that's your thing..." She casually shrugs as my eyes go wide.

"Damn," I curse, "you're right. That is much more fun. I'm going to have to keep that in mind for next time," I muse, already mentally preparing for the future.

"Well, then again, how many more next times do you think we have left?" she asks, the smile on her face slowly disappearing as my mind unfortunately follows her train of thought.

"I don't know, but is that really something we want to think about right now?" I ask. It may be selfish, but the idea of us ending and her moving out is something I've purposely avoided thinking about.

"No, but as fun as it is to play house, this can only go on for so long. We both know that. Eventually, I'm going to need to move on, and in just over a month, the annulment is going to go through. Us getting married will be nothing more than a silly memory that we can hopefully laugh about later."

I know she's right. I should be thinking about this, and normally I would make myself be the one to constantly remind both of us of the reality of things, but for once, it's been nice to follow in her footsteps and get swept up in the moment.

Instead of worrying about what comes next, I've allowed myself to focus on the here and now, letting go of the constant pressure to plan for the future—especially one that doesn't include her in it—at least not like this. Not in the way I want her to be.

"Well, it's not like we didn't know this was coming," I say, tilting my head to the other side. "Plus, aren't you usually the one to preach about letting go and not stressing over the stupid shit? What happened to living in the moment and saying 'fuck the consequences?'" I challenge.

She looks down at the still-closed notebook as she lets it fall into her lap. "I mean, sure, but I'm also not looking to leave here in a place where I'm worse off than when I showed up."

My brows crease. "And you feel like that's how this is going to end?"

She lifts a shoulder. "I don't know, maybe. I mean, right now everything is good," she says, casting her gaze upward as she meets my eyes. "But I'm scared too. You've somehow turned into my safety blanket, and I'm not sure what I'll do when things go back to how they were before, especially if you go back to hating me."

A frown tugs at my lips as I stare at her in disbelief. "I never hated you," I admit first and foremost. "And I never could.

Honestly, you've become one of my favorite people. From here on out, you're always going to have a place in my life, you have to know that. Sure, you might not always be my wife, but you'll always be my friend," I promise, even though every word I say somehow hits a little too hard, my heart breaking with each and every one.

I like having her as my wife, and while I understand there's a timeline for all of this, and everything I've told her is true, it doesn't mean I'm suddenly ready to let go.

The corner of her mouth lifts into a smile, even if it doesn't quite reach her eyes. "Well, maybe that means we should start being more strategic and smart about things and go back to acting like friends, if that's what we plan on being for one another."

I know she's right. I need to stop letting myself get lost in this, but even the suggestion makes my heart ache. I'm not ready to stop pretending, even if deep down I already know that what's been happening here has never been pretend—at least not for me.

"Well, does that mean we have to start that today?" I finally ask, the hollowness already filling my chest as I regret not only letting her move out of my grasp, but also letting it get to a place where this sort of conversation could happen. I'm not ready for this.

"Maybe we should," she admits, as I try to take solace in the fact that she looks just as depressed as I do right now over the mere idea of this.

"Or maybe—" I start, but she stands up and interrupts.

"Or maybe we protect what we have and stop. Stop all the pretending and just go back to being roommates. Isn't that what you wanted all along?" she asks, awkwardly folding her arms, sketchpad and all.

"Well, maybe it was at first, but things have changed since then," I argue, sitting up straight.

"Exactly. Things have changed, and I know that's because I pushed for this, but I really think we need to be smart here and start thinking about protecting ourselves."

"You don't need protection from me," I assure her, scooting to the edge of my seat, especially since I have no intention of being someone who could hurt her, not after witnessing all the pain she experienced from that douchebag Pete.

"I know I don't." She laughs with absolutely no hint of amusement. Opening the book in her hands, she turns to the page where she'd left off and tears it out. "It's myself I need protection from. We both know I've never been known for my smart decision-making, and I think it's time I finally start doing what I should, instead of what I want."

"What makes you so sure this is a smart decision?" I ask, the desperation seeping through, but I can't help it. If I had known those last few minutes would be the last time we got to act normal and be ourselves, I definitely would've gone about things differently.

"Believe me, when you've spent your entire life acting on impulse and ignoring the consequences until it's too late, you start to get a sense of when things are going to work out and when they won't. And with this being something I really don't want to do, that's exactly why I know I need to."

"Look, Vee, I'm not going to force you into something you don't want to do, but I'm not ready to call it quits. I want to keep exploring this. I want to see what can happen here."

"Until when? You get bored of me, or go back to finding me annoying?"

"I wouldn't—" I argue, but she holds up a hand to silence me.

"You don't know that, nor can I let it happen. I promised Blair I wouldn't let any of this affect our friendship, and if I let myself get hurt in all of this, that could change things, and not for the better."

"Why do you keep saying that you'd get hurt? I have no plans to hurt you or let you hurt yourself. I'm just not ready to let this end," I say as I stand up and take a step toward her. She once again holds out her hand and takes a step back.

"Believe me, Miles. This is for the best," she tries to assure me before finally holding out the paper she ripped from the sketchbook.

My eyes flick between the paper and her, but my curiosity wins out as I reach out and take it. As I hold it up, I'm stunned to see a perfectly rendered portrait of myself. Every detail is spot-on. It's so lifelike that, if I didn't know it was a sketch, I'd swear it was a photo someone had snapped with their phone.

"This is amazing," I tell her, truly meaning it.

"These days, you're all I think about. Hell, all day, every day, all I can think about is that stupidly handsome face of yours," she says, pointing toward me. "So, between classes, I started this sketch and finally took the time to finish it just now. But I'm starting to think I need something else to focus my time and energy on. I already left one unhealthy situation. I can't let myself jump right back into another."

My heart sinks. Is that really what this feels like to her? The last thing I ever want to be to anyone—especially her—is a source of pain. So, instead of voicing what I really feel and what I truly want, I swallow it down and nod. Maybe it is easier this way, even if every part of me is screaming to be honest with her.

"If this is really what you want and need, then that's what we'll do," I give in, despite the fact that my brain is yelling at me to put a stop to this. Then again, maybe that's my heart speaking, since usually my brain is a lot smarter than this.

"It is." She sighs, her shoulders falling in the process.

With one final dejected breath, I hold the drawing back toward her.

"Keep it," she directs, taking a step back as she taps the side of her forehead. "I already have the image seared right here," she softly offers with a weak smile before walking out of the room.

I run a hand over my face, trying to process what just happened. Did I really let her walk away? Did I just let the one woman who's truly made me feel something real and raw slip through my fingers? Then again, as much as I hate to admit it, maybe she's right. Not only is she at risk of getting hurt by all of this, but so am I. That aching pain in my chest? It's unmistakable, and for the first time, I think I'm fully experiencing what true heartbreak feels like.

39

VERONICA

"HEY YOU," I CALL out to Ford, beckoning him over as I wiggle my finger toward me. "It's hammer time," I joke, doing the famous dance. Thankfully he laughs at my lame attempt at a joke, even if he is shaking his head.

"So, where do you need me?" he asks.

"Right here. It's the perfect spot," I indicate, nodding toward one of Blair's amazing photo masterpieces before pointing to the wall and the spot I've picked for it. It's without a doubt, the best place for it to stand out and showcase just how bad ass of a photographer she is.

The three of us, well, four if you count Miles, have been working our asses off to get this place set up and running for Blair to have her grand opening tomorrow. However, I've done my best to avoid being around him, as we've both been working opposite shifts.

Not that he seems to mind, since it feels like we've both had the same goal—avoiding the apartment when the other is there. And if, for some reason we do both have to be there, we hide in our rooms, or at least that's what I've been doing

Maybe we could have kept this charade going. We still have a few weeks left before our annulment is granted, but I just can't do it. Letting myself fall for the wrong guy once was way too painful, and given how different things feel with Miles, and how much deeper the feelings go, it would truly devastate me. Hell, I'm already devastated, even if I'm doing a pretty good job of pretending like everything is fine.

"Okay, so how does this look?" Ford asks, stepping back from his work and tilting his head to the side.

"It's perfect." I nod, before scanning the rest of the building which has been sectioned off with unique sets and backgrounds. It really is coming together, and I couldn't be happier. Blair deserves to have the studio of her dreams. I may not be getting my happily ever after just yet, but at least I can find some comfort in the fact that I know she's getting hers.

"I think I'm in need of some coffee," Blair says, interrupting our admiration of her work.

"Well, I've never been one to turn down a coffee run, so I'm all for a small break," I agree, heading over to grab my bag from where I left it behind the front desk.

"What about you, babe?" Blair asks, wrapping her arms around Ford's middle as he does the same, dropping his forehead to meet hers.

"I think I'm good. I'll stay here and keep working, but if you want to grab me a muffin or something, I wouldn't say no to that," he tells her, before placing a kiss on the top of her head.

"Blegh," I tease, sticking out my tongue and wrinkling my nose.

Blair glances over, biting her lip. "Sorry," she apologizes, loosening her grip on Ford as he does the same.

I wave her off dismissively. Just because my love life sucks doesn't mean I need to go and ruin their fun. "I'm only kidding," I offer. "You two are adorable. You're couple goals, and I'm just salty that my love life sucks balls right about now."

"Couple goals, huh?" Ford asks, a boyish grin spreading across his face.

"Don't let it get to your head, Fordy boy. I'm still a bitter betty, and if you're not careful, I might just take it back."

"Aw, leave my man alone. Just let him have this one." Blair chuckles, standing on her tiptoes to give him one final peck before turning to grab her bag.

"Fine," I say, letting out an exaggerated breath. "You guys are the cutest, and honestly, I do actually mean it," I promise Blair, as I hold the door open for us to leave so we can make the short walk to The Steamy Bean.

"We are pretty cute, huh?" Blair asks, a dreamy tone to her voice.

"Yeah, yeah, quit rubbing it in," I tease, giving her arm a light shove.

Blair laughs as she loses her balance but recovers quickly. "Sorry," she apologizes before continuing. "I mean it does kind of suck," she muses as I glance over with a raised brow. "For a while there, I really thought things were going to work out with you and Miles, and we'd both have our dream men."

I let out a scoff. "Well, I'm pretty sure that ship has long since sailed."

"What really happened with that, anyway? I don't need to kick his ass, right?" she asks, and given the look on her face, I know she's serious.

I shake my head and cross my arms. "No, it's nothing like that. I was actually the one who put an end to things."

"Oh," she says, clearly taken aback. "I figured it was the opposite."

"Why?" I ask, my head rearing back, not sure if I should be offended or not.

She shrugs. "I don't know, but I suppose Miles has always been the type to self-sabotage and not let himself be happy. Given the way the two of you acted before everything got weird and awkward, it was as if the two of you couldn't stop touching or looking at each other. I guess I just thought you were feeling the same way about him, too."

"I was," I reply, a little too quickly and defensively, as we we reach the front of The Steamy Bean, which, thankfully for her, is only a few buildings away from hers. "And if I'm being honest, maybe I still am, but that's precisely why I couldn't keep doing it any longer."

Her mouth tips open, her brows crinkling together. "I don't get it," she says, looking and sounding a lot like her brother the night I chose to end things. "If you still care about him, then why end it?"

"I can't keep putting myself through this. I can't keep falling for someone who doesn't feel the same. A person can only endure so much heartbreak before they have to put themselves first," I say, my voice trembling as I reach for the handle to let us in.

Blair reaches out and stops me. "Wait, hold up. You don't think Miles feels the same way about you as you do about him?"

"No. He doesn't. There's no way in any world that Miles Bennett could ever feel for me the way I feel about him."

Blair's mouth drops open, closing her eyes as if composing herself as she shakes her head. "Come on, Ronnie. You're not stupid. There's no way you can't see the way my brother feels about you. Hell, I've never seen him look at anyone the way he looks at you. He's a love-smitten mess, and given the way he's been moping around ever since you pulled away, it only goes to show how hurt he is. He loves you, Ronnie. I know it."

I roll my eyes and fold my arms once more. "He doesn't *love* me."

"Okay fine," she concedes, tilting her head to the side. "Maybe love is a bit of a stretch, but I also wouldn't completely blow off the idea of it either. I've never seen him act like he does around you with anyone else. Hell, the guy hardly ever brings anyone home for me to meet, yet in front of our entire town, or at least the entire bar that night at Timberline, he called you his wife. That's not typical Miles behavior. Come on, you have to know that."

"Maybe so, but it's not like he wants me to stay his wife. It was just a mistake, and we've always known there was an expiration date on things, so why prolong it? Eventually, Miles would grow tired of me. We're two incredibly different people."

She doesn't look impressed as she reaches out and places her hands on my shoulders, giving me a light shake. "Are you even listening to yourself right now? Where is the Ronnie who follows her heart no matter what? The Ronnie who says, 'fuck the consequences'?" she asks.

"You mean the Ronnie who has an ex-fiancé and now a soon-to-be ex-husband? That Ronnie? Because that woman is tired of making mistakes and is finally growing up and looking to avoid all possible heartbreak. She can't take it anymore. *I* can't take it anymore. It's just too much."

She frowns. "I get that, but can I be honest with you? From experience, I can proudly attest that running away isn't the answer."

I turn to look away from her. "Just because it wasn't the answer for you doesn't mean it isn't the answer for me."

"And you really think that's true?" she asks, clearly unconvinced.

"Yes, I do. Just because things suddenly worked out for you doesn't mean it's all magically going to work out for me, too." Her frown deepens, guilt written across her features, but I can't worry about that. Right now, it's my heart I need to be looking out for. It's my heart that's on the line, and my heart that already feels broken beyond repair. "And that's fine. I'm not giving up on love entirely. So don't worry about that," I assure her, placing a hand on her arm. "I think my heart just needs a teeny tiny break, okay?"

She nods, her frown not relenting, but at least she no longer has that sad, pathetic puppy-dog look going on.

"Can we please get our coffee now?" I ask, forcing a smile.

"Yeah, we can," she agrees with a nod, linking her arm through mine before opening the door and leading us inside.

While I'm relieved to put the conversation behind us, her words linger, looping through my brain as the knot in my chest continues to tighten. Could his feelings be real? Maybe. I'm just not sure my heart is capable of giving it another chance. It's way too bruised and fragile and it feels like one wrong move could destroy it completely.

40

MILES

A RARE SMILE CROSSES my lips as I watch my sister give a speech before cutting the giant red ribbon with an equally amusing pair of oversized scissors. I clap my hands along with everyone else in the crowd.

I'll be the first to admit that the people of Evergreen Grove can be annoying as hell, especially when they insist on putting their noses where they don't belong, but one thing you can't deny is that they know how to rally around one of their own, especially since it looks like everyone from town—or at least most everyone—has made it a point to be here.

Local businesses have pitched in with goodies and drinks to celebrate, and Blair has set up a photo booth table, which, from the looks of it, is already a huge hit, with a giant line of people waiting for their turn

I know Blair has always felt like the odd one out and like she doesn't quite fit in, but given how the people have rallied around her, I can't help but hope this place now feels just as much like home for her as it does for me, especially since it's been such a relief to have her close by these past few months.

Making my way through the crowd, I head straight for the make shift bar, grab a drink and some popcorn, and set myself up as far away from the crowd as possible. While I'm here to show my support for my little sister, I plan on doing that from all the way over here. Plus, it isn't like I haven't spent the last eight weeks working my ass off to help make this dream come true for her.

Scanning the crowd, my eyes land on Veronica almost instinctively. Sure, it could be the striking pink floral dress, the matching heels, and white sweater that make her stand out, but deep down, I know it's more than that. She's magnetic. For the longest time, I thought we were mismatched magnets, constantly repelling each other, but now it all makes sense. It was always me resisting the pull that was always there—a pull I feel even now, despite how hard I'm trying to fight it.

I hate that I've had to keep my distance, especially when every moment apart feels like a battle to resist the feelings I so desperately want to surrender to. I know she wanted to end things before it got too deep, but I want nothing more than to keep diving in and exploring. Unfortunately, I can only go as far as she'll allow, even if everything inside me is screaming to do the opposite.

I suppose I can't fully blame her. I don't want to get hurt either. Hell, this distance is already killing me, and I can't even imagine how much worse it would be if we let this turn into a real relationship, only for it to come crashing down.

"Hey, man," Ford says, settling into the chair next to mine.

"Hey," I smile weakly, my attempt at being friendly as I tear my gaze away from the quirky brunette who has unsurprisingly taken over the photo booth. She poses in a princess crown and a giant pair of sunglasses as she poses next to what I assume is a group of her high school students.

"Taking a breather?" he asks, lifting his glass to his lips as he takes a sip.

"Something like that," I agree, not really in the mood for small talk. Then again, I've never been someone that can just open up and talk to anybody. Truth be told, the only person I've ever been able to do that with is Blair, and, well, Veronica, but I'm not so sure she counts anymore.

"I get that." He casually nods, his eyes scanning the crowd before he adjusts his glasses on his nose. "It can be a little over-whelming when the whole town shows up, but you have to admit, this is pretty damn cool, and Blair really deserves this and so much more."

"She does," I agree, doing my best to avoid looking back at the photo booth.

Ford clears his throat. "So..." he starts, and I glance his way. "Are you planning on talking to Ronnie tonight?"

"And what makes you think that's your business?"

I know I should cut Ford some slack—he's a good guy, and I'm grateful for the way he loves and treats Blair—but I'm just not in the mood to talk about this, especially not with my sister's nosy boyfriend. I get enough of that from her.

"Well." He fidgets, adjusting anxiously in his seat. "I guess it really isn't, but I know she misses you."

I raise an eyebrow. "How can she miss me? We live in the same apartment." Okay, I get it. I'm being a smart-ass, but he's being a nosy-ass, and to me, that's so much worse.

"You know what I mean. Plus, I'm serious. She's been miserable these past few weeks, and it's easy to pinpoint her shitty mood to the night she pulled away from things."

I set my drink next to the popcorn on the table and lift my palm to cover my face. "She told you guys?" I finally ask as I drop my hand into my lap.

"Well, she sort of tells Blair everything, and since I'm the obligatory third wheel, it just sort of happens that I get told too," he sheepishly admits, his eyes staring down at his glass.

"Figures," I say, shaking my head.

"Are you really going to let her get away that easy?" he presses on, and I shoot him a piercing glare.

"The only thing I'm letting her do is what she wants. I'm not going to force someone to be with me. That's not my style."

"But she does want to be with you. She's just scared she's going to end up hurt like every other time she's put her heart on the line. If you just told her how you felt, truly and honestly, I'm sure she'd change her mind. She wants this. I know she does."

My eyes scan the area once more, this time actively searching her out, and like usual, my eyes quickly find her, even though she's moved away from the photo booth.

I scoff. "If anyone is going to get hurt here, it's me. Hell, I'm pretty sure she already broke what was left of my heart, so maybe it's time everyone takes a step back and lets us figure our shit out on our own."

"Look, Miles," he continues, despite my protests, putting a hand on my shoulder. I glance down at his hand before looking back at him with a sharp stare. I'm not a touchy person, and I especially don't want to be touched by my little sister's goofy-ass boyfriend. He thankfully sees the error of his ways and removes his hand, but that doesn't stop him from continuing. "I'm not here to tell you what to do or how to live your life, but as someone who made a lot of bad choices in the love department, especially when I got a little too caught up in looking out for other people's feelings over my own, it left me with a lot of regrets, and I don't want that to happen to either of you. I really think you both need to stop acting like silly teenagers and talk this out like adults. I think you both owe it to yourselves."

I let out a small breath. The last person I want a stern speech from is Ford Hastings, but maybe he's right. I have regrets, and part of me knows that if I don't tell her how I feel and lay it on the line, I'll always wonder what if?

"We'll see," I say instead, not fully ready to admit that my sister's annoying little tag-along buddy turned boyfriend may have a good point.

He nods, a pleased smile appearing on his face. "Yeah, man. Just think about it," he agrees before standing up. "I'm, uh, going to find Blair, but I'll talk with you later." His usual awkward demeanor comes back with a vengeance, likely realizing that he just got a bit more stern with me, but if anything, it only makes me admire the guy a little more. It's about time he manned up and grew a pair.

I don't think I'll ever see myself becoming best friends with Ford, but I have to admit, he's a pretty good guy, and if my sister has to be with someone, I'm glad it's him.

My biggest issue now is that her "other person" is the very one I can't seem to get out of my head, and I'm not so sure that's a good thing. What if Ford has this all wrong? Veronica could have pushed me away for a reason, and as hard as I try to remind myself of that, my better judgment loses out. Taking a deep breath, I rise to my feet, deciding—for better or worse—to follow his advice.

My sister's grand opening may not be the best night for this sort of thing, but if I don't do it now, I'm not sure I ever will. Now more than ever, I know what needs to be done.

41

VERONICA

"THIS IS AMAZING. I can't believe you guys created all this in such a short amount of time," Gemma gushes as we walk through the various backgrounds.

"It was mostly all Blair and Ford, but yeah, it turned out pretty amazing, huh?" I ask, pride beaming on my face as I take in all the blood, sweat, and tears it took to get this place ready so quickly.

It's almost surreal to see this storefront now, transformed from the old model train shop into a professional photography studio, complete with its own darkroom. Just a few months ago, this place was nothing more than a rundown space with old shelves and cobwebs in every corner. But now, it's everything Blair dreamed of—and, most importantly, everything she deserves.

"It really did," Maeve agrees, her eyes also taking in all the decor. "I can't wait to bring my kids and get an updated family picture."

"Blair would absolutely love that," I say with a grin, as I beam with pride. It's incredible to see so many people eager to embrace her vision. Pouring all your money and life savings into a dream is one thing, but if nobody else sees it or wants it, what's the point? However, judging by the steady stream of familiar faces from around town showing up, it's clear Blair's dream isn't just going to work—it's going to flourish.

"Speaking of Blair, or rather, a Bennett, it looks like someone might be looking for you." Gemma smiles, her nose wrinkling in excitement.

I don't even have to turn around to know who she's talking about, but I also have to wonder if she's misinterpreting what's happening. These past few weeks he's been avoiding me, just as much as I've been avoiding him. I highly doubt he wants anything to do with me tonight—or ever, for that matter.

"God, he's fine. You lucky bitch," Gemma adds, her voice low enough before her face completely lights up. "Hi, Miles."

"Hey," his deep voice rings out, sending shivers down my spine. I hate that he still has this much of a hold on me, especially when I've been trying so hard to get over him.

Glancing over my shoulder, I force a smile in his direction, doing my best to play it cool.

"Hey," he repeats, this time speaking to me as his deep-blue eyes bore into mine.

"Hi," I reply, hating how quiet and breathy it sounds, but I can't help it. He still has me, even when I wish he didn't.

"Maybe we should give you a minute, yeah?" Maeve suggests, already reaching for Gemma's arm as she tugs her further into the studio.

"Have fun, you two," Gemma calls out in a sing-song voice, her and Maeve's soft giggles ringing out as they excuse themselves.

"Sorry about them," I apologize, turning to face him as I point over my shoulder with my thumb.

"No, it's fine. I *was* actually hoping we could have a moment to talk," he says.

My brows furrow. "Really?"

"Yeah, as long as that's okay. I know you've been wanting some distance..." he says, waiting for my answer.

"Oh, uh, yeah. That's fine," I hastily reply. Sure, I've been wanting, and even needing, the space, but now that I have his attention, I can't help but want to hold onto it for as long as I can.

"Maybe we could find somewhere a little more private?" he suggests, his gaze darting around the room. Though the space is reasonable for a photography studio, it's nowhere near large enough to comfortably accommodate the entire town. Thankfully, most guests are outside where the main festivities are happening, but the studio is still packed with curious onlookers, excited to see the new business.

"Yeah, sure. Everything okay?" I ask, still thrown off. He's had plenty of time to talk to me—we are roommates, after all—so what's so special about now?

"Oh, yeah. Everything's fine. I was just hoping we could talk about a few things."

The crease in my brow deepens, but I nod before spotting the door to the darkroom. "Maybe we could go in there?" I suggest, tilting my head toward the back of the studio.

While much of the place is open to the public, especially for the people to explore, that part has been marked as off-limits.

"Yeah, let's go," he agrees, his hand finding its place on the lower part of my back as he guides me through the small throng of people.

I open the door, step inside, and he follows, closing it behind us.

"So..." I begin, walking further into the small, darkened room before turning to face him. "What exactly did you want to talk about?"

"Us," he states, his eyes finding mine.

I fold my arms across my chest. "Us? What about us?" I ask, my voice shaky as I look down, no longer able to bear his piercing stare.

"I'm not ready for us to be over. I'm miserable without you," he bluntly confesses as I finally dare to glance in his direction.

"Miles—" I start, but he shakes his head and crosses the room, stopping in front of me.

"Vee," he says, his voice a raw and desperate plea. "I know you're scared. Hell, I'm scared too, but we can't let that fear hold us back. I don't just want to explore what we have; I need to. You've become more than a want, you're a necessity. Without you, everything feels shallow and pointless. I can't keep pretending I'm okay living without you, because I'm not. You've filled a void in me I didn't even know existed, and I refuse to go back to that kind of emptiness."

My mouth drops open as my eyes soften. "Miles—" I start again, but he takes another step forward and stops me from continuing.

"Let me just get this all out, okay?" he asks, and I nod in silent agreement. "I know that we've set ourselves up with a timeline and said that as soon as our elopement ends, so do we, but maybe we don't need to give ourselves a timeline, and maybe we don't even need to get an annulment."

"What?" I blurt, that being the last thing I expected to hear from him tonight.

"Well, I mean, we can if that's what you really want, but an annulment means that this," he says, pointing between the two of us, "never happened. And I don't like that, because what we have is real, and even if some day in the far and distant future we decide that we don't want to continue this, I don't want to pretend that we never happened, or that you weren't my wife. I love you, Veronica Prescott, and while maybe we don't need to act like some married couple, I'm not ready to throw everything away. I can't do that, and I hope you don't want to either."

I raise a hand to cover my mouth. I'm not a complete idiot. I knew he felt something for me, but I never could have imagined that he felt everything as strongly as I did. Hell, old Veronica probably would have guessed that the only ones he was truly ever capable of loving were Blair and Bubba.

"I love you too." I confess, my face splitting into a wide grin as I place my hands on his chest.

"Really?" he asks, carefully wrapping his arms around my middle as if I might suddenly break or disappear.

"Yes. Really," I promise, and before I can make the first move, he beats me to it, his lips hungrily pressing into mine. God, I've missed this.

It doesn't take long as he maneuvers us through the room until my back is pressed into the small countertop, and the two of us are nothing but a tangle of lips, tongues, and needy hands, clearly needing to make up for lost time.

"So you really love me?" he breathily asks, finally pulling his lips away from mine. He brushes some hair behind my ear before letting his hand rest on the side of my neck, his thumb brushing soft circles along my cheek.

"Yes. I really love you." I raise my hand to his cheek, making sure he's looking at me as I continue. "So, so much," I promise, needing him to truly hear it.

I know that he and Blair didn't have the easiest childhood, and I had to watch firsthand how his sister struggled with trust issues when it came to feeling loved or even lovable. However, the Bennetts are the most lovable people on this entire planet, and I feel so incredibly lucky to be the one who's gotten to experience something this real and intense with the both of them.

"So, what do you think about what I said about the whole annulment thing?" he asks, his still somewhat uncertain eyes searching mine.

"I think we should call our lawyers first thing Monday morning and put a stop to it." I smile, letting my hand slide back toward the nape of his neck as my fingertips curl into his hair.

"Are you sure? I don't want you to think—"

I speak before he can say more. "I'm sure. I'm beyond sure. In fact, I think it just came true."

His brows draw together in confusion. "What did?"

"My wish. Remember? At the wishing well in Disneyland. I told you I'd let you know when my wish came true, and it just did."

A smile tugs at the corner of his mouth. "You wished for me?"

"I mean, not *you* exactly, but in a roundabout way, I guess I sort of did." I casually shrug. "I wished for my real-life Prince Charming and my very own true happily ever after, and it looks like I've finally gotten everything I've ever wanted."

"Are you sure about that?" he asks, a deep chuckle accompanying his words. "I'm not so sure anyone has ever referred to me as a Prince Charming before. If anything, you're probably kissing yourself a frog."

"Maybe so, but if you remember, she turned that frog into a prince, so that's how I plan to look at it. Then again..." I trail off, my eyes scanning across his face, "I'd say you more closely resemble the Beast, which don't worry, that's a good thing. *Beauty and the Beast* has always been one of my favorites. Although, I think I prefer our story the best. Our love is one of a kind and way better than any silly fairytale. What we have is real. " I beam up at him.

"God, you're so adorable," he says, leaning down to kiss me once more.

"Right back at ya," I say once he's pulled back, even though he's still resting his forehead against mine.

"I still don't know if I'd go as far as calling myself a Prince Charming, but I will say I do like the person I become whenever you're around."

"That has nothing to do with me. That's who you've always been. I think I just make it easier for you to be your true self,"

I offer, since it's not like I'm forcing him to be someone else, or at least I certainly hope not.

"Well, either way, I'm just glad we're back on the same page. And I hope you know that I'm planning on doing everything in my power to make sure I never hurt you. My job from here on out is to protect you and your heart for the rest of my life," he promises,lifting his chin to kiss the top of my forehead.

"And I promise to protect yours as well," I assure him right back. "I know you like to pretend to be super tough, but deep down I know you're nothing but a big softy."

"Hey now," he says, an amused lilt to his tone. "Don't go around advertising that. I have a reputation to uphold."

"Don't worry, Broody Bennett. Your secret is safe with me," I promise. "Now, what do you say about us taking this whole thing public?"

Sure, the majority of the town knows, or at least thinks they do after the night at the Timberline, but now that things are officially official, I'm ready to truly announce, once and for all that we're together.

"Let's do it," he agrees, stepping back while also reaching for my hand. "I'm pretty sure they already do, but it's time to truly make sure everyone in this town knows that Veronica Prescott belongs to Miles Bennett, and if anyone messes with her, they're choosing to mess with me."

"Alright, whatever you say, Mr. Tough Guy," I tease, but honestly, I sort of love it. With Pete, it always felt like he wanted me because of who I was in the town or what my reputation could bring him, but with Miles, I finally feel like someone wants me for me, and that feels pretty damn special. "Lead the way," I say, pointing, as we walk out of the room, hand in hand—maybe not for the first time as Mr. and Mrs. Miles Bennett, but for the first time where it finally feels totally and completely real.

42

EPILOGUE

"I T'S SO CUTE!" VERONICA gushes from her seat next to me as we pull into the driveway of Blair and Ford's new place.

"I don't know," I muse, setting the car into park. "It was kind of nice having them live above Bob's Quick and Tasty Pizza. It was always so nice and convenient that whenever we left their last place we could stop in and grab a slice."

She rolls her eyes. "We're like, what, two blocks away? I'm pretty sure if we ever leave here hungry, we can still easily stop and grab something," she assures me as she opens her door and climbs out, fully taking in the details of their new place. "If anything, we should just be happy Blair is finally settling in and putting down some roots."

She's not wrong. My sister had talked about escaping Evergreen Grove since we were little kids, and the second she turned eighteen, she had made that a reality, but after returning for what should have been Veronica's wedding, and reuniting with Ford, all that changed.

As her big brother, it's always been my job to support her as long as she was happy. If leaving this place was what it took, then I had to be okay with it. But now, seeing her genuinely happy here for the first time, it's a relief.

Walking around the car, I reach for Veronica's hand and link my fingers through hers.

"It's kind of weird, though, right?" I ask. "I'm not sure I ever pictured Blair as the settling down and living in a cookie cutter house type."

While the place isn't huge, it matches many of the other houses here in Evergreen, with a nice white picket fence and flowers lining the small pathway toward the front door.

"Well, that's only because she had other priorities. But now our girl has gone and found herself the love and her life, and that tends to change things. I mean, look at you," she muses, waving toward me as we walk the cobblestone path toward the bright red front door.

"What about me?" I ask, straightening up, even though part of me already suspects I know the answer.

"You're whipped," she casually suggests, as if she didn't just drop a bomb, and raises her hand to knock.

"Excuse me?" I ask with a small scoff. "I am not whipped."

Before she can answer, the front door opens, and my younger sister beams at us, a giant smile plastered on her face. Not only did she and Ford just purchase their first home, but her business is thriving as well.

"Hey guys," she practically squeals, leaning in to give us both a hug.

"So, sis, what's new?" Blair asks, turning her attention toward Veronica as I try not to roll my eyes. They love that they get to call themselves sisters, especially since we've still done nothing to put an end to our marriage.

"Well, I was just telling your brother here that he is, in fact, pretty whipped," Veronica casually states as she lets herself inside.

I let out a small grunt. "I am not."

Blair looks toward me with knowing eyes. "I hate to say it, but my sister here has a point. You're pretty fucking whipped."

"Alright, whatever. You two keep living in this dreamworld of yours. I mean, what else is new?" I joke, taking a step forward to follow them, taking in the new digs. "This is nice," I quickly add, ready for a change of subject.

"You think so?" Blair asks, a nervous lilt in her tone. Even with the nerves, it's obvious she's fully ready to happily show off her new place.

"It's adorable," my wife gushes, wrapping an arm around Blair's waist and leaning in for another hug.

"It still needs some work, and we want to paint a few of the rooms. Obviously, I'm going to need your expertise on where to hang a few things, but we're pretty happy with it."

"And you should be. This is amazing," I add, moving to the other side of my sister, draping an arm around her shoulder. "We're so incredibly happy for you."

"Thanks, guys." Blair smiles, tilting to lean against both of us for a quick moment before finally pulling away. "So, Ford is out back grilling, and if I'm being honest, I'm a bit worried that he's going to burn everything. So maybe you could do us all a favor and head out back and join him. I'm pretty sure we'd all be forever grateful," she pleads, turning toward me, batting her signature puppy-dog eyes in my direction. "And while you do that, I can finish giving Ronnie the rest of the tour."

"Oh, so I don't get a tour?" I ask, crossing my arms.

She lets out a small huff. "You'll get one eventually, and you're always welcome to join, but that might also mean we end up with some extra well-done steaks." She casually shrugs.

"Well, we can't have that now, can we?" I deadpan, resisting the urge to roll my eyes once again.

"Thank you, babe," Veronica says, giving me an appeasing smile before leaning up to press a kiss to my lips. We both let it linger, likely for a bit too long as my hand snakes around her waist

Blair clears her throat. "Um, and you two thought Ford and I were bad?"

Veronica's cheeks blossom into a beautiful rosy pink color. "Sorry."

"I'm not," I simply state, leaning in to press my lips to hers one more time before finally forcing myself back.

"Well, I guess I'm even more grateful that I'm choosing to separate the two of you. Geez, you're like two dogs in heat," she jokes, motioning her head toward the back of the house. "Just head out back that way. You'll see the sliding glass door," she explains.

I'm incredibly tempted to lean in for another kiss, but I resist, at least this time. There will be plenty of time for me to kiss and be near my wife later.

"See you soon," Veronica says, her eyes staying locked with mine before Blair finally yanks her away.

"Oh my God, you two. Stop being so damn cute." Blair laughs, shaking her head as she leads my wife in the opposite direction. My eyes follow them for as long as I can, especially with the great view I have of Veronica's perfectly round ass, but as they walk into one of the bedrooms, I finally make my way toward the back door.

Ford has definitely grown on me, but I can't say I'm thrilled about spending more one-on-one time with him. Maybe the women are right, and I truly am a bit whipped because I'd happily follow Veronica around like her own personal lap dog. Then again, I'd follow her anywhere. Still, I suppose it's good for her to have some girl time with her best friend, especially since I've been monopolizing most of her free time as of late. I should feel guilty about that... but I don't. Not even a little.

"Hey, Miles," Ford greets me as I slide the door open, lifting a hand in greeting before adjusting his glasses.

"Hey." I nod, shutting the door behind me before making my way toward the grill, where luckily, the steaks don't appear to be on fire or even burning.

"You get the tour already?" he asks, flipping a steak.

"Actually, no. I got booted from the tour in favor of making sure you don't burn or overcook anything."

"Fair enough." He chuckles, not taking offense. "Actually," he starts again, his voice lowering, "I was hoping to get you alone today."

My brows knit together. "Oh, yeah?"

"Yeah. And I hope it's okay that I'm coming to you about this, but I know how important you are to Blair, and this just felt like an important step, so I wanted to come to you before I moved forward with things," he explains, setting the spatula down and turning to face me. "As you know, I love your sister, and while I don't have a specific date planned yet, I know I want to marry her, and before I officially ask her to be my wife, I wanted to make sure I had your blessing."

Ford may not be my favorite person, but it's never been because I didn't feel that he was worthy of my sister. If anything, I've always known he's exactly the person she needs.

"Blair has never needed my blessing for anything she's ever done in her life," I start, noticing the obvious nervous beads of sweat dripping from Ford's forehead as he nods, but I keep going. "But I really appreciate the gesture, and I know it will mean a lot to Blair as well. So, of course you have my blessing. Just keep doing what you're doing, making her happy, and we'll be good." I nod, holding out my hand for him to shake.

Ford bypasses my hand and pulls me into a hug. I freeze, never having been a fan of physical affection, especially not from my sister's nerdy boyfriend, but I decide to give this one to him as I loosely drape my arms around him as I give his back a small pat.

"Whoa," Veronica's voice calls out as the back door slides open. "Ford, you aren't making a play for my husband, are you?"

"No," Ford says, quickly jumping back. "Of course not. We were just, uh..." he rambles, clearly not great at hiding or keeping secrets.

"I was just telling him congrats on the new place," I offer instead, as Veronica slides in next to me, her hand slipping around my waist while I drape mine over her shoulder.

"Aw, that's so cute," she gushes, beaming up at me with a giant smile.

"Well, I'm a cute guy, what can I say?" I shrug.

"Oh God, is this going to last all night, you two?" Blair teases, moving to stand next to Ford.

"Oh whatever, you two were just as bad," she reminds my sister. While they may have chilled out a tiny bit with the public displays of affection, it's clear the two still can't take their hands or eyes off each other, especially as they stand in a stance similar to ours.

"Well, that's only because we have a lot of time that we need to make up for," Blair objects.

"And we don't?" Veronica jokingly interrupts. "If anything, Miles here has a lot to make up for, especially since, for the longest time he was so mean to me," she teases, looking up at me with a small pout.

"Yeah, yeah," I say, trying to brush it off, but she's not wrong. Even more, it's something I plan to do. I will spend every day for the rest of my life making sure she knows how much I love her and how big of an idiot I was for not seeing what was right in front of me all along.

"On that note," Ford says, clearing his throat. "It's looking like the steaks are ready," he adds, sending me a nod. I have a feeling he did that on purpose, especially after I saved him not too long before. Okay, so maybe Ford isn't actually that bad. Maybe I do need to cut him a little more slack.

"Alright, you two can head inside, and I'll help Ford bring everything in," Blair suggests, and we listen and follow her lead.

For as long as I can remember, I've always figured that my little sister's friends weren't my people, and I'd constantly been annoyed by them, but as the night goes on, I can't help but smile to myself. As a big brother, all one can ever want for their younger sibling is to find someone who will treat them right, and as I watch Ford and Blair interact, I know that's exactly what she's found.

As for Vee... God, I couldn't have been more wrong about the woman she is. Then again, maybe I just wasn't ready for her, but I sure as hell am now.

We've had long conversations about not getting divorced, and have both agreed that when the time is right, I'll give her a real proposal along with a vow renewal ceremony—one where she can finally experience the wedding she's always dreamed of and deserved.

I can't say I'm a big wedding type of guy, but if that's what Veronica wants, that's exactly what she'll get. In fact, my plan is to spend the rest of my life making sure she gets to live the happily-ever-after fairytale kind of love she's always dreamed of.

It's only fair, since as she smiles up at me from her seat beside me at the table, it's clear she's already made all my dreams come true. Now, I get the privilege of spending the rest of our lives making sure I fulfill every one of hers too.

Thank You For Reading

Thank you for taking the chance on this Indie Author. Being able to write these characters and tell their story is a dream come true. It means the world to me that you took the time to read my book. If you enjoyed this story, and would like to further support me, please consider leaving an honest review on Amazon and Goodreads.

Acknowledgements

I can't believe this is now the third book I've put out into the world, and there is no way I would have been able to do it without so many and important people in my life.

The first person I have to thank, like always, is my husband Naldo. I couldn't do this without you. I know I can be a lot to handle, but you continually love and support me. You were one of the first to believe that I could do this, and not only would this book not exist without your support, but none of the others.

Next, is my sweet little kiddos. I know it's rough, and likely annoying when I lock myself up in my room to write, but you always give me the time and space I need to make this all possible. It also means the world to me when you get excited when each new step comes up in the process. I love hearing all your sweet questions and comments about when my next book will come out.

I also want to thank my bestie, and platonic soulmate, Kaele. Thanks for being a constant support and cheerleader. Your friendship and support truly keep me going.

I also couldn't do any of this without my sweet friend and proofreader, Britt. I truly mean it when I say I couldn't do this without you. The mistakes you catch, and the suggestions you make, truly turn me into a better writer. I'm so lucky and blessed to have a friend like you, and I'm so glad you're a part of my life.